The Song *of* Freedom

A HISTORICAL MYSTERY NOVEL BY

D.N. GOODSPEED

Cover artwork by J.R. Gork

ISBN 978-1-961093-22-5 (Softcover Book)
ISBN 978-1-961093-23-2 (eBook)

Published by Silversmith Press–Houston, Texas
www.silversmithpress.com

SILVERSMITH
PRESS

To my son, Ben; too tender for this world.

In his honor and for those reading this that have ever or now considered taking their lives, please let this book inspire you to keep fighting and work through the pain and suffering. At age seventy seven and hopefully beyond, I survived that kind of depression, but lost a beautiful son.

Let this book reach out to you and touch you in pleasant ways and not be laid aside.

DNG
February 2025

Acknowledgments

John Gork (JR) was the "wind beneath my wings" on this project. He amazes me with his insights and strength and helps me see the forest from the trees. That mastery to give the story that thirty-three-thousand-foot altitude perspective to give the reader a feeling of being included at every step of the way in this Song of Freedom project. And thank you from the bottom of my heart for your incredible book cover artwork!

Also a big thanks to Chuck DeVries; a lifelong friend and fellow classmate from my older brother's class. To new associates Roger DeHaan for technical support and Mark DeVries who helped with the Civil War portion and was a great inspiration. These men gave me invaluable insight and suggestions that kept me on the path.

Thanks to Joanna Hunt-Boyer and Chris Boyer who were the first great publishing team to track the essence of what this project was really about and turned this humble 'writer' into a real writer. I highly recommend this team to anyone. Thanks to Carrie Sloan as a great coordinator and encourager. Thank you to my friends who pre-read my manuscript and provided feedback, and thank you to my editors.

Last but not least you, the reader whom I feel connected to. We must all fight the good fight to save this wonderful country in its hour of need. Let us make it our finest hour and not go quietly into the night but share our love with the rest of creation, self-government, liberty, freedom, and law.

Contents

Introduction 8

Part One - First Generation Builders 10

Yale 1759 11

Metamorphosis 20

Retribution 24

Dr. Franklin's Warning to Gold Nathan 42

The Day After the Meeting 68

After Franklin's Death 78

Memories From the Past 85

Battle Aftermath 88

Friday, 13th October, 1797 91

A Mother's Love 102

New England's Season Without Summer 121

A Peculiar Burial and the Noose 128

Endless Winter and a Match Made in Heaven 141

Part Two - Second Generation Builders 150

Slippery Sam 151

"Fly, Little Bird Fly!" 160

One Loose Cannon 172

Rochester, Massachusetts 178

Goodspeed's Landing 184

Fifteen Years After Their Western Migration 194

Twenty-Three Years After the Goodspeed's
Western Migration 205

The Athens Station 211

Goodspeed's Landing 218

Calvin Goodspeed 227

Part Three - Last Generation Builders 234

Another Mysterious Death 235

The Missouri Compromise of 1850 243

Last Routine Excursions on the Mississippi 264

Ballot Box Stuffing, Corruption, Riots, and
Bank Collapse 281

Secessionitis and War Drums 287

Part Four - The Determined Generals 302

An Impactful Letter 303

Lincoln Plans for War 307

The Request: Early August 330

A Partner's Final Farewell 343

Atlanta Campaign 353

One Final Adventure 363

Crabs in a Bucket 375

Appendix 394

Introduction

Song Of Freedom is a story about how my ship build-er ancestors, and three determined generals, saved America. These courageous men were driven by rugged individualism, their deep-rooted faith and an instinc-tive desire to stand up for what is right: The elements that have helped to make this once God-fearing nation great. My intention is that this book will inspire young freedom loving Americans into action! [1]

The Builders: Nathan Goodspeed, known also as Gold Nathan, or Corporal Nathan, was founder of Good-speed's Landing and a shipbuilder, dry goods busi-nessman, Revolutionary War soldier, and patriarch. He saved the Nathan Hale School in East Haddam, just af-ter Hale was martyred, executed by British Authority. A warrior from the American Revolution, he was ruthless and demonstrated great foresight to outsmart and al-ways be one step ahead of the Maryland Gang and died a natural old death in 1818. Joseph Goodspeed was Gold

---

1 Author's Note: From 1500 to 1850 around 11 million people were transported from Africa to the Americas. These slaves, usually captured and sold by other African tribes, were taken across the Atlantic, mostly to Brazil and the Caribbean Islands. If they arrived in America, originally, they became indentured servants; if they arrived elsewhere, they became slaves. Anthony Johnson, a black man, was the first to own a slave in the United States in 1641. Anthony changed all that for blacks as court records show! Before the woke mob gets offended, the judge who sided with Johnson may have been a corrupt white judge, so I'll give credit for that. However, that's tantamount to Supreme Court justices refusing to look at proof of stolen elections and take responsibility for righteous decisions, thereby not upholding the Constitution and disenfranchising the majority of American voters. I'm sure God is going to hold such judges accountable one day.

Nathan's surviving son who took over as ship builder after Nathan's death in 1818. Joseph was much later found dead in his office at Christmas 1848 with "no apparent signs of struggle," a sudden death.

The Generals: Major General Henry Halleck was the driving strategic Union war planner whom history unfairly treated as Grant's and Sherman's tormentor; when, in fact, he protected both from the press and remained their beloved mentor and friend. Major General U.S. Grant who crushed the rebellion. General Sherman who demolished the institution of slavery, was staunchly military, as well as a businessman and banker who stopped a major California bank run early in his career and was later noted as the first "modern day" general. He was also the first real successful community organizer born in the nineteenth century.

The Readers: You are a much-valued patriot audience of all races, creeds and colors, whom I love like a brother! You are on the best of honor rolls to save America yet again.

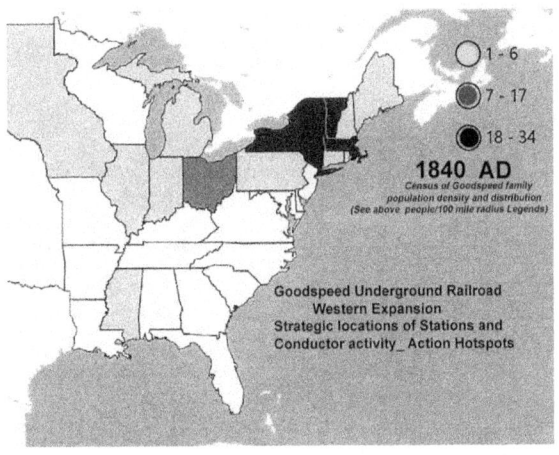

PART ONE

The First Generation Builders

CHAPTER ONE

Yale 1759

Nathan, quick to come into the world but being too tender for this world, struggled with deep depression, life taken from him, a loving grandfather Ebenezer of old age, and loving father Moses of unexpected cause, most recent. When Nymphas Marston the older witness to all this tragedy, saved his life from suicide Nathan found a reason for living and achieved greatness in other ways. He lived a long productive life instead of a short one and didn't die until old age of 83 from "general decay." He even out lived fellow Yale friends Nathan Hale, and his mentor Nymphas Marston.

The night of that attempt, the campus mood this night was at variance with student Nathan's, and when he survived, grew up overnight through this harrowing night. He then became known to the world as "Gold Nathan," a man of the world, skilled, and confident who accomplished many things in his life.

This night was dark and raining on and off, reflecting

his mood of confusion and anxiety. On nights like this the top drawers of his desk stuck and would especially get on his nerves. On better days he would pay little or no attention to this annoyance, but not this particular gloomy night.

Nathan left his window open for fresh air because stew had been served in the dorm, and although it was a rich good smell, it was still overpowering to Nathan. It distracted him in his depressed state and looked sourly at his untouched soup.

"Cheap stone soup!" he grumbled.

Nathan now was in his small study. The floors were scrupulously scrubbed and unlike most males, he prided himself in keeping it so to maintain control on his own world. Several chairs surrounded his study area because he often had company that included the Hale brothers, including Nathan Hale who was Nathan's closest friend, and his old mentor Nymphas Marston, graduate of 1749, who was now finishing up further studies and sharing that same floor and hallway with Nathan and the Hale brothers.

Nathan was very quite as he listened to the brothers who belonged to the Yale Literary Debate Society. Tonight, they were debating the Ethics of Slavery and the conversation was becoming quite animated. They turned to real challenges their little colony faced.

Great Britain demanded the colonies pay the huge war debt for French and Indian wars; and by not complying became their own Crown's enemy. The New England and the Island of Great Britain citizens were all subjects of the crown; the colonists were finding themselves unequally subject to Crown rules!

Agitated, still self absorbed in deep suffering, Nathan it was only about his soup, while the group was intently focused on the debate.

"This soup is stone soup. I guess the only kind this college can afford to give us."

Nathan Hale, as usual encouraging Goodspeed to join in, said, "Hear, hear!" even though he wondered what the connection was to their current concerns.

Fiat currency of the slave trade. Home bound traders and sailors returning from Jamaica, when they were drunk, got careless and infected their own Rhode Island with counterfeit gold doubloons that their own scheming traders had minted that weighed a quarter less that the real doubloon.

"Yes, I had a friend," Nathan Hale added "who didn't realize he had one of those counterfeit coins and nearly got killed in a bar fight and strung up."

"Taxation without representation" was not quite the cry yet but it was getting close, and people were painfully aware of all that. Inflation itself became a more sadistic evil form of taxation so it wouldn't be long before the nation would explode when markets were crushed, and they'd asked for independence from the crown as a last resort.

The conversation, debate now really, deteriorated when another Hale brother added to the fray.

"Yes, the Articles of Confederation won't keep us safe from starving. The Tory Party talk conservative, mock our blood and sacrifice we gave to them in war behind-closed-doors deals with spurious speculators, power hungry tyrants...and getting fat!"

Nathan Goodspeed got up and threw what remained of his cold unfinished soup into the fire grate with disgust. Depressed, cooped up indoors, his friends sometimes intimidated him. He returned to his desk without a word; a mood that Nathan Hale grew somewhat apprehensive about.

"Tories surely love their slaves; thank God that trade is slowly dying."

"Thank God our northern climate isn't like in the South, or that would spread up here and then we'd be no different morally than they are."

But the conversation was interrupted when another Hale brother entered the chambers excitedly saying that they were cooking and making maple sugar candy outdoors under a shelter.

But Nathan, still quiet at his desk, stroked his ink quill pen absentmindedly till he accidentally spilled it much to his own discomfort.

"Oh quick," Nymphas said, "Somebody grab a towel!" Which to more general laughter several rushed to produce so to relieve poor Nathan's distress.

Nymphas too, like Nathan Hale, had been closely observing Nathan's behavior.

Hale noted this and praised God silently that Marston was here at Yale and staying temporarily with them.

His business was more in Barnstable where he was getting more involved with politics and testing the waters, debating with such figures as the famous loyalist Massachusetts politician Timothy Ruggles.

Nathan's mood swings and less time participating in the discussions, alarmed Nathan Hale and Marston more and more.

Nathan Hale knew Marston himself had a history of depression but as a result Nymphs had learned to control his anger and drinking habits as a result.

The conversation turned back to the excitement of the maple sugar candy production. Goodspeed showed some slight interest, being technically minded, which was why he, Marston and Hale usually hung out together.

Goodspeed also had a deep passionate interest in patents and inventions like Marston. Astronomy was also one of their intense passions, along with philosophical discussions of the unknown, the metaphysical, and Judaeo-Christian strong beliefs of right and wrong.

But this particular night both Hale and Marston sensed that it was not a good time to pick up that conversation with Nathan.

One Hale brother came back into the room and said, "We need volunteers. We're getting down to the sugar where the stirring gets harder. Any volunteers?"

Nathan Hale shook his head wanting to stay with Nathan Goodspeed and hoping that Marston would stick around also. It was nearing midnight and Marston, older than Nathan Hale and Goodspeed, started to yawn, then looked at the friendly Hale intruder, smiled, but shook his head.

"I want to keep my eye on these two." He dismissed the other with a wink, a smile, and a nod.

This was of course a hint to the other, still seated beside Nathan Hale, to take his leave. For the first time this brother looked at Goodspeed, then noticed his mood, and understood what was coming up.

Now alone with just his friends Nathan unloaded his pent-up emotions.

"I never felt this bad, my friends. It's like I'm in a deep hole I can never climb out of! Why do we talk of who we can trust, or don't trust, when the British compel us to not even think about abolishing black slavery as they fill their coffers? We do indeed live in a whore society! I'm going to end it."

"Don't say that!" Hale pleaded.

"What are your feelings, Marston? Pray, speak to him!"

Marston looked firmly into the man's suffering soul with no regard to Hale's plea and said coldly without blinking, "Boredom!"

A shocked moment of silence hung in the room till Nathan G. jumped out of his chair.

"Even you two, my trusted friends, have turned on me! Be gone now, both of you!" he yelled.

The next night was calm with no rain yet still overcast and oppressive, but all was quiet in the dorm with most asleep at the late hour.

Nathan Hale awakened from a sound sleep with a jolt.

"Come on, we've got work to do. Be quick about it!" The urgent voice was Marston.

Without waiting Nymphas rushed out of the room to the adjoining room. Dazed, Hale quickly stumbled after him.

"Oh my GOD!" Hale yelled. Outside there were suddenly flashes of lightning which revealed a disturbing scene. From a rafter Nathan had hung himself but was still struggling, his eyes starting to bulge. Hurriedly, Marston lit a lamp.

"Catch him!" Nymphas yelled, as he quickly ran behind the victim. In the shadows created by the lamp, he whipped his sharpened sword out of its scabbard and with one deft stroke cut Nathan down. He fell against Hale's waiting but trembling arms.

The room was brighter now as Nathan Goodspeed was roughly thrown down by Nymphas and into Goodspeed's chair behind his study desk.

Then Nymphas, to Hale's alarm, pull out his pistol, cocked it, and jammed it close to the suicide victim's left forehead. It was a massive .50 caliber browned long barrel of British design.

Both Hale and Goodspeed were crying, but Nymphas remained cold and with measured coolness spoke to the victim.

"Answer me! Is life worth living? And how is your soul?! Answer me now!"

Goodspeed broke down crying, as Nymphas was hoping.

No one present in that room noticed that Nymphas' hand was starting to tremble, let alone that the pistol was only half-cocked. Nymphas started to tear himself, but bit his lip knowing that his cold demeanor was the only possible device that could save Nathan's life.

"You're not alone, nor do you really want me to end your suffering. Yes, your father, our beloved Moses, was poisoned. I could see it in your eyes last night, but rest assured we all now know the truth. By who (?) we don't know right now but, I assure you we are investigating!".

Nymphas looked up at Nathan Hale. He gave him a wink, softened and compassionate, Nymphas now raised and relaxed the pistol's hammer carefully to its rest position. Then he hugged Nathan Goodspeed to calm his trembling and comfort the crying figure.

The room was now totally silent. The three men, like statues, could have been a sculpture study.

"How is your soul now, Nathan? Why not make your concerns charged with a sense of providential purpose rather than worry?" the whisper seemed to come from somewhere other than its author Nymphas.

The hand of the sitting statue moved. At first imperceptibly then deliberately, slowly but surely, and laid the instrument of self-destruction aside as a smile slowly developed.

Nymphas and the other Nathan, blinking but without further obvious expression, looked pleased.

It was a short time later, as if transformed from student Nathan, now Gold Nathan suddenly emerged, dawning for the first time in history and throwing pure radiant sunlight on what otherwise could have been a very dark night!

And another whisper, spiritual in nature, seemed to come out of nowhere and from nowhere; some unknown ethereal source enveloped all three of them, lost only in time, eternity, or space.

"Well done!" it spoke, then accompanied by a strong wind, the curtain fluttered, moving freely with dowel weights that Gold Nathan himself had fashioned and woven into the base of each curtain. The dormitory window was open, although it was still the dead of night. All three men were shocked. None of them expected the whisper or the wind!

Metamorphosis

From Nathan the Student to Gold Nathan the Ship Builder: "Blessed are we whose lives were saved on the West banks of the Connecticut River, and a sense of purpose gained among four story buildings dominated by cathedral towers; and men in their early short black top hats dressed in black wearing light-colored breeches were out to be social and to save the world, riders on show horses, elegant carriages for two traced the dirt trails of this beautiful campus paradise."

Marston turned around on their walk and looked sharply and suspiciously at his young companion Nathan Goodspeed.

"You're pretty chipper for a young man who tried to hang himself last night, aren't you?"

"I'll be honest, sir, Moses' will witnessed by brothers, but never signed and dated makes me feel like doing something to keep my mind off problems and to avoid thinking about things that upset me today," Nathan responded. After a brief pause, he continued.

"Like a carriage ride upriver! Let's join Nathan; he's talking about being a teacher as you know and wants to see a school in East Haddam upriver. It won't be far and might do me some good."

"Only under one condition: that you won't kill yourself tonight," Nymphas responded dryly but with a twinkle in his eye.

"That shall not happen!" Nathan vowed, "We'll be on the road tonight with Hale; and seventeen miles, you know a stay is in order at some roadside, especially if we make it a round trip to be back and start fresh in time for classes next week."

"Sure, I have no problems with that," said Marston, breathing in and enjoying the fresh spring air with hints of lemon sachet from a passing carriage. "In fact, I'm rather curious myself to find out what he's up to."

1777 - Time Passes

A quarter century had passed found Nathan in his thirties a believer and committed, tempered by military service and a brutal war to stay the course.

In those formative times early on was his attempted suicide, then the very next day he fell in love with a culture that turned his anxieties to purpose at East Haddam on his first visit. Both Hale and the school visit had inspired Gold Nathan to weep with tears of joy on the banks of the Connecticut River. School children of both races were learning the same subjects and being taught forbidden skills contrary to British Authority. But unlike Barnstable, where Gold Nathan felt confined to British tyranny at close quarters, he longed to go back to where their oppressive presence was not present and people of all races, creeds and colors were at liberty to think for themselves. So, time would always draw Gold Nathan back to those beloved banks of the Connecticut River often found with either Hale or Marston or both.

After the horrendous Boston Massacre where one black and several others were killed by British soldiers, Nathan had seen enough and now more or less took solitude in his beloved adopted state of Connecticut.

In 1772 he was in Barnstable, where he was born, long enough to court and married Mary Kellogg. Her Christian virtue and strong will but healing nature tempered his once destructive nature forever.

Then in 1776, on the gut punch of finding out that Nathan Hale had been lynched by the British he joined the Connecticut Militia, and he and his wife never looked back at Barnstable.

"Oh Marston, I'm so sad, but at the same time so happy too to see you once again and to be married to a beautiful woman!"

"I missed you too my friend," Marston responded.

They were standing on the misty banks of the Connecticut River watching the herons and higher up overhead a "v" flight of geese, the sounds of the rear wing team encouraging the gaggle and silent lead to maintain formation and speed most definitely caught the two men's attention. The air was so fresh and clean, all surrounded by peace and tranquility, including the two men watching the geese...and what's more they knew it in their souls. But both felt lonely without a word missing their beloved friend Nathan Hale.

"It just isn't the same, is it?" Nymphas commented. The surviving Nathan, knowing exactly what he meant, replied, "No it's not the same. My mother is gone. My grandfather is gone. My dad gone... a poison mystery."

He turned and looked at Marston, and said "Then your mother before you, another mystery!"

Then that strong wind of old came once again, a breath of fall, Marston, the chill, Nathan the winter. Last he added, "Then, only I, shall be left, alone, to stand for all of us that were!"

Nymphas replied, "I know. My mother, your Aunt Lidia, after my father, then me." Eye to eye, both men nodded and said their final good byes.

CHAPTER THREE

Retribution

1788

About this time Pennsylvania dweller Dirty Abe flitted back and forth from Boston and the Maryland slave plantation rice beds. Politics and poison were his trade. To Dr. Ben Franklin he was known as Abraham Lincoln. To crime families and Goodspeed's landing he was known as Dirty Abe.

From those rice beds came methyl iodide extracted and concentrated at levels to work as a sedative or poison. A man in shadows who preferred sipping Madeira in smoke-stained walls, dark and dirty taverns, sulked by day and worked by night with cronies that hated America and creation itself.

Before 1788 Nathan after the final 'good byes' went on to found Goodspeed's landing in Connecticut to build warships used against the British, with Marston's support that contributed greatly to Great Britain's ultimate defeat, during the American Revolution. "Why not take out Gold Nathan first before Marston?" the pockmarked thug asked, referring to himself who, with a waiter's help, ministered the poison to Marston at Marston's own tavern in Boston.

Abe answered, "Because Marston, turned businessman to politician, I am afraid, was the only one who would have defeated Timothy Ruggles in a fair election; Ruggles buys influence for slave traffic and drugs."

After another sip of his Madeira, "So Marston had to go. Understand?"

The worthless guy indicated that he did, in evil affirmation and the sound of their glasses clinked together.

"'We the people' be damned! So, we made it look like a seizure," he answered so dryly that it made even the thug shudder in open admiration.

"When the time is right," Abe darkly emphasized. "We'll get his friend Nathan, knowing his history, make it look like a suicide." The flash of a dying flame from their table candle caught a glint of dark light in evil eyes. Nymphas Marston died on his 60 birthday, a Boston constitutional convention lead delegate!

Dr. Benjamin Franklin and Nathan's Response to Retribution

Nathan Goodspeed was amazed when the great, international acclaimed man of science, action and proven patriotism, Dr. Benjamin Franklin, out of nowhere sent him a letter of Marque.

"What on earth is it about me that he wants to see me, about my dear friend Marston's death?"

It was one thing to get a letter of Marque from the esteemed gentleman. But quite another to actually receive an audience invite to personally meet the man!" Dr. Franklin, "Don't look so nervous, young man, it's only me." His natural smile immediately put Nathan at ease.

"Allow me to ask you a personal question?' Ben paused and waited for Nathan to respond. Nathan nodded.

"You once tried to kill yourself, I understand?"

Nathan was embarrassed but cautiously nodded.

"What made you decide not to, then go on to become such a very successful man of action in life?"

The curiosity on Dr. Franklin's part was genuine and warm, as the man leaned forward, demonstrated all the warmth of a great listener put Nathan even at further ease. Nathan noted that there was a glint of admiration and recognition in Benjamin's eyes.

"You may call me Ben." He said with a chuckle read his mind, which endeared Nathan to the man forever as a close friend and confident.

"I knew your mentor Nymphas very well, God rest his soul."

"So you know everything?"

Ben nodded. "That terrible night, as Nymphas was at deaths door, I also met your privateer cousin Samuel Goodspeed, the spy James Armistead the black, with my journalist, who brought me that awful news who prompted me to reveal what I should have printed in

September. But now pray tell me what convicted you to not be suicidal?"

"As I hung from that rafter, terror was replaced by peace, so to answer your question

First, I knew Nymphas was coming to rescue me after I was filled with the Holy Spirit."

Ben leaned in with keen interest.

"And," Nathan further encouraged continued, "the gift of divine prophesy entered my soul..."

"Excellent!" Benjamin exclaimed, "Indeed what struck me was that your prophetic conversation with your last contact with Marston, he shared with me."

Ben with emphasis, "Tell me where we are at now, in your opinion, young man!"

"That it was not obedient and a mistake, with all due respect, sir, to not have included Jefferson's grievance of the crown's barbaric cruel practice of slave transport in the Declaration of Independence... And now, some sort of resolution in our new constitution of the sovereignty of God and his son Jesus Christ. The Scottish Covenanters advised Gen. Washington, about that if the weak Articles of Confederation were ever replaced by our stronger Constitution, blessed for all time, or cursed if not included!"

Ben was thunderstruck.

Nathan with intensity added, "Right then and there we lost a valuable opportunity to put the matter of not just our race, but ALL races to consider, that, indeed all men are created equal in the eyes of our creator! I now prophesize will haunt America thru all times until the end!"

Nathan surprised the old man further, when he took, out of his pocket; two carefully wrapped separately deck of playing cards.

"These cards," Nathan explained "were passed down to me from my dad, Moses, also poisoned like Nymphas, from founders, Roger and Alice Layton Goodspeed, 1639. The oldest, here is a deck depicting the coat of arms of the European sovereigns and states, to remind Roger of the importance of national identity and the need that ultimately led us to break free from tyranny of the Crown, as my father, Moses, and his dad Ebenezer would say to me over and over, to claim as the thirteen United States of America our independence. Indeed way ahead of their time!

Under God, Dr. Franklin knew my three times removed grandfather, Privateer Samuel Goodspeed and the journalist, mentioned earlier who urged Dr. Ben to print an article that might have, in a remiss Franklin's own words, "Saved Marston's life.

So, dear reader, we will pick up with them here, as a recap, time wise, slightly out of order but in close proximity, and directly related to the poisoning of Marston at the Boston convention!

When the journalist came back to Boston for the second week, he found that they had tricked Marston's delegation to move the convention from the town hall to the Church on Long Lane, closer to the taverns that Nymphas owned and frequented often!

As the journalist approached the church and the tavern, he heard the terrible news of Nymphas' seizure.

The same symptoms the journalist witnessed with Ben, now Nymphas had far worse, drifting in and out of consciousness. Instead of recording the second week for history to remember, he and Samuel found themselves in shock doing what they could to claim guardianship over the stricken man and rescue him from danger.

Nymphas was now dying and Ben in bad health and pain, was still determined to fight the good fight. He was in constant pain because of gout, which Dr. Rush told Ben might be from poison as well. The convention that ended in September of the previous year.

With Armistead's assistance he sat down at his secretary.

"Of the twenty-three votes against constitution ratification here, James Marshall and William Brown had nothing to do with the Article of Minority Dissent." Ben, now in front of his small audience, drew a line through their names and proceeded to review all other names until he got to the last six that he would identify as "persons of interest".

Ben took out his own notes and from them for his company wrote three names on a blank page: *William Findley, John Smilie, Robert Whitehill.*

"These were the only speakers against the convention! At least I'll give them credit for being honest...but make no mistake..."

Then Ben recorded three more names of persons of interest: *Adam Orth, Nicholas Lutz, Abraham Lincoln.*

"Dirty Abe!" Dr. Franklin muttered with such disdain and force that no listener could miss his convictions of what this man was capable of doing, even murder.

"These last three are very evil and in my own article twice I list their names as friends of worthless paper money and religious bigots. I should know, they attacked even my adopted Quaker faith."

"My friend was kind enough to add in their Dissent Article that these men were also opponents to the liberty and independence of our new Republic. For that I thanked him."

Ben looked up at Samuel and the journalist.

"Between my convention and now this mess, I rebelled against the Crown's attitude on slavery and every species of traffic in the persons of our fellow men. I firmly believe that Negros are equal to us whites and are entitled to all liberties that other Americans enjoy!"

"Even so these cowards still signed this document, so at least I give them credit for that!" Dr. Franklin closed his eyes as another wave of pain caused him to momentarily clench his teeth. "Come on boys. Let's give the folks in Philadelphia something of interest to read![2]

A Forgotten Image from History, Pennsylvania Gazette - Weekly circulation: Wednesday, January 23, 1788

On the following pages are the receipts of Franklin's article to read. An article once seen cannot be unseen.

Then as now! The Constitution and Bill of Rights was universally attacked.

---

2 Author's Note: Later Franklin made his view clear in a letter to then Vice President Adams and the Congress in 1790.

Then as now! Attacking Washington founders with falsehood and lies by those that claimed to love liberty.

Then as now! Flooded markets with non-backed paper money to serve the dual purpose of supporting evil programs that undermined freedoms, targeted commerce and farmers to create dependency on corrupt governments.

Then as now! Targeted any religious sect that did not support the status quo.

Then as now! Always was some kind of deep state connection or secret society and news from domestic enemy sources!

IN the lift of the fignors of the proteft of the minority of the Convention againft the fœderal conftitution, we find six----(and THREE of them the only fpeakers againft it in the Convention) whofe names are upon record as the friends of *paper money*, and the advocates for the late unjuft *tefti-law* of Penafylvania, which for near *ten* years excluded the *Quakers*, *Menonifts*, *Moravians*, and feveral other fects fcrupulous againft war, from a reprefentation in our government.

In the minutes of the fecond feffion of the Ninth General Affembly of the commonwealth of Pennfylvania, we find in the 212th page the following perfons among the YEAS, who voted for the emiffion of paper money, which has, by its depreciation, fo much injured the trade and manufactures of the ftate, and which, by impairing its funds, has weakened the ftrength of our government, and thereby deftroyed the hopes and fupport of the public creditors. The perfons are, *William Findley*, *John Smilie*, *Robert Whitehill*, *Adam Orth*, *Nicholas Lutz*, *Abraham Lincoln*.

In the 301d page of the fame book, we find a report, declaring the Quakers, Moravians, &c. who, from confcientious fcruples, declined taking part in the war, to be " enemies to liberty and the rights of mankind---Britifh fubjects, aliens and cowards---who had no fhare in the declaration of independence, in the formation of our conftitution, or in eftablifhing them by ARMS;" which report is agreed to, as appears in the lift of the YEAS, by the fame *William Findley*, *John Smilie*, *Robert Whitehill*, *Adam Orth*, *Nicholas Lutz*, *Abraham Lincoln*.

Thefe men certainly are not in earneft, when they talk and write of *liberty*, and of the facred rights of *confcience*. Their conduct contradicts all their fpeeches and publications; and if they were truly fenfible of their folly and wickednefs in oppofing the new government, inftead of trying to excite a civil war (in which they will bear no more part than they did in the late war with Great-Britain) they ought rather to acknowledge, with gratitude, the lenity of their fellow-citizens, in permitting them to live among us with impunity, after thus transgreffing and violating the great principles of liberty, government and confcience.

In the Centinel, No. XI. we are told that General Washington (under God the deliverer of our country) is a poor creature, with many *conftitutional* infirmities; and that he has, from ambitious motives, united with the *confpirators* of Delaware, Pennfylvania, New-Jerfey and Connecticut, to enflave his country.--- Can human nature fink fo low as to be guilty of fuch bafe ingratitude to a man to whom America owes her independence and liberties ? or will the more grateful fons of America fuffer the author of fuch a declaration to continue to infult their opinions and feelings ? There was a time, when the liberties of our country were at the mercy of this great and good man---There was a time when a defrauded and clamorous army, devoted to his will, and a Congrefs without power or credit, would have rendered it an eafy matter for him to have eftablifhed a monarchy in the United States. But how nobly did he behave in this alarming crifis of our affairs. He compofed the turbulent and punifhed the mutinous fpirit of the army. He ftrengthened by his influence the hands of Congrefs, and finally bequeathed, as his laft legacy to his country, his parting advice, to form fuch a union as would for ever perpetuate her liberties.

In the fame Centinel we are told, that *anarchy* and a *civil war* are lefs evils than the defpotifm (as he calls it) of the new government. It would be an affront to the underftandings of my readers to controvert thefe two opinions---I fhall only afk the author of them, whether he will rifk himfelf, at the head of a company of his Carlifle *white* boys, in cafe he fhould fucceed in his beloved fcheme of exciting a civil war, or whether he would not rather fhelter himfelf under a fafe office, as he did during the late war, until the bloody ftorm was over ?

I with the public creditors to look to themfelves. The funding fyftem of Pennfylvania is on its laft legs. It cannot exift another year, without convulfing our ftate. All the diftrefs, oppreffion, fpeculation, idlenefs, peculation in government,----and bankruptcies, not of merchants only, but of *tradefmen* and *farmers* (a thing unheard of before, and unknown in other countries) are owing to the funding law. Pennfylvania has affumed a million and an half of dollars in certificates, above her quota of the public debt. It is only by adopting the fœderal government that this enormous, unequal and oppreffive burthen can be taken off our fhoulders, and the ftate refcued out of the hands of fpeculators, fharpers and public defaulters. It is, moreover, only from a fœderal treafury that the public creditors, of all defcriptions, can expect fubftantial and permanent juftice.

A CITIZEN OF PHILADELPHIA.

Seen here as published in its entirety by Ben Franklin the morning of the journalist's and Samuel's early morning visit.

Wednesday, February 6th, 1788 - Early Morning

Samuel Goodspeed had returned to Boston. He wanted to see the celebration now that both states had ratified the Constitution. It was the only thing that could compel Samuel to leave Nymphas' bedside in Barnstable.

Sam heard bells ring out and the noise of firecrackers from where he was standing on the porch of his Brattle Street apartment. He took himself back in time to a similar patriotic moment after the British blockaded Boston and Washington's return.

He remembered something from that time that he now took out of his pocket, a yellowed copy of a slip his ship master had given him.

The captain had argued with Samuel Crocker on their return trip after that blockade. Tight fisted clerk Samuel disputed their cargo list, Samuel Goodspeed noticed John Hancock's name on a page opposite the inventory list dated July 17th, 1776. Samuel thumbed back was thrilled to see the Barnstable entry "In Congress, July 4, 1776, Declaration by the Representatives of the United States in General Congress Assembled," transcribed by the same 'red faced' clerk.

"What are you doing there, lad?" Crocker barked at Samuel who jumped back.

"Is this...?" Samuel started.

"Yes, it is!" Crocker laughed. "Don't grime it up with your filthy paws, lad."

The captain grinned, already knowing about that historic entry next to his inventory list.

"Go ahead and have a closer look if you like," said Sam Crocker, the men now continuing a more amiable discussion about compensation.

There Samuel made a vow.

"If I ever get back from this adventure, and marry Sylvia, I'll want our names entered here!" he decreed and softly jabbed the blank page after the inventory. Ten years later on February 15, 1786, on the day of their wedding, he and Sylvia did just that.

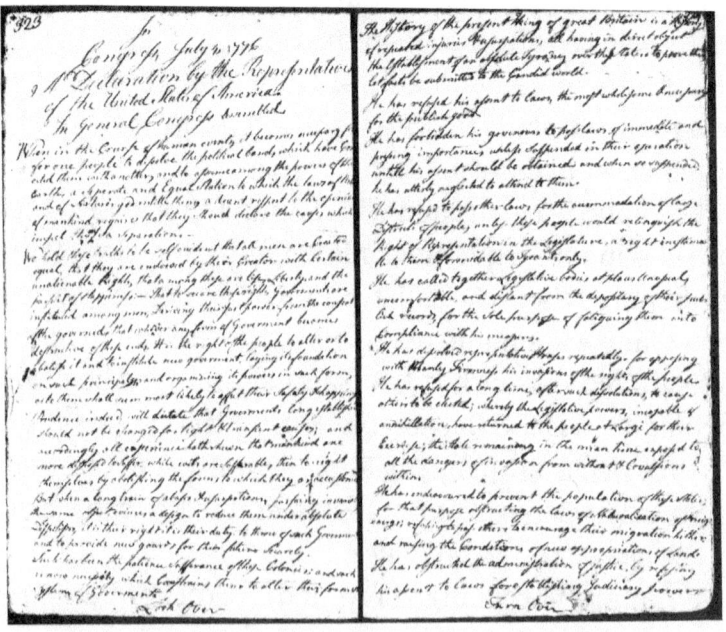

After leaving the meeting house his master took out a churchwarden pipe.

"Well Sam, thanks to you, we saved our business. Our whale oil in exchange for imported flour from the southern states paid us well, but good coffee not so much."

Samuel was not used to compliments from this man.

"I'm promoting you, young man. This is not the first time you have helped me. This time we salvaged our losses in the Caribbean, cheap patrons that they are!"

Samuel was unsure how to respond to the captain's newfound faith, nonetheless he ventured an answer.

"Sam Crocker got less than he wanted and gave what he could, while we accepted less than we had hoped for. But we made up the margin of loss down in the Dry Tortugas."

"Yep," the captain responded, then suddenly stopped walking. The skipper turned to evaluate Sam through a cloud of smoke, then finally asked, "How is your soul, lad?"

"Sir?" Sam inquired, embarrassed.

"How...is...your...soul?"

"Sir, I felt proud seeing our Declaration. Under God our trials small and of no substance," Samuel replied, then tested their new relationship. "Much like the cloud around your head."

Sam waited. The man convulsed in a laugh that developed into a roar of appreciation.

"Oh, bless me! Will wonders never cease! You were the only one that never complained, even when you smashed your hand in the hatch."

"Yep!" Samuel responded.

"Also, when you saw the man fall in with the sharks and lose his leg, without hesitation you threw yourself in there with a tethered line. I thought I had seen the last of both of you."

Samuel "Yes, I know! You left it to the crew to heave us in."

"You, facing death, were more alive than those on the deck with their bare faces hanging out!" Then he added, "You're a special breed of cat! That's why you're taking over as first mate!"

Samuel saw the ship master's hands go into his pockets. Finally, he grunted with satisfaction. He took out a worn thick envelope, unfolded it and removed a parchment with a broken seal and opened it to read, but first he respectfully emptied his pipe.

"From Recorder Josiah Crocker whom I requested made a copy for me," he began, then waving the Council Order that Samuel had seen before the other Crocker yelled at him, the captain continued to read.

"Ordered that the Declaration of Independence shall be printed and a copy be sent to the minutes of each parish, of every Denomination, within this State; and that they are whereby required to read the Same to their respective Congregation as soon as Divine Service is ended, in the afternoon on the first Lord's day after they Shall have received and offer Such publication thereof to deliver the said Declaration to the Clerks of their Several Towns, or Districts Who are hereby required to record the Same in their respective Town, or

District blocks, there to remain as a perpetual memorial thereof.

And for the support of the declaration, with a firm reliance on the Protection of Divine Providence, we mutually pledge to each other our Lives, our Fortunes, and our Sacred Honor.

Signed by Order and in Behalf of the Congress
John Hancock, President.
Attest Charles Thompson Secretary.
In Council July 17th, 1776."

After refolding, the captain put the circular in Samuel's breast pocket and spoke.

"Now that is putting it all on the line!" he said, then patting it, added, "Keep it close to your heart, lad! It is now yours to complement a brave spirit. Share it with only those you trust."

The captain motioned with a wave.

"Come on, Sam, we have much work to do!"

Samuel heard the parade coming now and refolded the old copy. Sylvia came out and hugged his arm to watch the festivities.

"Jane's now two and such a cute girl. Do you think Silver Nathan and Thankful will have a boy next?"[3]

"If they do, I'll wager they will name him Jabez," he responded, both watching the approaching parade.

"Why not Nathan after himself?"

He looked at Sylvia and continued. "Before his older

---

3 Author's Note: Samuel's father John was called "Pewter John" to distinguish him from his first cousin "Silver John".

brother Solomon was tragically killed in the war, there was another son even before Solomon, who was still born whose name would have been Jabez."

"How sad!" Sylvia said, softly caressing Samuel's arm. Then after a moment's reflection, "So why didn't they name their second born Jabez instead of Thomas? Where did the name Thomas come from?"

"You're a Goodspeed, dear kissing cousin. I'm surprised you don't know!"

"Oh, that's right, it was Thankful's father's last name, who died in an English prison of war ship"

He nodded solemnly.

"Very sad!" Sylvia, tearing up, still gently pressed his arm.

The approaching procession now broke out in Yankee Doodle. Samuel's eyes narrowed as he listened carefully to the new lyrics. The parade looked more like ruffians than parade participants.

"The 'vention did in Boston meet.
The State House could not hold 'em
So, then they went to Fed'ral Street..."

Samuel wondered now. Brattle Street was where Nymphas had the Convention moved to at that church by the same name. This realization caught Samuel by surprise.

And there the truth was told 'em...
And ev'ry morning went to prayer,
And then began disputing,

Till oppositions silenced were,
By arguments refuting.
Now politicians of all kinds,
Who are not yet decided,
May see how Yankees speak their minds,
And yet are not divided.
So here I end my Fed'ral song...
Composed of sixteen verses.

"My God! It was composed of sixteen verses... Sixteen days!" Samuel realized, exclaiming under his breaths so passionately that Sylvia turned to look at him. *May agriculture flourish long and commerce fill our purses!"*

"Dear, excuse me!" Samuel said softly.

Bystanders cheered the song's conclusion. Others folded arms and smugly grinned. Samuel walked quickly along the boardwalk until a cane pressed his chest.

"Stop, Samuel."

"James! Those aren't sixteen verses they're talking about! Those are days and..."

"Easy brother! Yes! Sixteen days since he was poisoned; and yes, it is a warning for us niggers and folks like you."

"The first three verses are aimed directly at Nymphas and his delegation!" Samuel hissed then added "And the first line is a lie about not enough space..."

James finish the thought, "Because in the convention records the reason was about poor acoustics. Yes, we know all that!"

Samuel calmed down to listen.

"Ben, Benjamin Rush, the journalist and the rest of

our group has been following this for days. Obviously, it is no surprise to you now as well. Those people in the procession and some groups in the crowd you noticed are connected. They're all thugs, bought and paid for."

Sylvia, smiling at James, caught up with her husband.

"I was worried you were going to get yourself killed. My oldest brother, Ansel, married Lidia Marston whose uncle was Nymphas Marston. So, patience dear, we all have an axe to grind in this affair!"

Now James tipped his hat and excused himself, bowing to Sylvia.

"Take care! We're all at a dangerous crossroads and the powers that be are not going to let a little ratification stand in their way. Count on it! This was also an angry response to Ben's article from Abe and the gang! We have much work to do!"

Franklin dispatched a letter of marque to Corporal Nathan Goodspeed who had the resources at Goodspeed's landing, to conduct an investigation into the murder mystery. Franklin knew that Nathan too had an "axe to grind" in this affair.

Nathan, already primed by sadness, loss, and righteous wrath, fired back an immediate reply: *I want Dr. Benjamin Rush to be part of this investigative crew along with our friend and associate James A.*

—Respectfully your trusted servant, Corp. Nathan Goodspeed

Nymphas Marston, son of Lydia, another Goodspeed, eventually died. Ben himself was in the twilight of his own life, and in just less than three years he, would be gone as well.

Nymphas Marston's Tombstone reads:

"In Memory of Nymphas Marston, Esq. who died Feb'y 11th 1788 on the anniversary of his birth aged 60 Sobriety and attention to his studies marked the course of his academic education received at Yale College, the honours of which were conferred on him in the years 1749 and 1752. In 1760 he was appointed as Magistrate. For a long course of years, he sustained the first offices in the town and was of their delegates at the Conven-  *tion for ratifying the Fed-eral Constitution where he was seized with the disor-der which put an end to his life. He was a fearer of God, a serious but not a bigoted Christian. He was moderate in prosperity and patient in adversity, a kind husband, fond parent & indulgent master in his house, affa-ble to his neighbors, generous to his friends and relatives, charitable to the poor and just to all."*

Dr. Franklin's Warning to Gold Nathan

Oh, Connecticut how lovely is your Sound and Shores
The Sons of Liberty have a tale to tell
And God's Author a story to sell!

DNG

Friday July 4, 1788 - East Haddam, Connecticut: Corporal Nathan's Meeting

"There was murder in their eyes! In which God lives for there is murder in all our hearts! God is love and he who abides in love abides in God."

Old Thomas Goodspeed, who followed the sea for many years, knew Gold Nathan. In 1763, he was captain of the sloop *Desire* which made trips between Boston and the Connecticut River. He was still thus engaged as late as 1768. He died before Nymphas Marston's memorial meeting.

Flashback – 1770

"Corp. Nathan, what do you need from me to help you?" inquired Thomas.

Nathan looked out at the bay by the mouth of his river, the sun just the right angles off the bay to blind him, almost washing out the outline of the generous man before him.

"Lumber for more ships. I want to help America in what's coming. They don't know me yet, but will!"

"What's coming? You mean independence?" Thomas asked.

"We'll get war before we get independence, I'm afraid, and recon before this current decade's over!" Gold responded.

"You've got it then. This load in my hold is for you today and I guess my other loyalist client is just going to have to wait! Liberty and freedom must come first!" Thomas laughed.

On that beautiful day Thomas had welcome news for Corp. Nathan. Both heard the sweet soft sounds of a lute. A man with a short grey top hat, a Yale man, played a lute to a young attractive woman.

"By the way," Thomas turned back to Nathan. "Marston told me to stop here first..." he winked. "Don't let your loyalist competition get anything more!"

Thus, on the banks of Long Island Sound Goodspeed's landing was born, with just a wink and a nod.

Meanwhile back at Gold Nathan's office on that grey July 4th Marston Memorial meeting, those in attendance at Nathan's office recorded their positions on ratifying the constitution.

Barnstable .... /
Shearjashub Browne, Esq., ... *Yea*
Nymphas Marston, ... *(a ghost Yea!)*

Sandwich .... /
Dr. Thomas Smith, ... *Nay*
Mr. Thomas Nye, ... *Nay*

Yarmouth .... /
D. Thatcher, Esq., ... *Yea*
Capt. Jonathan Howes, Yea

Hardwick .... /
Hon. Solomon Freeman, ... *Yea*
Capt. Kimball Clark, ... *Yea*

Wellfleet—Rev. Levi Whitman, ... *Yea*
Falmouth—Capt. Joseph Palmer, ... *Yea*

Sandwich, a strong Loyalist community, cast the only Nay vote.

These concerned surviving delegates were first to attend Marston's memorial that Corp. Nathan conducted, and surprisingly, all did show up angry and in earnest.

Mr. Nye spokesman concluded. "That night Brattle Street was a mess, broken whiskey bottles and litter. And on one street corner there was a pig's head wrapped in that Philadelphia Gazette article."

No investigation. None arrested. And one hushed autopsy performed on Marston,. Demands for the missing report made. "What report? Only a 'seizure'", they said.

One server where Nymphas had his last dinner sixteen days earlier was also found dead, naked under a pillow!"

Thomas Nye spoke aside to old Nathan and hissed, "The sons of bitches tried framing me, though I voted 'nay'!"

"The only county targeted!" decried Dr. Thomas Smith. "Any 'yeas' singled out!?" he questioned.

"No. Only 'nays'!"

"They're covering their tracks," Nathan remarked. "Welcome to our side!"

Now Thomas Nye and Capt. Joseph Palmer from Falmouth were laughing.

"What's so funny?" Thomas Smith asked.

"I'll never forget when I was a guest at his estate during the war. The soldiers called out from below the defense of Falmouth. On their return home they called upon Marston, and after accepting his bountiful hospitalities, gave vent to their patriotism by firing a salute in the house, shattering the plaster in the dining room," Thomas Nye explained.

"Marston had responded 'Ye be pardoned if only you

gents would carry out your zeal in shattering the ranks of the common enemy!'" Nye recalled.

"Now that's funny!" Nathan laughed.

It was now July and the rest of the family members and friends filed in.

Enter Silver Nathan and Thankful. Her husband was tall, thin, and handsome and the woman looked small beside him, but in the company of women stood taller.

Next came Samuel and Sylvia, who were "kissing cousins".

Shearjashub and Elizabeth Ruggles Goodspeed followed. Shear was in many ways a remarkable man, a revolutionary war hero. He possessed enormous strength, such that seeing two men tugging at a large stone without being able to raise it to the wall they were building, he picked it up and placed where it was needed. He is said to have once lifted and carried for some distance a dead hog weighing 450 pounds.

Wife Elizabeth had brown hair which was always in a tight bun with a ribbon. Elizabeth was broad like her husband Shear and didn't look anything like her Tory cousin Bathsheba Ruggles Spooner, who was very beautiful and intelligent, till they executed her for murdering her husband in a most dreadful way.[4]

Their eight-year-old son Seth came with them and in just ten years he became a man of high moral standards

---

[4] Author's Note: Bathsheba's criminal history, a blank in family records, was never mentioned by the family historian. Historian and author, Weston Arthur Goodspeed, in 1907 A.D., apparently avoided the awful controversy, a dark stain.

and was equally broad and mighty, too. Seth was later credited with the following quote.

"I was born when my country was in trouble and would die when it was in trouble." From the end of the Revolution to beginning of the Civil War, Capt. Seth would always put America first and had that instinctive desire to fight for what was right!

Son, like father, later acquired a thirst for military glory and spying. The son also inherited the physical features of his famous strong persuasive Loyalist cousin Timothy Ruggles, who was Marston's political opponent. Shear, with all these rugged features would make Seth a great spy, for the patriots would always mistake him for a Loyalist spy during the War of 1812, earning him the honor rank captain. Hence, throughout the rest of his life was known as Capt. Seth.

Loyalist Timothy Dwight Ruggles

Patriot spy and thug Capt. Seth Goodspeed

Gideon Goodspeed from Dutchess County, New York, attended with older brother Lieutenant Nathanial Goodspeed from Ulster County.

Lt. Nathanial founded the grist mill that supplied the American Continental Army during the war. He was sad and worn like his old military staff coat he now proudly wore at the July meeting.

Many the others either came to East Haddam from nearby Rhode Island or further up north New York.

With all present, Nathan started the meeting. "You represent the community Nymphas will be missed by the most," he began.

Someone interrupted. "I called enlisting support at Franklin's request to investigate Marston's death!"

He laughed, looking at old Dr. Franklin, who applauded enthusiastically.

"Is that your young son Seth?" he asked, turning to Shear. "How old is he?"

"Eight. Old enough to enlist!" Shear laughed.

"My word. He may be the first man to volunteer also! We'll have to wait for him to get older before this investigation starts!"

There was more laughter and amiable protests.

"Well, let's get started. Later some awards for your service in the war of freedom! Then I'll share dreams, call for volunteers and conclude. But first, Dr. Franklin shall start, then I'll call on Silver Nathan, and how the war impacted their lives. And finally, Mary's tribute to Nathan Hale for which Goodspeed's landing was launched."

Dr. Franklin slowly stood up.

"It was in the schoolhouse at Goodspeed's landing that you and Captain Elijah Attwood preserved where Nathan Hale taught before his martyrdom. You implemented our suggestion, providing Negro education that the Crown suppressed.

"Now Tory holdovers, starting at the May Philadelphia Constitutional Convention, fight a new war to tear up the Constitution, to create monetary chaos and to tarnish the aging Washington's reputation!

"They framed 'nay' voters to create division after the vote and shifted the blame to Marston's delegation of Sandwich 'nay' voters for the very poisoning they orchestrated!

"But now we share a dream. The dream Corp. Nathan had when he protested the Yankee killing of British prisoners surrendering after Nathan Hale's martyrdom. Nathan was escorted back here by Capt. Attwood. Attwood later married one of your Goodspeeds to preserve the old schoolhouse in Nathan's memory. He started building ships as a military necessity which was both providential and appropriate for future generations to remember our sacrifices!"

Ben now stopped talking and moments slipped by.

Was Ben having a stroke? Even Dr. Benjamin Rush got concerned. It was like Dr. Ben Franklin was staring at something beyond the room.

Without looking at anyone Ben finally started to speak as if in a trance.

"They called me the sage of the convention." His eyes

narrowed. "I was delivered to that body in a sedan chair and the only one who signed that document in tears. I set the convention rules, said often that we were there to confer but not contend."

"Nathan! With providential help you overcame worry one night at Yale...didn't you?!"

Gold Nathan was too shocked and didn't know that anyone still alive could have known that!

"Did Marston tell you about that night?" Nathan stumbled.

Franklin replied, "What night?" Nathan audibly gasped.

"Nathan, I've got a message for you! A warning! Bathsheba's disgrace and execution angered the Maryland Gang. They were counting on Timothy's future. But now overnight, with the war over, Timothy had no future. So with Marston out, you're next Nathan for retributions. Take care in all you do and places you go and people you seek!"

Now everyone, including Rush, thought to themselves, *What warning?*

"With providential purpose fate chose Marston to die instead of you, though you should have strategically been the one to go first! God must be watching over you, the ship-builder!"

Nathan shuddered.

"So be careful. Your life's as much in danger as it was during the war, and we must hang together...a republic if we can keep it!'"

Ben received a huge round of applause.

"I'm tired now and will give back to you the floor, Nathan." Ben then sat down. Dr. Rush patted Ben's weary hand, as everyone broke out in applause, tears, and deeply heartfelt cheers.

Nathan, spoke "Ben you weren't called the 'sage of the convention' for nothing!"

Next, Nathan encouraged Thankful Thomas to address the group.

Thankful's beautiful quiet voice resonated in the room.

"My father died on a British prisoner of war ship during the War," she started.

"That's a horrible way to die and we never found him to bury. The fate these brave men faced with conditions so terrible. After the war, Nathan and I married January of '82. We named our first-born Solomon after my husband's brother who was buried in a small mass grave with his best friend Abraham Tayler in Marston Mills. They died as volunteer privateers on a secret mission to Fort Ticonderoga sent to rescue our retreating sentries evacuating the fort. My husband Nathan was only thirteen at the time of his older brother Solomon's death, and five years younger than Abraham was at twenty. Nymphas' kindness will be remembered," Thankful finished, crying, then sat down.

Silver Nathan got up from a creaky wooden fan-back chair. The room now was very quiet.

"When loved ones become a memory, memories become a treasure. You might say I married Thankful because we both shared a sad tale about that war. We were too young to participate in it directly. The coroner was in haste to bury the remains. He simply called all their deaths a drowning and placed the bodies in a small mass grave. Their only marker was a small twin grave-stone that Nymphas had found, the like of which was usually reserved for stillborn twins. Nathan collected his thoughts and continued.

"They were shelled on. Somebody who knew my parents recovered their bodies from the smashed boat, then found a local butcher who packed their corpses in salt for the long hot journey back to Barnstable. That trip took weeks.

"Nymphas did the best he could to make it a hero's welcome, but it was horrible. Nymphas was a comfort to our poor family, covered all expenses and arrangements. There were no permanent tributes; for fear of an enemy who could do such terrible things to the honored dead. Like with Councilman Warren after the battle of Lexington, when they spit and pissed on his hacked-up body. Shear here witnessed that himself from secure cover after the fight when every other patriot fell back in retreat. So, yes, after the war we married. My love of the sea and our happy marriage made us forget for a time the horrors of war. Nymphas' death made us feel their hate all over again!"

Dr. Rush then made eye contact with the older Nathan. Thus prompted Nathan, got up to speak.

"My apology Nathan, Dr. Rush is frustrated and angry as well. Frustrated that the coroner who performed the autopsy found nothing suspicious and lost the records."

"In other words, the coroner lied!" Dr. Rush growled. Over the angry murmurs, and vain calls for another autopsy, Silver Nathan shouted to the group.

"Who wants to join us, since we'll never get a second report?"

Shear's eight-year-old son Seth jumped up raised his hand to volunteer causing general laughter. Thankful's husband now regaining some of his composure, turned back to Nathan, who could barely withhold tears; the very man he wanted to recruit.

"We're here to serve whenever you call us!"

Corp. Nathan then instructed Samuel and Sylvia to please keep their remarks short in order to call on Shearjashub and Elizabeth. Due to the sensitive nature of Elizabeth's relationship with her notorious cousin he felt it would be more relevant for the purpose of getting more volunteers.

More importantly that the notorious cousin was the very reason the whole Nathanial line of the Barnstable's founding forebears, Rodger and Alice Layton, was disgraced.

Gideon and Lt. Nathaniel Goodspeed who both have just joined us from the Eastern New York region especially would be motivated to find more volunteers for the investigation.

Corp. Nathan addressed Elizabeth first.

"We know that some say your cousin was evil, and some say she was a victim of abuse and made a few bad choices along the way."

Elizabeth sadly shook her head and spoke quietly.

"Nathan, we knew there was fighting between them, mostly over how bad Joshua Spooner was managing money. Our offer was always there for the option of protection if it ever came to that, but her only bad choice was getting pregnant by a soldier she was taking care of. She was banking on Loyalist support for killing her Yankee husband, but because of General Burgoyne's embarrassment over the massacre of Jane McCrea by Loyalist Indian troops, there was a compromise whereby the Loyalists withdrew support for her trial. The truth is no one wanted to see a pregnant woman hang, and not one, but three, judges were involved with a jury in the ultimate decision." She sadly looked off.

Nathan motioned Shear to continue in her place.

"My patriotic wife's cousin Bathsheba was a Tory like her famous dad Timothy, and like the mobs, she had murder in her eyes," Shear began. "My wife's disgraced cousin hurt all of us by her actions. Any line other than Nathaniel Goodspeed's found missing in action was honored. Our line wasn't. We were automatically labeled deserters!" Shear looked at Gideon, spat and sat down.

"Gideon let's end with you. Please tell us your story of Tom, the son of the old sea captain that gave me a start in this patriotic business and of his dad, now long gone," Nathan encouraged as Gideon rose to speak.

The curtains fluttered and the scene faded as Gideon started to tell a similar tale of Thomas and his military adventures. Nathan was caught up in the telling.

The voice coming to Nathan's mind first was Thomas' father, following the sea and talking about catching striped bass as Nathan stared out his office window. The curtains fluttered gently on that mild mid-summer day chasing off a fly on the windowsill.

The voice then changed, in Nathan's vision, from Thomas' dad praising the beauty of the Sound and the Connecticut River to Thomas' son who previously had a conversation with him in this very room just before Thomas and Cousin Nathaniel fled to New Brunswick.

"There were only three of us when our father, Thomas whom we loved, died in '74, leaving Simeon who was thirteen and me just a year younger," Gideon continued.

"We all missed the skipper dearly! Our lives were shattered when he died. Then we found ourselves relocated to Uncle Joseph's farm. Joseph was put in charge of us since our mother Puella was gone as well," he wept.

"At age fifteen, Simeon did something stupid and Uncle Joe let him enlist.

Simeon only fifteen! Anyway, young Simeon, in the winter of '77 died at Valley Forge, wracked by exposure! Didn't even see his seventeenth birthday. I wished I could have been with him or died with him!

"Well, that started my guilt and anger which only got worse. I transferred my anger onto British soldiers, which was stupid! Why couldn't I challenge my own guilt? Nothing anybody could have done would add a day to his life.

"The military asked for volunteers. Against the better angels of my nature an idea had been sparked. A grisly military maneuver had been successfully executed in the South by Francis Marion's troops."

"Why did you volunteer then?" Old Nathan asked.

"For revenge's sake." Thomas shrugged, now older and wiser and combat experienced.

"Anyway," Thomas continued, "we drilled the exercise. It took a week to perfect and get right. We would fake a retreat. We were to fake retreating our last round from our muskets, dreadful muskets stolen from the enemy. It would be a slow run to trick the enemy to get closer. Then we'd turn at a particular moment and bang! We were the heroes of the regiment even before the event itself, before blood had ever been spilt."

Dr. Benjamin Rush had been there as well. He rose to share more of the story. He was also requested to work in Rhode Island that fall. As the crash of battle commenced, the rescue teams appeared, and the bloody work began. Rush had smiled to keep morale up among his staff and it worked. Those present marveled at the old man's ability to sustain the pressure and horrors without never once appearing to grow weak or falter. He kept his own spirits up along with the rest of his staff's.

In the third hour, a pale young man, gaunt and covered with dried blood and the smoke of battle came into the confines of one of the tents where Dr. Benjamin Rush was working, with another man accompanying him. Benjamin rushed to the pale man but then noticed fresh blood on the other man and quickly attended him first.

"Name!" he asked as he tore the man's bloody shirt open.

"Goodspeed, Thomas," the gaunt man replied.

"Your charge, Thomas?" Rush asked as he worked on his partner.

"Nathaniel, my cousin, sir," Thomas replied.

"Aide, take this man out; process for cleaning routine compress and patch. Nothing serious."

Then turning back to Tom, Dr. Rush asked, "Are you alright? You're pale."

"Yes, I think ...no, I'm fine".

"Then go with your cousin. Stay with him."

Then Rush was quickly off somewhere else, leaving only the aide to guide Tom and his cousin Nathan to a less busy location.

Tom looked up at Nathan who was crying along with him. He considered the situation.

In August, an angry man enlists at age 18. September, that angry young man brutally kills a British soldier, iron-ically too late to stop the very image of his dead brother's face! God! Thomas' thoughts moved him. *Death changes a man. More so that man who draws blood in vengeance. It kills both its recipient as well as its sender! ...God!*

The battle raged on, but it was over for Thomas. He knew he would die if he went back. He soon lost track of Nathaniel and time. He had murdered a good man in front of God! There was a spiritual lock on every trigger of every muzzle loader on the field. He did not even know what had happened to the rifle he had used or where he last had it.

The only memory he had was the soldier's face before and his face after he had... then his mind would shut off in a thick cloud of silence.

After a time, he came back to the medical outpost and collapsed by a tree that still had leaves and trunk and limbs all intact.

"Is that you, Thomas?" he heard a man's soft voice as in a dream. "Thomas!" the voice called, more insistent and louder.

The earth started moving then shaking. "Thomas, wake up, you must stay awake!"

He knew now that it was not a dream but the voice of the medical man. He would have gotten up with a start, but hands restrained him from getting up too quickly.

"Now, now, take it easy, there." Tom recognized the voice.

"Benjamin," Tom mused.

"That is correct. Thomas, can you open your eyes?" the voice implored.

"If I ever have a son," Thomas said, slowly opening his eyes, "I am going to name him Benjamin."

"I would consider that an honor and a privilege! Thank you! Now slowly get up," the voice instructed.

"He is dead!" Thomas blurted out.

"Who's dead?" the voice asked.

"My eyes!" suddenly Thomas cried, blinking his eyes rapidly.

"Can you see?" the friendly voice asked.

"My eyes, doctor, I cannot see," Thomas said more, as if drugged not panicked.

"There, there. Relax," the friendly voice continued, "Your vision will return. This too shall pass. Just sit up for a while and we will just talk. You've been through a lot of stress today young man."

"How did you know my name was Benjamin?" the voice continued.

That was a mystery even to Thomas, but as a distraction it served to calm him down immediately. "How did you know my name was Thomas?" he countered.

The man laughed. "I take good notes."

"The dried blood is still on your face." He felt Dr. Rush's hand rubbing his forehead, then more carefully around his nose and eyes.

"Where did…" He stopped himself from completing the question for fear it would bring bad memories back to the patient. But in the process of the rubbing Thomas began seeing things, blurry at first, but then quickly gained focus, mesmerized by the hands rubbing his face.

"When I said, 'He is dead,' that was for the man I killed."

"I see." Then Thomas saw the man's eyes focus in on his eyes.

"Oh, I see that you can see again," the doctor responded. Dr. Rush slowly moved his finger from side to side and up and down to observe Thomas' tracking response.

"Saul is now Paul" he chuckled.

"Now comes the hard part," Thomas continued.

"What do you mean?" the doctor asked.

"I have to live with that," the man confessed. The doctor inclined his head like a bird encountering something interesting. "I mean, I murdered someone, someone who reminded me of my brother!" he cried.

"There, there, there. Do not cry. That is what you were trained to do and there's no shame. War is wasteful and that is one of the first lessons a veteran must learn immediately if he's got any heart at all and wants to survive.

"And you have plenty of heart," Rush added embracing Thomas. "There, there, have a good cry. I was hoping you could have done that earlier when I first saw you. I knew something was wrong when I asked you earlier if you were all right."

"You remember," Thomas added dourly.

"Yes, I remember," Benjamin responded, drawing back to a more formal doctor patient posture, smiled then nodding. "Riddles always keep my attention until I can solve them."

Gideon continued saying something and now Gold Nathan attention snapped back to the present because he heard Gideon used his name.

"Nathan, Dr. Rush found Thomas for he had passed out under a tree..." Gideon interjected then continued.

"Dr. Rush over there comforted him. I broke down then, too, given that same insane assignment in New York; further south but I was still stinging from the embarrassment of Bathsheba's treachery and conscientiously refused the order...Probably wouldn't have otherwise!" Gideon then laughed bitterly.

"For my reward, when I left my unit, I was labeled a deserter, even when serving as long as Shear over there! My other brothers were all killed or missing in action because of that harlot's actions, and we were labeled deserters!"

Many were tarnished by the harlot's actions. Bathsheba had tried to poison her Yankee husband and take his life. Later, by having some British thugs beat her husband to death then stuff him in their own well when she found out that she was pregnant.

Later in life, after that terrible experience, Thomas learned to forgive and love his enemies. He named his son Benjamin, after Dr. Rush who comforted him on that terrible day, as Thomas had promised lying blind on the battlefield.

After his discharge, he found his war buddy Nathaniel wandering the countryside of Rhode Island. One night Nathaniel almost got killed in a knife fight but, fortunately Thomas being bigger and stronger, saved him. They made great campfires and talked about their boyhood friends and games they used to play.

After the knife fight, they found themselves working on the road of their many aimless travels. It was Dr. Rush who recognized Thomas and Nathaniel immediately. This particular day and evening when they all together witnessed another woman being tared and feathered. They worked the whole night into the next day to save her life from asphyxiation. They removed tar with solvent and carefully used towels until the victim had enough bare skin to breath and survive.

During that month Dr. Benjamin Rush tried to talk them into staying in America but understood them when they finally decided that they were going to leave America forever. It was just at the close of the Revolution when the nineteen-year-old moved to New Brunswick.

Later in his new country Thomas found, courted and married Lois and they had that son he named Benjamin. The father found the Lord through that same son, and like his son, later became a Baptist. But the biggest irony of all is that from eyewitness accounts, it was recollected that he said later, notwithstanding his service with the rebels, that his sympathies were with the British in the Revolutionary struggle.

Nymphas' memorial moved forward and in the final ceremony of the meeting Ben Franklin got up to address the wrongs that had been cast on the Nathaniel line.

"Lt. Nathaniel, we honor your service. You provided bread from your grist-mill on Fishkill Creek for the Continental Army. You did that in spite of your grief for your younger brothers who were lost in battle and unfairly branded as deserters. Let us now make amends!

"Again, thank you for your service and support! Allow us to extend to you and the other members of your distinguished line, full title and honor to the following land in Dutchess County, New York, where to you, Lieutenant, the following said lands, under date of 1788, Vol. LV, page 24, Certificate No. 12, Lt. Nathaniel is granted Lot 163 of 430 acres, in Chemung Town for his Revolutionary services. To Samuel, other lands in Pawlet, Vermont, for your work as a Privateer to do with as you see fit. And Shear, and to you, Elizabeth, other land in Montgomery, Vermont," Nathan continued.

"We know in his memory, and Nathan Hale's, that even if we succeed with the 3/5 Compromise to limit voting opposition and get it to stop for all transatlantic activity on cruel slave transportation by 1808, as agreed, that we will still be a long way from abolishing slavery in America. That probably cost Marston his life, along with his inspiring me to continue building ships!"

There was more applause and more tears.

"Slavery and indentured servitude is the law of the land by the Northwest Ordinance passed a year ago in July, but plans to build canals with James Wilson's help, to start establishing secret fugitive slave routes north of the Ohio River, are underway, as I speak."

Samuel raised his hand, "Question!"

"Samuel," the speaker acknowledged.

"Why do you think that's important since slavery in America is slowly dying anyway? Won't 1808 cessation of transatlantic black slave transport from Africa stop that growth?" Samuel awaited an answer.

"Good question, but recent intelligence indicates otherwise."

"How so?"

Nathan replied, "The English already have a machine that can quickly and efficiently remove cotton seeds, which currently, in America, is the only obstacle to limiting the amount, quality and quantity of cotton produced, which we know is causing the slave market to shrink," he continued.

"But once we're clever enough and resourceful enough, as Americans are, to figure out how they are doing it, and start doing it here, cotton production will inevitably soar. So, the black slave population will suddenly be in demand."

With a smile Samuel raised his hand again.

"It will have to be a very deep canal to get my ships through, Nathan!" he offered.

Corp. Nathan laughed and smiled.

"Marston, Franklin, Rush and I saw something that was written up that got our attention at the Philadelphia Convention. We, among other delegates saw from the banks a fire engine boat test demonstration and were amazed with what we saw. The damned thing moves and can haul cargo and do so quickly, even in shallower waters."

"Good Lord!" some in the room erupted.

Samuel turned, suddenly very animated, "How soon?"

Nathan chuckled. "We're working on it now." The entire group broke out in applause.

Now as planned, Mary Kellogg Goodspeed had the honor of closing. She began casually.

"Does anyone know when striped bass season starts?" she asked the audience.

"Spring," someone in the back answered. Chuckling was heard.

"Good, I see we have a native here!" she retorted. More laughter. "Great. And the rest of the year?" she asked, but unable to keep herself from laughing.

"No, terrible!" someone else answered. It was one of their boat fitters answering, no doubt!

"Correct!" Mary smiled. "So, where would we find Nathan Hale in the spring?"

"Mouth of the Connecticut!" several voices answered.

"Doing what?" she prompted.

"Fishing for stripers!" The crowd responded in near unison.

By this time Mary had the entire assembly in the palm of her hand, as she had intended. Gold Nathan always marveled at how fast she could captivate a group.

Even grumpy Gideon was starting to catch on and enjoyed it. Days of war and betrayal started to dissolve, at least at this one meeting on this special day.

"Now let's be solemn for a spell and know why I'm here..." Mary's voice held their attention.

"About a hundred years ago my great grandpa Sammy Kellogg was out with Sarah, his pa's first wife, and his only brother when they were killed by Indians out in the woods. A bad place to be!

"But one Indian brave who didn't like killing took his hawk warned off the other excited Indians, managed to stop the others from killing young Samuel."

Mary's casual mannerisms in the telling caused some in the audience to start laughing before their wives stopped them. But Mary just smiled and finished.

Her tone shifted now. She got serious when she talked

about the balance of how freedom was never free and exploring had its costs. Then she launched into a tale about how the schoolhouse was restored after Nathan Hale's death and what that taught.

September 1776 – Nathan Hale's Final Day

A Loyalist cousin, Samuel Hale, close to Queen's Ranger Major Robert Roger turned Nathan Hale in. Then Queen's Ranger Roger turned Nathan directly in to British General William Howe. Being held for spying, the authorities learned about his aversion to battle as motivation for spying instead of killing.

At this point General Howe recommended release, and for a while it looked like that was what they were actually going to do.

But later on Saturday the 21st, they had provost marshal, Captain Cunningham question him. Captain Cunningham told Nathan that they were not going to hang Nathan but tried to get him to spy for them in exchange for a death sentence.

"Sir, with all due respect," Nathan Hale bravely and boldly responded, "based on moral principles and ethics of slavery under British authority to not be allowed to educate Negros, I decline the invite and choose death instead!"

In a last attempt to change his mind, the captain tore up the letters that Captain Hale had given him to give to his mother, in front of him. Nathan simply bowed politely and asked to be excused.

Nathan's final words, at his execution were, "I only regret that I have but one life to give for my country."

So now Gold Nathan had been warned by Dr. Franklin, as described earlier, in that meeting. Besides that, there was still another challenge waiting for him. It was a struggle that hit him very hard, planned out by an enemy who never sleeps.

The Day After the Meeting

Massachusetts founding father, Roger Goodspeed and Alice Layton Goodspeed's first-born son was Nathaniel, from which the unfairly treated line started. Founder Roger Goodspeed's last male son named Ebenezer, the sixth child, was a totally different story.

Ebenezer, born December 1655, the second to last child, grew up and turned out to be a remarkable man, ahead of his time. He put his daughters through college at Yale which in those days was highly unusual indeed. He lived to be over one hundred years old.

So Gold Nathan's fortunes were about to bear fruit to the next generation, delivering a nation from slavery, long after his passing.

In the dog days of summer 1777, Nymphas helped the poor family of a humble sea-faring background to restore their dignity. It was discovered in the author's research that Christopher Tayler, the deceased Abraham's Tayler's dad, avenged his son's death by volunteering for a secret mission, much like the one rescue mission at Fort Ticonderoga where young Solomon Goodspeed and Abraham died, in a vain rescue attempt of those patriot occupants. In an attempt to recapture another fort in Rhode Island, under similar circumstances, Christopher Tayler, age sixty-one, made him the oldest soldier of the Goodspeed and Tayler clan. No other record of service found; showed that Christopher was on a one-time secret mission.

Back to Nathan, he woke up feeling great. He praised God for the opportunity to restore the dignity of the Nathaniel line, with generous land grants of compensation, from Dr. Franklin's office. Nathan got up early for another appointment.

Flies buzzed on the open windowsill of his study. It was the start of a beautiful clear morning. An early wind dispersed the flies, moving the lace curtains back.

He was meeting with another creative visitor, Eli Whitney.[5]

Eli was at Yale. Eli was a young and promising Yankee from Massachusetts and was five years away from making cotton gins a serious production tool.

---

5 Author's Note: אוּרים ותמים (Hebrew; 'Ûrîm wə-Tummîm), Yale's motto in English "Light and truth" which in Ebenezer's mind stood for the light of Christ and truth of His resurrection to set the captive free from sin. And for a time that was true while today's philosophers, including Marx had and opposite interpretation of what "light and truth" meant. Or perhaps the founders of the college had too great a love for kings and men that the college was dedicated upon and perhaps of more materialistic concerns in which this author finds very troubling in this current day and age with founding of another sinister institution the current college promotes: Skull and Bones. (To which this author's distant cousins had a certain controversial affiliation with, who later became presidents of this country) That by the close of the 18th century some awesome leaders were produced with strong propensity to Judeo Christian service and philosophy. Their kind spirit and strong belief in limited government(s), free enterprise, individual freedom, and an instinctive desire to stand up for what was right: As Ebenezer modeled himself to be "remembered and revered".

Soon sounds of churning carriage wheels were heard on the gravel, then the expectant rap on the front door of the adjoining hall outside the only entryway to Nathan's study. Eli Whitney, that morning had just come up from Yale on invitation from Nathan.

"What are your plans when you graduate?" the older man inquired.

"Tutoring down South in a lucrative area," Eli responded with a wink. "I'll be tutoring the widow and family of Revolutionary War hero General Nathanael Greene. I'm invited to Mrs. Greene's Georgia farm, where I will be working on the cotton gin with the plantation manager, Phineas Miller."

"Be in the world not of the world," Nathan laughed as he quoted the scripture.

"I know, master," Eli mocked, then grew serious as the meeting prompted.

"You know that down there...Where is it you're going to be tutoring?" Nathan queried.

"Georgia."

"Near Savannah?"

"Hopefully."

Nathan smiled, "Not warm enough here?"

"I don't mind the heat like you do," Eli followed. Nathan frowned.

"Don't expect to be making a fortune anytime soon. Why don't you stay up here where resources abound? It will be hard for me to support you with you living down there, you know!" As like Clinton De Witt, Gold Nathan supported other inventors and builders, like Eli Whitney.

Nathan continued after Eli nodded.

"I'm not anxious to make the South prosperous in slave cotton trading but I'm wondering how you're coming."

"I'm able to produce screens and fine gear teeth cheap enough, and close to copying British gins with improvements," the young inventor reported.

"Good!" Nathan leaned forward. "Now how about building me engines on a mass production scale for that Connecticut River yonder?"

"Oh, you plan on doing it yourself, Nathan?" Eli asked, playing dumb.

Nathan countered. "No, but I have associates that can make parts quicker and cheaper. And cheaper also means lighter engines."

Nathan knew that one problem solved by Eli would create another problem; to promote slavery by the enemy. But he saw in Whitney the solution which would eventually be the answer; promote mass production in the north and military might to slow or stop the will of the "friends of slavery" if it ever came to civil war or strife.

Nathan warned Eli that he would keep him on a starvation diet as far as becoming rich on the cotton gin project was concerned.

Although the meeting ended on friendly terms, Eli made weak excuses for the benefits and merits of cotton production and played down the reality of human suffering as just "rumors" and "highly exaggerated claims".

August 1788 - Doctor Breadcrumb and Doctor Baker

Now there was an overwhelming challenge. With no more investigative volunteers, Nathan's troubles weren't over.

Although he had built many ships, most now needed to be dry-docked. Nathan was forced to build up his fleet, but in peace time there was no real demand. To build enough ships to establish communication from the Chesapeake to Long Island Sound he needed money enough to build a massive number of ships which were estimated to take seven years to build! Nathan would also have to deal with his own personal health and safety risk issues from the gang.

"You look pale. I think you need to see a doctor," said Mary.

"No. I'm not...I'm fine," was his quick response.

"You look terrible!" she rebutted.

Nathan knew the discussion was over! Especially when she went over to the matte painted board in the kitchen and in upper case with chalk and a flourish dashed off the word "PERIOD!!!" then dramatically erased everything, including groceries and chore lists, off that board in order to get his attention.

At this point Nathan knew he was in trouble! Especially when she broke the chalk stick in the process!

Doctor Thaddeus Breadcrumb's office attendant not liking Nathan's remark about the dubious doctor's name, coldly replied,

"I beg your pardon! It's 'THE' Doctor Thaddeus Breadcrumb to you, sir!"

Nathan cringed,

as the surly male attendant pointed to the Doctor's study, "The door is open!"

Dr. Thaddeus curtly voice curtly rang out, as Nathan meekly entered the room and offered Nathan a seat and as curtly retorted, having overheard him "My bread-crumbs do save lives!"

Nathan humbly nodded with guilt, as charged by both the receptionist and the doctor himself.

"What is the nature of your visit?" the doctor continued.

"I'm pale they say," Nathan explained.

"I see you do look pale. How long did they say?" The doctor's chair creaked.

"I don't know."

The doctor leaned back, "Soreness of joints or pain?"

"Sometimes." Nathan replied.

The doctor took a file from a shelf and read it with a frown of concentration.

Then he looked up, "I think, that you have diabetes. Do you have any relatives that have had it?"

"Yes", Nathan responded "a cousin."

The doctor's eyes narrowed.

"If you diet and exercise, and eat fruit, vegetables, avoid drink and eat only fish...then there is still hope."

"Thanks for being forthright," Nathan said as in a bad dream. He knew that diabetes was a death sentence wherein the patient only had a few months.

How can I get anything done? he thought to himself in total despair.

When he told Mary, she cried. But at least they were both happy about just one thing. No matter how despaired he got, they both knew he would never take his life even though one time they both knew that he was stupid enough to try! Telling no one, he made a vow: to carry on with the mission!

He and his wife went to church more often. He started a library and along with a well-worn Geneva Bible collected classics like the Italian Divine Comedy, Shakespeare, Foxe's Book of the Martyrs, and Moliere plays. The Rise and Progress of Religion in the Soul was a manuscript copy which was his favorite since Nymphas had personally given him. That tome had influenced William Wilberforce the abolitionist, as it did Nathan, after its author's recent death while Nathan was still a student at Yale.

For Nathan and his wife, the weeks became a month, and the months a year. One day when it looked like he was going to make it to his second year his wife began questioning his diagnosis.

"Hey, Breadcrumb! Get a second opinion!" she blurted, revealing her honest negative opinion of the doctor. She had heard rumors about him all this time.

Shaking his head, he looked up and just smiled, knowing that would trigger a reaction. She stormed over to the kitchen matte board.

"You're driving me crazy!" she said, but this time without erasing his chore list. She wrote in big enough font for the neighbors to read, "GET TRACKING!!!"

Then she sent him packing.

"Go visit Doctor Stephen Baker. I've heard good things about him. Now go, or you won't get dinner tonight!"

Nathan obediently did just that, laughing all that way, but looking over his shoulder nonetheless heeding Dr. Franklin's warning from previously.

Dr. Stephen had no attendant.

"How long ago was that prognosis?" he asked with a grin.

"Almost two years," Nathan answered.

"Almost two years," the doctor repeated to keep himself from laughing. He hadn't asked Nathan the usual questions because he knew something that Nathan didn't know.

"Well, I'm afraid you're definitely going to live. So, what do you need me for?"

"I don't have diabetes then?" the patient queried.

"Nope!" The new 'real' doctor laughed, giving Nathan an even broader smile. The doctor's chair creaked as he leaned forward. He patted Nathan's knee and spoke.

"Dr. Breadcrumb is gone," the doctor informed him.

"What!?" Nathan recoiled.

"Didn't you hear? He and his assistant are gone. They both left town." The doctor's chair creaked again as he leaned back. "Your Dr. Breadcrumb was a fraud."

"So, I guess I'm back to just having to worry about getting killed and building a fleet," he said sarcastically, but his relief was palpable.

When he told Mary, she marched back to the matte painted board and chalked, "GOOD!!!"

The next day when he went into the kitchen Nathan read on the board, "MORE TIME IN YARD, LESS IN LIBRARY!" Then Nathan noticed a limerick Mary had cut out from a newspaper, and had left the poem where he usually ate breakfast. He laughed as he read:

A farmer's dog came into town;
his Christian name was "Runt."
No noble pedigree had he,
but piddling was his stunt.
And as he strutted down the street,
'twas beautiful to see
His work on every lamppost,
his mark on every tree.
He watered every gateway, too,
and never missed a post,
For piddlin' was his specialty
and piddlin' was his boast.
The city curs looked on amazed
with deep and jealous rage
To see a simple country dog,
the piddler of his age
They smelled him over one by one,
then smelled him two by two.
While noble "Runt" in high disdain
stood still till they were through.
Then, just to show the whole shebang
he didn't give a damn,
He went into the butcher shop and salted down a ham.
Yet all the while this country dog did never wink or grin,
But blithely piddled out of town as he had piddled in

The city dogs a convention held
to ask, "What did defeat us?"
But no one ever put them wise,
that "Runt" had diabetes!

The good doctor Stephan eventually befriended Nathan and later joined Nathan's inner circle after Dr. Franklin's death in 1790, when they discovered that Dr. Breadcrumb was a fake name after all. He and his so called male assistant had disappeared from the community, but the worst revelation of all: Nathan's earlier symptoms were actually poison induced to delay his own production schedule and investigation!

Dirty Abe, the poison assassin, and the fake doctor meet

"So, what you're telling me is he got a second opinion?" Abe asked, trembling.
The thug named Thaddeus but wasn't... nodded.

After Franklin's Death

1797

In August, with the fleet finally made ready, Nathan and Samuel met back in Corp. Nathan's office. James Armistead Lafayette was seated in a dark corner and Corp. Nathan was at his desk, with the curtains drawn for security: This wasn't to be an ordinary meeting.

This was young Nathan's first assignment. James was their lead agent.

"Welcome Nathan!" the boss said.

In silence Gold Nathan studied the departed Solomon's younger brother, Nathan; the old man's hands clasped together, his elbows on the arms of the tall-backed chair.

Drawn curtains and James' silence had its intended effect. This was going to be a dangerous assignment. Slowly Corp. Nathan leaned forward in the old creaking swivel chair until his forearms rested on his massive desk. A dark sky reduced light in the room and rain audibly fell on the panes. It was raining all the way down the North Atlantic to the Chesapeake.

"We're aware of suspicious activity at one of the Maryland's estuary rice plantations."

James' chair also creaked. In the corner's darkness as he added to Corp. Nathan's statement, without getting up. "Methyl iodide is a naturally occurring substance from rice beds and works as a sedative. If further concentrated a poison." He then added," Abe and the mysterious Dr. Thaddeus were also spotted there. The day-workers in the field behave like ghosts, no laughter or drumming at night, very odd!" he shivered. "There are no slave graveyards, sea burials only, again, very odd!!"

Gold Nathan joined in, "We want to get remains for our medical team to examine. And since this is Maryland, where neither of you have ever been seen, we will send you," Nathan proposed.

"It will be dangerous work done at night, under terrible conditions, done alone off skiff diving platforms with underwater diving bells. Messy work, with remains in various stages of decomposition. Poison remains down to the bone!" he warned. "You will be watched and surrounded by death on every side!"

The oppressive rain increased in intensity so that further conversation was now difficult. Corp. Nathan spoke louder.

"Will you accept this assignment?" he asked. The rain now was competing with voices, however both Samuel and Silver Nathan simply nodded. The looks in their eyes validated that Nathan had picked the right men for the assignment. The instinctive desire to stand up for what is right influenced all present so thickly one could have cut it with a knife.

"Good!" A contract from hell was set in stone and thunder and lightning now ratified the deal!

Corp. Nathan laughed to break the solemnity of the meeting and signal that they were done.

Corp. Nathan called Samuel and Nathan back into his study. James was elsewhere. The curtains were now drawn open, greeted by an early evening August breeze.

"This is the last time I'll order anyone into so dangerous an assignment," who compressed his lips and spoke quietly. "Are you sure you want to go through with this and leave Thankful and your family?"

"Without question, Nathan," the younger Nathan replied, eyes tearing. "I told you earlier to call me. So here I am."

The older Nathan smiled. "And so you did Nathan! Thank you...so you did. God speed to both of you!"

When Nathan told Thankful he was going to sea she was troubled. When they named their one child 'Nathan', out of nowhere she asked, "Who will live after you Nathan?" She wanted to take it back. But he shrugged and laughed "We're older now, dear; and no one lasts forever. Hush! Don't cry, it's a good name and it's time."

On the eve of leaving this final time they would ever

be together, she placed his hand over her hardening abdomen, and said simply,

"I'll name this one Elijah. Save a nation!"

How did she know it would be a boy? he thought.

"Women know these things, dear, especially now having named our last Nathan after you," she answered as though she had read his mind.

They had named every child after their parental families, with only one exception, Rebecca! Oddly the one on whom bad times would especially fall!

The first child was named after his father Nathan's older brother Solomon, who died for independence with his friend Abraham Tayler during the evacuation of a fort July 7, 1777.

The second was named Thomas after Thankful's father's last name, who died on a prisoner of war ship, in some godforsaken harbor.

Husband and wife, with tears of joy, hugged on those two sacred occasions when they named those successive newborns. With the names of those soldiers who had made the ultimate sacrifice!

The third was to be Jabez, after Nathan's dad, but she turned out to be a girl! So close as they could come, they named her Jane!

The next, Jabez of course, but sadly, he was born on the eve of Marston's mysterious death.

Now the fifth was named Rebecca, the last female child. Why not Thankful? Why not after herself? Thankful would honor Nathan but not her own name. Nathan?! Alas! With that came enmity between mother and daughter! Thankful, had you only known that grief was heading your way particularly with this one sweet, beautiful child.

What's in a name? Everything! It would have been something for the child to hold on to in times of trouble.

Then finally came Nathan, named after his father.

The couple hugged just a little longer, embraced one last time, and bid their good-byes.

Oct. 11, 1797

Wednesday evening Corp. Nathan waited for the messages to start conveying up the coast from Maryland by light, horse, or pigeon. His mind was on two issues this particular night. The last salvage mission of the remains recovered had already told the story. This final night he was glad and relieved that it was finally coming to a close.

The second issue was his intern Eli Whitney, who in '92 finally made the breakthrough on the cotton gin and was gradually changing the world for the worse; and giving friends of slavery a second wind!

On Nathan's desk lay an angry letter from Eli. He had discovered that Nathan had been behind the rumor that Whitney had stolen the idea for the cotton gin from British inventors in the South. Worse than that, Nathan openly promoted the notion that Whitney's models were damaging the cotton fibers during the ginning process. So, the English and Irish Southern planters now refused to buy cotton ginned on Whitney and Miller's machines.

Other enterprises were quick to copy the simplicity of the process and violate Eli's patent. Neither partner could afford to prosecute!

There was deep contrast to the lives of those involved. One side was aspiring to become rich and famous on the backs of mankind, and the other two, brave privateers, who, along with their resource teams, were now risking their lives for freedom's sake, on the open waters.

Somewhere off the Shores of Maryland –
Early Evening

Samuel and Silver Nathan were in 56°F water. They both had on warmer wax which was impregnated gear with small weights sewn into the waist-seamed jackets. Armistead's privateer ship lay just up the shipping lane with lamps poised to transmit the first night message. Side shields were in place because Abe's men would be on sentry duty.

Seth, now eighteen and every bit as big and muscular a man as his father, had great empathy for the men in cold water. He stood heavily equipped with two other armed privateers with muskets, rifles, ropes, and tackle.

Aboard the gun vessel, James prayed for Samuel and Nathan. He nodded to the semaphore operator to send the first message. The "MEN IN BELL" message went up the coast, by light, horse, and pigeon.

Samuel and Nathan were in the diving bell, took their last gulp of air and oriented themselves to the deep.

"Targets spotted," they signaled one another. They could make out the canvas straps and on one corpse saw the ball weight iron ankle bands. They would have to dive.

With experience and plenty of lead it didn't take long to secure their find, then they were back in the bell and inhaling another gulp of the now stale lamp air. They transferred the shrouded bodies to another set of hooks and yanked hard on skiff lines to signal the crank operators to lift once the drag hooks were disengaged from the straps.

With one last gulp of air they swam up over the bell top, grabbed the lifelines to the skiff, and pulled hand over hand to the surface.

The skiff lamp was lit and trained down on them for first time in the mission, but now cast a blood chilling red caution beam of light. As they reached the surface, they heard muffled sounds of ordinance and men shouting.

Up line, Armistead saw the flashes then heard the delayed rifle and musket shots. He didn't need to give the operator the last message who already signaled: "ENEMY ENGAGEMENT!"

What was a retrieval mission suddenly became a rescue operation. Sails unfurled and James' gunship was now on its way, rushing to the endangered skiff.

Memories From the Past

When Corp. Nathan first saw the "MEN IN BELL" message, there had been a two-hour delay from the time when the message was sent. To Nathan and Mary, it seemed only within minutes after that came the dreaded "ENEMY ENGAGEMENT" message. Nathan started praying in his quiet study as though the battle was going on all around him

Rain pelted the window. The next messages came ten minutes later and caused Nathan and Mary to drop to their knees and Nathan to cry out.

"MINOR WOUNDS>>> >>>NATHAN MISSING>>>"

The sound of the rain increased, now filling the room with its sounds the same way it had when Nathan made that terrible contract in stone with Silver Nathan and Samuel! And now with the bad weather moving in so quickly it became impossible to receive further lamp signals!

In this moment even thunder and lightning raged like a battle cry!

Silver Nathan had taken a mortal hit from one enemy cannon ball that was fired before Armistead's ship could reach them to interdict. It shattered parts of the skiff. Samuel, just behind him, was the only one that saw him go down.

Corp. Nathan, an experienced war veteran, knew exactly what had happened.

Once the gathering of servants was dismissed, Nathan and Mary freely grieved. Later, after Mary had retired and the weather had cleared, Nathan sent the last message down line: "SEA BURIAL>>> >>>CONFIDENTIAL>>> >>>REPORT TO BASE>>> >>>OVER"

Earlier that morning just before dawn, Nathan was very depressed in his study and tried to open the left top drawer. To his irritation he found it sticking and squeaking as he took Marston's pistol out, the very one given him so many years earlier. He placed it to his left, closed the offending drawer, and was reminded of his Yale days.

Then quietly opened the desk door on the right and took from the top shelf a filled cut-glass brandy decanter. He calmly got up, walked over, and closed the office door, locked it, then went back and sat down. *Fill the tumbler one third full*, he thought to himself.

Let it be emphasized that he rarely, if ever, drank, so these actions would have alarmed anyone that knew him looking into his study window at this early hour of the day.

From that day forward, there would be no Gold Nathan or Silver Nathan. From that day on there was just Old Nathan.

In tears, he swirled the brandy tumbler and regarded the legs dancing therein. He paused without taking a sip and placed it down on the desk then reached over slowly. He took the pistol, drew back the hammer, then one click with fingers on the trigger guard, raised the deadly fifty caliber barrel to his left temple.

Battle Aftermath

As the privateer vessel pulled up alongside the skiff, the enemy's cannon put into submission, the shooting stopped. Samuel, still at the side of the damaged skiff, handed back his pistol.

"Give me a rock!" he said angrily, then took the rock and plunged it beneath the surface.

Atop, the men concentrated on where Samuel had dived. The skiff crew was so focused, they ignored James' hailing from the ship's forecastle. The skiff crew members and wounded survivors were indisposed to respond. The quartermaster was about to hail again but Lafayette motioned him to silence.

"We'll get you next time!" cried a voice from a shore bull horn.

Aside to his cronies Abe hissed, "Was that him our ball hit?" he relished with a hideous grin.

On the skiff, Seth aimed his musket toward the voice and fired a shot so close it parted the hairs on the top of Abe's head with a dull whirling buzz. An inch lower would have removed the top of his skull. Abe hit the dirt and made a mess! Even his men laughed at him.

Seth boomed back louder than the bullhorn could, "We'll be waiting for you, you coward!"

Someone on Abe's side blew a booger to stifle a laugh. The word "coward" had triggered him. Those aboard the skiff laughed, too. Suddenly Samuel's head broke the surface.

"Help me! I've got him!" When they all saw Nathan's body many of them cried.

James, saddened, informed the skiff crew of the last message he just received in a soft voice, "Burial will be at sea, those are our orders."

East Haddam

The office windowpanes were violently blown in and woke everybody up. Nathan jumped up and aimed the massive pistol, the second click for business at the demolished window.

"Don't shoot master, it's only me!" a trembling voice announced.

"Madagascar, what the hell are you doing, my friend?!" Nathan yelled. The Black man leaned and looked in to explain.

"I thought you were going to kill yourself!"

"Good God, no... wait. I hear someone pounding on the door!" Nathan started.

Madagascar was a prince who was captured by a rival black tribe and sold twice to European mercenaries; then later sold to a good woman in America who bought his freedom. However, the man chose to work for Nathan to pay the woman back. He was angry at the village he once loved, so he took the slave ship's name and never looked back.

Red Sky at Morning

With the red dawn of day, they made departure preparations. The crew secured the dead, the diving bell, and other equipment, and ordinance, they weighed anchor, now drifting quickly out to sea. The medical team was packed up and now aboard. All were homeward bound.

A few miles up, in deeper water, the ship could come closer to the shore. There they heard cries. Scanning the shoreline James spotted an emaciated lone black youth in dirty rags.

"Man overboard!" James barked.

Friday, 13th October, 1797

The ships arrived in early evening at Goodspeed's landing. They dominated the harbor and became a floating city.

Thankful, as Nathan's guest, had received the tragic news from Madagascar, escorted from Barnstable. Nathan's burial at sea was from Block Island Sound off the shores of Rhode Island to Goodspeed's landing. It was a long and sentimental journey for a tired stressed soul.

When Samuel got off the ship, Thankful Thomas approached him.

"My dear, dear friend, if only I could have been with him," she added now drying her eyes; his, too, and even laughed at Samuel's own pathetic condition.

Dr. Benjamin Rush talked with Nathan at that evening's meeting.

"I have another close friend. His name is Johann August Arfvedson and he thinks he can identify what the unknown metal in the salt is. This chloride substance controls depression, which would explain the calm serenity of the inmates of this plantation. It wasn't just general amiability of a good slave plantation, but if anything, a good cover-up for slavers. That allowed them to get away with more serious crimes of abuse."

Nathan sat back in his chair now, looking first at the boy then smiled, and grew serious looking over at the marines who also attended the meeting.

"Who'd you say you found in the brush?"

"One of Abe's grandsons. No weapons found on him. The one who wounded the lad had the good sense to shoot and then scoot. For all we know that one who got away may have shot the grandson and the boy! Our Marine from the launch said he heard two shots. When we rushed the forest, we just caught glimpses, but by that time, he'd gotten too far away to apprehend or shoot."

"So, you're saying they might have had two active shooters?" Nathan queried.

"We've identified them, but they've identified us," the man replied. Nathan whistled.

After the meeting, Nathan spoke to Thankful and Samuel.

"Thankful, Abe now has a vendetta, 'an eye for and eye and a tooth for a tooth!'" Nathan explained.

Madagascar had left the room but entered now.

"What is it?" Nathan asked him.

"You've got a visitor," the man announced.

"Well, who is it?" he demanded.

"Eli Whitney."

Nathan welcomed the distraction. He wished to give himself more time to think of a better plan for Thankful. Nathan nodded at his bodyguard to let Whitney enter.

"Thankful, I'm so deeply sorry to hear about your loss and offer you my condolences. How are you holding up?" the young Whitney said, offering sincere condolences.

Nathan allowed this conversation to proceed as they already knew each other.

Eli continued, "This coming June, I'll be signing a contract with the U.S. government to deliver 10,000 muskets," he reported and the other two exclaimed and gave their congratulations.

Now Eli said, "I've got intelligence for you, Nathan."

"What sort of intelligence?" Nathan now sat up in his creaky chair.

"Madagascar, are you catching this?" His bodyguard came back into the room.

"What? That your investigations in Maryland is not so secret anymore? Word spreads quickly."

Nathan tilted his head. "So how are you hearing about all this on the road coming up?"

"I came up through Maryland to Congress Hall in Philadelphia on this arms production and procurement business," he continued. "I have contacts, like you, in every state south of the Ohio River including Maryland. Hotbed contacts in the cotton gin trade, you might say. Some folks are uncomfortable in Maryland, if not unhappy! So I rented the fastest horse and carriage I could get! And came up quick, on this detour, to warn you. And to warn your guests as well!"

Nathan nodded for Eli to continue.

"The rumors are specific and included you, Thankful. The friends of slavery are working to starve you of all financial support. It has begun Nathan! Once I shared all the intelligence that I had with Madagascar and James, they decided you'd want to know and interrupted this meeting."

James Armistead Lafayette entered the room looking gravely at Nathan. Nathan whistled.

"Without funds from your husband's income, Thankful, you would be in trouble, I'm gathering, now that Nathan is gone, and no longer a source of income. I can only imagine what these vindictive villains are plotting! Pray continue, Eli!"

"That's all of it. You've got it, boss," Eli responded.

A Week Later

"Even a man like you, Nathan, who battled depression early and then climbed out of it is a unique strength and rare blessing!" Mary was at it again!

"Let's take stock."

Chalk in hand, Mary turns to her board and simply writes: "41"

"Your age when Hale died. Long before anything like that happened to you! Are you with me so far?"

Back to the board: "43"

"Our son, the joy in your life, and great business partner turns 19. Then: "53"

"You lose Nymphas."

At this point, depressed Nathan starts to feel silly. He starts laughing in spite of himself at what a joy of a wife she was with her magical clownish ways.

"So, let's move on!" she says. "62"

Old Nathan now raised his hands in surrender.

"Yes, I know! Silver Nathan."

Mary smiles, takes the stick with index fingers and thumbs and breaks it.

"Sure, you've got dependents and a widow, but cheer up old man; her eldest three can take care of themselves!"

"But you're stupid enough to blame yourself! Of those three you only have to concentrate on the little girl and the newborn, because Nathan is being taken care of by Samuel and Sylvia." Nathan shrugs.

"It should have been us taking care of him and the girl...perhaps the baby too." Mary explodes.

"Alright, then why don't you?" Her words capture his full attention. "Nathan! look at me!" she continued.

"You own a huge fleet, a third of which are going to be worthless, while the other third will follow shortly and will rot even in dry dock!" she challenged.

"That means I've got to sell them!" he replied.

"No!" Mary stomps her foot and leans over him. "You sell the best ones first and get the most money. Then sell the next best to the Navy, like Eli suggested!"

Nathan frowns, "Then I'm left with the ones that are no good!"

"No, darling, you sell the remainder for their scrap content! And start over!"

"Doing what?" he asked incredulously.

Slowly she turned and offered him a bright smile.

"Build fire boats" she said, smiling triumphantly. "Because it's your dream!"

"Take what you can to support Thankful's family. Pay spies to look after those you can't, and we'll come out of this just fine, because indentured time is only for a season. But love lasts forever!"

As Nathan walked out onto the porch, he could smell the sweet-scented spring honeysuckle that was starting to bloom over white pickets. He saw Joseph, relaxed and sitting casually on the steps leaning back on one of the white balustrades quite comfortable, smiling like a tiger at him.

"Mary's put you up to something."

"Now I've been thinking!" Joseph smirked as Nathan rolled his eyes.

"You know dad, with characteristic energy and ambition I, your son, will push every department in my business," he began.

"Oh, it's your business now!" his father retorted.

And so the conversation went. Withal the father would live to see his son grow into a successful businessman. In '04, he would open a store. In '15, after his mother's passing, he would, at age 37 move across the beautiful flowing Connecticut River. There he would build a combination store and joiner shop for building steam ships. Nathan lived to see all that happen, then fade into history. A free man, to meet up with Hale, Marston, Silver and his secret weapon, Mary Kellogg.

"You know dad, I've been thinking"... into the eternities... of broken chalk sticks, stripped bass, maple syrup, chairs that would never creak and drawers that would never stick.

The death of Thankful's husband, in '97' made it necessary to bind out his children. This scattered them forever separated some of them, and left all to their own resources.

1802 - Face in the Crowd

"Leave my family alone!" Thankful cried as those animals took her last child away. Samuel, bloodied and trembling, stood beside her.

But Elijah was an amazing child. At that moment his master grabbed him and he faced the crowd and yelled, "If Negros are not free...how can we be?"

His master slapped him, then struck Samuel who made a protective lunge. Before things could get any uglier,

Seth's face in the crowd, unnoticed by anyone else, got their attention and saved the day.

That evening the stranger shadowed the master's house. Hierarchy, not hypocrisy, was this evil man's game and children were his pawns.

Seth, the stranger, listened to Elijah yelling and the young maid crying. The man inside had killed other servants, but the man on the outside was no amateur either. His curious mission was to protect Elijah, and to disable this monster, in that house, if the occasion called for it.

The verbally abused children were safe for the time being. The owner finally went to bed and Seth left. The wind howled, gently tapping the leaded panes, and leaves swept down the narrow lonely street.

Seth spent his tenure in an apartment nearby this cruel master's dwelling. One time, Seth even went over and warned this man not to harm Elijah or the maid. In '07, the man finally met his fate when the maid fell in love with another man who also was an indentured servant, like her and Elijah.

Author's Note (Legal point): Indentured servants by law could not marry during terms of indentured service. The master during those periods of service literally owned the servant which led to hostility in this case.

That night, Seth propped his door open, pushing the chair closer to the door. The indentured man spent more time calling on the maid and as their relationship deepened, arguments became more heated with the master.

For such a time as this, Seth, Corp. Nathan and Thankful, had made plans to rescue and transfer young Elijah. That night a blanket hung as a makeshift door to reduce the chill. Transfer ship privateers from Goodspeed's landing now stood by waiting for action in the alley. The massive silver candle sconce sat where it always had been in the master's establishment as noted early on by the spy Seth.

At 10 p.m., the boy Elijah was scared and angry when the argument got heated and the master pulled a knife.

"So, you want to marry my servant? We'll test your loyalty behind that curtain!" his voice rang out. This action prompted Seth who to get up from his chair who selected, for the occasion, a darker jacket which he never wore. Then he checked ordinance and moved out into the street. He pressed near the door, then opened it more, and slipped into the shadows. By the window, Seth the privateer spy, saw silhouettes. The old man held a knife to the man's throat.

Elijah and the young woman thimbled. Seth's eyes narrowed.

"You really want to marry her?" the sadistic man asked. "Why don't you tell her then?" the old man mocked.

Don't! For God's sake, don't, the spy wanted to yell.

"Will you marry meeeeeeee..." the lover sang,

Silhouette... knife... blood... then the young woman shrieked.

From the woman's confused perspective, two men rushed her. One was the old man, the other a stranger, the spy Seth, pushed an angry Elijah out of the way. The old man grabbed her first, but the stranger attacked the old man. The young maid cried out the first time in fright, the second time in confusion. Capt. Seth struck the old master with the massive sconce, crushed, with a disabling blow the throat. The same blow snapped the victim's spine, intended to permanently parallelize. A very brutal, and devastating blow as planned. He then deftly made an incision and put a tube in the master's throat as the old man fell down, paralyzed.

Next Seth rushed in a vain attempt to save the young woman's boyfriend behind the curtain but disappointed soon came back now helped her over to a chair. It was then she realized he was there to help both her and rescue Elijah.

"You are safe, darling. Listen to me carefully. I am here to protect you and take the boy to a better place. Now pay attention. We don't have much time. The man on the floor can't hurt you anymore. Understand?"

He gave the woman time to nod. "I'll get someone to help you, understand?" Another nod. The spy nodded, too.

"You are doing very well. Now listen, for I must go but will return. You will tell whoever asks that you were attacked by a gang, both you and the old man and your visitor. You must lie, just this once, for God and country!"

After calming her down and telling her all this, Seth left with the boy. He took Elijah to the alley where they were waiting to take him to the ship.

Seth rushed back to his apartment and changed back into his other lighter colored coat. He banged on doors for "help" and went back to keep the old man alive and breathing. He took credit for being a "good neighbor".

He even won compliments from the arriving doctor for taking care of 'the patient"! The patient was in no condition after that ever to contradict or refute Seth and died later from a stroke he suffered from his injuries.

A Mother's Love

Elijah, now rescued, had lived on half rations and was weak and suffered from whooping cough. Thankful, his mother, though worried about the whereabouts of her youngest daughter, Rebecca, paid Elijah secret visits. He was a ship runaway, hiding from the law and the gang.

"In these times Elijah, find love! I believe in God who loves us as much as He loves America. The Lord put us here for a purpose. You never knew your father, but he and my mother called me 'Thankful', especially after my father Thomas died, since that was the only name he called me. He lovingly used only that name. I, like you son, am always singing and thankful even in the worst of times"

The War of 1812

Blessed is the nation whose God is the Lord,
The people he chose for His inheritance."

From the Great Lakes to New Orleans
From British landing to Goodspeed's landing
From Americans bearing the Flag to
J6 Americans singing Imprisoned
This author saw now what Frances Scott Key saw then,
sang the same song, in their peril,
The Star Spangled Banner.

1809 - James Madison Wins Election

Madison's family was jubilant with his victory over Jefferson after bitter campaigning. Afterward, they were friends, brothers. Following his election, he instructed Congress to prepare for war. In response to Britain trying to induce Americans from remaining neutral.

New England protesters misunderstood the word "prepare" and thought he meant war, but that wasn't true. They referred to his resistive countermeasures as "Madison's War," although in the developing western frontier the War Hawks also misunderstood the word "prepare" and actually wanted war.

His wife Dolly was also furious with him, but not for Madison's actions or the label that was given her husband but something closer to home.

Abigail Adams, wife of John Adams, was not happy either, when they were out for a lady's tea after Madison's first day in office.

"Do you remember when we were younger how upset I was with John?" Abigail asked pointedly.

The question put Dolly on the alert, when she saw the intense look her friend gave her. She had seen that look before when anything was the least bit out of place, and this time she already knew what it was.

"You mean that painting of you when we were younger?" she responded.

Abigail didn't even have to nod.

James was seated at his desk when he heard his office door slam. He looked up at his wife and when he saw her angry face, he knew he was in trouble, although about what he had no idea.

"Hello dear. Guess what?" she said through clenched teeth. "Abigail invited me to the art show this morning!"

James knew what was coming and he braced himself. He was a short man but the anticipated storm he knew headed his way made him shorter yet and he paled, much to Dolly's grim satisfaction.

"What were you thinking? I'm the talk of the town!" she cried and burst into tears.

James didn't know what to do. If he tried to hug her, he feared she'd get violent. So, he did the only thing a rational husband would do, dodge and make excuses.

Try to act angry, he said to himself. He made a fist and brought it down emphatically on his desk, taking care not to overdo it, for that would only make matters worse.

"He publicly insulted me! He called me a hermaphrodite!" Madison defended, banking on the fact that Dolly herself had been offended by Jefferson's remarks during their recent campaign; but he could see that she wasn't buying it.

"I don't care!" she stammered. Her statement made James even more apprehensive about how badly he had injured her dignity.[6]

"Listen to me," she said, "When I allowed you to have that artist paint my image, I never thought that like Abigail you would ever pull the same stunt with me!" She was now less hysterical so he thought he could get up and go over to comfort her.

"Why did you do that?" Dolly demanded.

"It was only one artist!" he tried to reassure her, but then realized that was a lie which knowing she also knew was an even a bigger mistake than anything else he had said.

She tore herself away from his embrace.

"You might as well have painted me naked!" she yelled, "And no! It's every other portrait artist in Washington; the whole gallery was full of that trash. I was never so embarrassed in all my life!"

And so the conversation went. His parting comment after he quickly grabbed his hat was simply, "I'm sorry. I didn't realize that you would be so offended. I won't let it happen again!" He gave her a quick kiss then out the door James went.

---

6 Women's dresses with low cut exposure of their breasts was the rage in that era. It didn't last long because the men loved it while their women hated it, for the most part. Abigail and Dolly were both members of the haters, of men's portrait games. An 1846AD image of Dolly in later years revealing a woman that preferred more modest lace up to the neck-chin line!

June 1812

On that date, buoyed by the arrival of "war hawk" representatives, the United States formally declared war for the first time in the nation's history. Citizens in the Northeast opposed the idea, but many others were enthusiastic about the nation's "Second War of Independence."

Ironically, the British Parliament was planning to repeal trade restrictions. By the time the ship carrying news of the declaration of war reached Great Britain, almost a month and a half after war had been declared, the restrictions had been repealed. The British, however, after hearing of the declaration, chose to wait and see how the Americans would react to the repeal. The Americans, after hearing of the repeal, were still unsure how Great Britain would react to the declaration of war although one of the main causes for war had vanished. The fighting began.

Early 1813 – White House

President Madison looked at John Armstrong, his Secretary of War.

"Not much to report James," the Secretary began.

"There wasn't much to report last year either, John," the President responded.

"Don't get discouraged, James. No news is good news."

"Well, with the exception that we lost a fort, the beaver trade, all the Great Lakes trade stock, and travel lanes around the straits, I believe we're doing remarkably well." James spoke quietly but with a certain tone of polite sarcasm.

Late Summer 1814 - British Invasion of the Chesapeake

It was known that General Jackson was the only real fighter, but other skirmishes were suddenly on the rise. After the invasion of Russia that year, French troops declined in Spain and Napoleon lost momentum in Europe. It became obvious that Britain now posed a bigger threat to America.

"But our Navy's stronger thanks to New England shipbuilders like Goodspeed's landing is still able to supply but for how long?" William Jones had declared.

August 19 - The Battle of Bladensburg

An expeditionary force of 4,500 hardened British troops under command of General Robert Ross landed at Benedict, Maryland and began a lightning-fast campaign. After routing Maryland militia at the Battle of Bladensburg, Ross's men were now the first serious incursion into American territory. Nobody was sure exactly where Ross' troops were going to strike next.

August 24, 1814 - The Burning of Washington

British troops under command of Vice Admiral Cockburn and Major General Ross marched into Washington D.C. as the next strike after their victory over American forces at Bladensburg, Maryland. Earlier in the day Dolly Madison was having her staff prepare a wine dinner. The troops came swiftly to Washington taking everyone by surprise and interrupted the First Lady's routines and carefully planned dinner

This unlike the first year of war was no longer comic theater! British troops were hardened and seasoned, many of them twenty-year veterans of war. Every civilian wondered how it could be possible for peace negotiations to be going on in Europe at this perilous moment.

From the Journal of Paul Jennings, Chief Negro Server for Dolly Madison, we learn what actually happened after the night of that mightily disrupted dinner.

"Everything was left to General Armstrong, Secretary of war, who ridiculed the idea that there was any danger. But, in August, the enemy had gotten so near, there could be no doubt of their intentions. Great alarm existed, and some feeble preparations for defenses were made. Com. Barney's flotilla was stripped of men, who were placed in battery, at Bladensburg, where they fought splendidly. A large part of his men were tall, strapping Negroes, mixed with white sailors and marines. Mr. Madison reviewed them just before the fight, asked Com. Barney if his "negroes would not run on the approach of the

British?" No sir," said Barney, "they don't know how to run; they will die by their guns first." They fought till a large part of them were killed or wounded; and Barney himself wounded and taken prisoner."[7]

Dolly Madison had ordered dinner to be ready at three. Paul Jennings, chief server for Dolly, set the table, and brought up the ale, cider, and wine, and placed them in the coolers, as all the President's Cabinet and several military gentlemen and strangers were expected.

While waiting for the dinner to begin, Sukey, the house-servant, was by the chamber window when James Smith, a free colored man who had accompanied Mr. Madison to Bladensburg, galloped up to the house.

"Clear out, clear out! General Armstrong has ordered a retreat!" the rider waved his hat as he cried out.

Confusion broke out.

Mrs. Madison ordered her carriage, and passing through the dining-room, caught up what silver she could crowd into her old-fashioned reticule, and then jumped into the chariot with her servant girl Sukey, and Daniel Carroll, who took charge of them. When the British did arrive hours later, they would eat the very dinner, and drink the wines, that our witness Jennings had prepared.

John Suse, a French door-keeper, and Magraw, the President's gardener, took Washington's large portrait down and sent it off on a wagon, along with some large

---

7 Author's Note: "No sir, they don't know how to run; they will die by their guns first!" That's the difference between sunshine patriots and warriors! The ongoing battle between liberty and tyranny, where patriots regardless of race, creed or color were perfectly willing to make the ultimate sacrifice!

silver urns and such other valuables as could be hastily removed.

People were running in every direction. John Freeman, Negro butler, drove off in the coaches with wife, child, and servant, and with a feather bed lashed behind the coaches. All the furniture was saved, except part of the silver and the portrait of Washington, which by then had already been taken away in the other wagon that John Suse and Magraw left in.

John Suse and Magraw returned hours later in the empty wagon and watched the invading soldiers eat the rest of the dinner and drink the wine that had been prepared for Madison's party.

"Did you take a portrait?" soldiers rudely asked of the returning servants and pointed to a conspicuously large rectangular outline on a bare wall.

"What portrait?" was the servants only reply. Then, politely as any good host would do, the astute servants changed the subject.

"More wine, gentlemen?"

A wiser soldier sneered but accepted the generous offer of more wine.

"What was that portrait?" a third soldier asked with his mouth full of food, but again the answer was the same.

"What portrait?" The cheeky Frenchman smiled not giving a button what the invaders thought. He was bold not to hide his French accent and satisfied just to rub it in! This would distract these Brits from asking where the First Lady and President stayed or had gone. He would never disclose any information, even if it cost him his life!

But the soldiers respected his measure and knew with this brave defiant sort it would be in vain to pursue further.

John Suse later had the gall to press further, till finally the invading company left. Suse had them believing and being fearful that Madison might have had a countermeasure prepared to have someone like the Marquis de Lafayette, Pirate Jean Lafitte, or perhaps Napoleon himself, sail up the bay and spoil their dinner. That caused the troops to excuse themselves like gentlemen and leave the rest of the wine behind, which was the Frenchman's intent all along.

When the news of peace arrived, Jennings, and the rest were crazy with joy."

Miss Sally Coles, Dolly's cousin, came to the head of the stairs, crying out, "Peace! Peace!" and told John Freeman, the butler, to serve out wine liberally to the servants and others.

"I played the President's March on the violin. John Suse and some others were drunk for two days, and such another joyful time was never seen in Washington. Mr. Madison and all his Cabinet were as pleased as any but did not show their joy in this manner." Paul wrote.[8]

---

8 Author's Note: Often history likes to either vilify or make our founding fathers bigger than life. For example, historians tended to glorify Dolly Madison the night George Washington's portrait was saved from being destroyed or desecrated by the invading British troops. One account has her giving elaborate instructions to her staff to either save Washington's portrait or burn it before the invaders could. Another account has her taking a knife and cutting Washington's canvas portrait out and physically taking it away during the hazing of Washington D.C. by Ross's Troops. And quite frankly, this author was personally disappointed that neither account was accurate upon reviewing the direct eyewitness account by her Negro servant, Paul Jennings. But then I realized there was a much richer 'America First' theme here.

Here, Paul's above account gives full credit to the brave servants who actually saved George Washington's portrait on their own without their masters prompting. It was John Suse and Magraw, the President's gardener, who actually took Washington's portrait down and saved who should get full credit and honor for this.

The Madison family was a slave owning family but their attitude toward their servants has a kind of "Gone With the Wind" and, quite frankly, "America first" quality that restores some of the beauty to what once was. And again, they gave full credit in its retelling, and honor to the servants who actually saved George Washington's portrait on their own accord without their masters' prompting!

That is a real "America First" expression, right down to the grass roots level!

These men of both races had a mind of their own, were created equal, and were very patriotic. They didn't need to be told what to do for they possessed that instinctive desire to stand up for what is right!

September 12, 1814

On this day Major General Robert Ross of the invading British forces was killed in action.

September 13, 1814 - Fort Henry

Quoted from Paul Harvey the following: Francis Scott Key was a lawyer in Baltimore where in 1814 the vicious conflict between Britain and America had now dramatically escalated. They had protracted many prisoners on both sides and Armstrong sent Key to the British government to negotiate an exchange. When they reached a conclusion that men could be exchanged on a one-to-one basis, Francis went down below in the boats. "Men I've got news for you. Tonight you will be free men. Tonight, I have negotiated successfully to take you out of this filth and out of your chains!" Key told the astonished men. But as he went back up on deck, the admiral approached him. "We have a slight problem. We will still honor our commitment to release these men, but it will all be academic after tonight." "What do you mean?" Francis Key asked. "Well, Mr. Key, after tonight we will lay an ultimatum upon the colonies. Your people will either lay down the colors or we're going to remove that fort from the face of the earth!" "And how are you going to do that?" Francis Key queried. "Scan the horizon of the sea. That's the entire British war fleet. All of the gun power is being called upon to demolish that fort. It will be within striking distance in a matter of about two hours. The war is over. These men will be free anyway," the admiral explained. "You can't shell that fort!" Key said. "That's a large fort and it's filled primarily with women and children! It's not a military fort!" "If they will lower that flag on the rampart, the shelling will stop immediately and they'll now be under British rule," the admiral said. Francis Scott Key went down, and the prisoners asked, "How many ships?" "Hundreds," he answered reluctantly. As the ships got closer, Francis Scott Key went back on top, and said "Men, I'll shout down to you what's going on as we watch." As twilight began to fall, as the haze fell over the ocean as it does at sunset and soon. "Tell us where the flag is! Is the flag still flying over the rampart? Tell us!" the prisoners implored from below. Key watched intently and relayed information to them as he observed. One hour...Two hours...Three hours into the shelling. Every hour, Francis Scott Key would report down to the men. "It's still up! It's not down! The flag is not down!" "Your people are insane!" the admiral declared incredulously. "What's the matter with them!? Don't they understand?" "What sets the American Christian patriot apart from all others in the world is he will die on his feet before he will live on his knees!" Key said. When sunrise came there was a heavy mist hanging over the land. Francis immediately went into Fort Henry and found the flagpole. He learned that each time the flag had fallen, the men, although knowing that all of the British guns were trained on them, walked over and held it up. He said that what held that flagpole in place at that unusual angle were patriots' bodies. He later penned the lyrics:

"Oh, say can you see
by the dawn's early light...

What so proudly we hailed
at the twilight's last gleaming...
O'er the rocket's red glare...
The bombs bursting in air...
Gave proof through the night...
That the flag was still there!
Oh, say does that star spangled banner yet fly and wave
For the land of the free and the brave...
That death was demanded...
The price it was paid!"

Fewer Goodspeeds would serve in this war than in the previous. Those that joined the conflict did so to prove something Twenty-nine had served in the preceding war, however fewer than half that number would serve in 1812. Except for Isaac and Luther, the brothers who had served in the previous, the rest were new recruits.

These particular men were fighting for one reason only: For honor to replace dishonor in Nathaniel's line.

In this category was the only person that fates chose to kill in that war. That was John Goodspeed, who was from the neighborhood and connected to this author's line. The line of Nathaniel and Ebenezer Goodspeed.

That dark night John Goodspeed of Dutchess County had the misfortune of facing the same fate as young Solomon and friend Abraham Tayler had at Fort Ticonderoga in '77.

But in his case, unlike Solomon and Abraham, he barely survived. John was one of those rare few who hadn't died, but probably would have been better off if he had.

Capt. Seth had also served in that war, and certainly by this time, had seen enough of strife!

Francis Scott Key looked down at the mangled men hauled on stretchers from the fort to a platform to triage. One man among those injured caught Francis' attention.

"Take care!" he said, for he noticed, unlike the others, this man wore a tattered and bloodied uniform; he was a soldier.

"Who are you, can you talk?" Key asked, leaning over him. The man groaned, tilted his head and with great effort said something so faint Francis had to lean forward to catch it.

"John..." was all he spoke.

Francis looked at the other survivors in the mass, then back at the orderly.

"Please, sir, carefully remove this one or he won't make it. I'll help you port him over to my carriage," he instructed.

"He'll need a lot of treatment," the orderly remarked and shrugged. But several veterans now freed by Scott quickly came over to assist. All worked to take him to a safer place.

Also standing close by were two privateers, Samuel Goodspeed and Capt. Seth and they too joined in the transport.

"Wait," said Samuel. "I know this man!" He carefully cleaned the blood and grit from his face. "John? Is that you!?"

The weak man nodded then coughed up blood. Seth then recognized him too. "Dear Lord," was all he said.

Seth turned to Samuel.

"Wasn't your Great Grandfather also John's Great Great Grandfather?" he spoke softly. Now both men wept and vowed passionately to take care of him as their last act of war!

General Andrew Jackson played a major role, in the south, against the British foothold there in the south to interdict with the heaviest British enchantment of ruthless, seasoned, professional soldiers. He proved to be one of the only effective, fighters bar none, with what he was about to accomplish, in pure cussedness and valor. Some might condemn General Jackson for what he did to the native American Indians later and the Trail of Tears, but tell the man's story and one might understand.

Like young Elijah, he too was treated terribly as a young, indentured slave to the British troops. One example told of a soldier who took his saber and twice viciously slashed young Andrew's face when he refused to polish the officer's boots. He carried the scars for life.

The British had invaded the Carolinas and Jackson's homestead. They killed his mother and two brothers in front of him, leaving him with a lifelong hostility toward Great Britain and their Indian allies.

But unlike Andrew Jackson, Elijah, despite his own emotional scars, would grow up to learn how to overcome this intense bitterness and hatred.

Always pray for our leaders no matter what we think but be willing to stand up for what is right!

1814 – The Battle of New Orleans

"Hey, Crumbs!" Mary's affectionate way to mock and stay strong with innuendos of a previous quack doctor, got his attention from her sickbed without losing her good humor and without scaring the poor man to death.

"What?" Nathan came in smiling, but not without a lump in his throat. She died two days later on May 16, 1814, before Jackson's final push of British forces from New Orleans.

And, as Joseph promised his father a month before, he now at twenty-seven, with characteristic energy and ambition, would build steamships in her memory, fulfilling the father's dream and vision.

In early December, to help cheer up his dad, he started moving the operation to the other side of the river and was well into the process. He opened a store in a building he had refurbished into a joiner's shop.

"Hey, Crumbs!" The nickname now echoed her spirit and lifted his dad's spirit. He was reading a newspaper during his lunch break in that building, across the river from the honeysuckle vines in winter repose.

"What?" Nathan came in from the joiner side and smiled at Joseph, but still with that same feeling every time Joseph pulled that trick. As a matter of fact, he now laughed for the first time since Mary Kellogg's death.

That laugh surprised his son. But then he laughed himself and returned to the newspaper. Pointed at the newspaper he continued, "Today's December 1st, right?"

Checking his time cognizance caused his father to roll his eyes.

"Get to the point son!" Nathan said.

"Well, it says here, old man, that Gen. Andrew Jackson's at it again!" Joseph relayed.

"What? Tell me more," Nathan demanded.

"Well, do you remember back in recent autumn? When Pakenham sailed into the Gulf of Mexico?" Joseph set the stage.

"Get to the point son!"

"Well, General Andrew Jackson's going to the defense of the city against those bastards!"

"What city would that be?" Nathan queried.

"Oh, stop that!" Joseph laughed, "You know damned well what city. He's going to take it to Pakenham's ships with his own armada, thanks to Goodspeed's landing!"

"You're kidding!?" Nathan exclaimed.

Then Nathan broke out into a fast jig and surprised Joseph even further.

"Awesome, old man!" Joseph just laughed.

Now it was Nathan's turn to have fun with his son, so he pulled out a freshly minted coin and handed it to Joseph.

"Here take it!"

"What's this, besides a large cent?" he remarked but quickly took it, being a good businessman like his dad.

"See a resemblance? You met her once." Joseph studied the coin.

"Oh tut, it does! We met her in Washington. After the British sacked Washington, then Ross that bastard died! That scowl and bonnet!" Joseph shook his head. "Beautiful Dolly, about to give them a thrashing in New Orleans!"

This time both father and son did a jig with glee.

The War is Over!

The Madison's servant Paul Jennings wrote:

"After the news of peace, and of General Jackson's victory at New Orleans, which reached here about the same time, there were great illuminations. We moved into the Seven Buildings, Corner of 19th-street and Pennsylvania Avenue, and while there, General Jackson came on with his wife, to whom numerous dinner-parties and levees were given. Mr. Madison also held levees every Wednesday evening, at which wine, punch, coffee, ice-cream, & etc., were liberally served."

New England's Season Without Summer

1815

On April 5th a massive volcanic eruption occurred on Mount Tambora, located on the island of Sumbawa in southern Indonesia. It was reported at the location and time that 15,000 were instantly killed and another 65,000 died soon after from disease and starvation. Tons of ash was thrown into the stratosphere and blocked the sunlight, lowering temperatures globally.

Napoleon's troops met a very cold Waterloo, killing many!

Maryland Gang[9]

A crackling fire burned in the hearth. A new face, Dirty Abe was no longer the center of attention and was given a smaller table in a dark corner, far from the warmth.

Abe cowered, nursing his red wine. They had murdered his grandson and demoted him, but cut him enough slack to prove himself. The truth of it was he would sell his own grandson for power, and they all knew that, and there they kept him, which Abe feared.

So, in the long winter they planned their payback. Ranks had swelled and they were more organized and vicious than ever.

"We spotted Samuel in Baltimore," Tom McCreary spoke to his motley gathering as he leaned forward at the greasy table.

"Capt. Seth was also there with an injured relative named John from the fort." He leaned further forward. "And Francis Key was with them!"

Tom pounded the table in anger, "The war's over... it's back to scratch."

"Waiter," he called, irritated, then turned and yelled, "More rum!"

The Gang respected this man, Tom McCreary. He glared at Abe, cowering in the dark and yelled.

---

9 Here in the 1800s we begin to see the dawn of the secret society PSYOPS 'patsy' concept that would have far reaching consequences far into America's future.
Like Lee Harvey Oswald in the early 60s of the twentieth century; 'Dirty Abe' was the Maryland Gang's mark then!

"You let that boy get away!" But Abe had just enough 'spine' and pushed back.

"Well, that boy made a friend while we had him, a boy named Joseph C. Miller."

"Do tell!" McCreary demanded as he slugged down his tumbler of rum. Now empty, he slammed the glass down violently. "Waiter!"

Sufferings of John - Autumn 1815

John, from Dutchess County New York, was confined in Baltimore and needed relief. Three strange messengers delivered three separate notes, one each to Thankful, Samuel, and Seth. Thankful had volunteered to care for the cruel dying master, another one of the gang's sinister associates.

The hate-filled friends of slavery from Maryland saw an opportunity to finally destroy this family and so insisted that she and Samuel come in John's "hour of need."

Seth recognized the trap, but finding Thankful resolute, Capt. Seth rushed to notify Nathan of potential danger. Before she left, she again visited Elijah on the ship.

"In '08, after being rescued, I was given my first assignment," he said. "I was assigned to the captain's team for charity and salvage work. The '07 storm that hit Boston Harbor recorded tides that were higher than ever experienced in fifty years. All cellars on the east side of Broad Street were flooded, killing thousands of rats that spread disease."

Thankful shuddered as he continued.

"Lumber wharves in the west portion of town were damaged and inventory was scattered and lost," he said. "When we got there, I started learning carpentry, along with rebuilding."

"Did you work with your oldest brother?" she asked. He nodded, smiling. "How did that make you feel?"

She could see him for once visibly relaxed. He nodded and offered a bigger smile that went straight to her heart.

"I love my new life, but..." Elijah knit his brows. "There is one thing that puzzled me. It doesn't make sense."

"What's that?"

"How exactly did my father die? Solomon, my oldest brother, said he died at sea. What does that mean?" Elijah looked to her for an answer. The question stopped Thankful cold. Suddenly she realized that Elijah would not have known.

"Oh no!" She broke down in tears.

"What?" Elijah got up and hugged her.

"Son."

"Yes?"

She looked at him. There was no other way to tell him, pain overwhelmed her. The injustice of it all!

"He was killed," she said. "He... was... murdered!"

They were in Thankful's kitchen... a small cottage by the sea. The sound of the waves on the shore could be heard and a stiff wind boomed on the shoreline.

"Samuel, you're going to go back to John alone. I won't be able to go with you"

"What's wrong, Thankful?" Samuel puzzled.

"Sam, I just told a man his father was murdered!" She burst into tears. Samuel understood.

"Why didn't we think of this before?"

The sound of pounding waves soothed them as they hugged. Too busy living, each felt terribly sorry for the other. Each felt sorry for the son, and felt sorry for each other, then the boy again! More booming resounded upon that lonely beach that was once filled with many familiar voices from the past. So many memories and other sounds.

Samuel nodded.

"I'll go talk to him, and Cousin John will have to tough it out on his own a bit." Then both of them broke down and cried.

Capt. Seth knew that things had changed with the Maryland gang. He applied what they had learned at the Long Island Sound meeting. Now there were two active shooters! The organization was tooled in poison and growing in numbers. Where was Rebecca? That was a tragic problem that bothered and haunted all of them and haunted their thoughts. Was she well? Was she still alive? Was the gang involved in that, too?

In late 1815 to early 1816, Elijah excelled in hard work and enthusiasm for his duties. In contrast to his past, he felt not only grateful but blessed. It was, however, time for him to adjust to the truth of his dad's murder. He learned that to understand others was more powerful than trying to get others to understand him. So, in a few short weeks Elijah went from a lost orphan boy to a man of the world!

He was given the tools from two wonderful teachers: how to survive, to know his enemies, and how the game was played. This, of course, would require a trip to Boston so that he could be debriefed by Capt. Seth. It was a longer trip to East Haddam for Nathan's input, but promises made must be promises kept.

Elijah enjoyed charity work. He was ruthless and bold enough to stop incidents when outnumbered, but by then the law found him. When asked where his captors were, he just stared them down and told them that he had killed them all. They believed him and never bothered him again.

Meanwhile, a nurse worked with Samuel and Thankful gave John a gradual overdose of metal salt with enough arsenic to kill. At least Thankful and Sam had come to their senses on the Messengers but found a nurse that was yet another gang plant!

John's death was messy. Both demoralized, the unsuspecting couple returned home. Thankful was puzzled by Samuel's weakening condition. She attributed his change to depression over his distant cousin's violent end. The nurse gave them some "medicine" for Samuel to take to "help him" with depression when they returned home.

Samuel experienced a bad growing season and started worrying about next summer because there was no surplus crop to store. Summer went directly into winter;

where trees hadn't even changed color. Much damage occurred to his apple crop from an early massive snow weighing down branches that broke the trees. Silvia noticed Samuel's loss of energy into the New Year.

Sam had turned fifty-nine in December. In early April, Samuel developed severe tremor attacks. No one ever suspected the "medication"! They prayed for sunshine but with each passing day things only worsened. Spring was three to four degrees colder than average in previous years. Then in April, with the heavy snows, Samuel's health quickly deteriorated. He became bedridden and died April 16, 1816.

For the first time in years almost all of Thankful's entire family had been reunited. They payed respect to their distant cousin and closest friend Samuel. Surrounded by family, Thankful held dear her children, Solomon, Thomas, Jane, Jabez, (Rebecca the only one not present). Nathan and Elijah were also present. The ubiquitous snow was unrelenting and weighed down heavily on the community, spiritually as well as physically, collapsing roofs and making many market lanes totally impassable.

A Peculiar Burial and the Noose

In dreams, Elijah saw a youth he identified as himself, racked with coughs and filled with visions of a Negro mother with a child. Their master tried to force himself on her but she resisted, then in spite, the man sold the wife and children into the Deep South, separating man from woman and woman from child. Then the man fled in despair to the north, crossing the Potomac to freedom on Christmas Eve at night.

A knock and the vision changed. Two men, whose black images were covered with ash from head to toe, neared a hot steamship boiler, their bodies now placed in separate straw lined boxes and nailed shut. Yet, their physical sufferings were endured, for their hearts were lifted up with hope and they preceded north to freedom.

The knock revealed another vision. Uncertain whether a man, child, black, white, Native American, or possibly even himself was running in thick brush, away from some pursuing danger.

He awoke in a cold sweat, no stranger to visions. It had been a while since the last occurrence. Now fully awake Elijah speculated this was the result of being in unfamiliar surroundings, since he had spent the night in Samuel's guest cabin, now the widow Sylvia's estate.

Elijah remembered whooping cough and its recuperation period after being inoculated. Thank God for that timely medical development. The nightmares always reminded him of what he had endured; those occasional beatings and slow starvation from only being given half rations before his deliverance.

Elijah toweled his face. Unlike other visions from before, the dreams were typical, but the knocking was something new. Elijah went to the door. He looked for footprints and did notice some that were quickly being covered by falling snow in its unrelenting intensity, especially for this time of year. He put a pot on the hot stove for coffee, pulled his shirt on, then quickly made his bed. Dawn was just breaking. It was time to be on his way; a long return to Boston, his ship, and to his loyal crew.

Banging on the door interrupted his thoughts, but came as a welcome distraction. He opened the door. He was pleasantly surprised to greet visitors among whom was Mashpee Chatham, an Indian he knew.

"Elijah, we thought you were dead! I'm glad to see you among the living," said his oldest brother Solomon with a chuckle.

"Was that you who knocked earlier, brother?" Elijah asked, pretending irritation.

"The Alpha and the Omega!" The Indian mocked his old friend.

Then Elijah recalled the rest of his dream. Everyone had noted his look of surprise, including the Indian.

"What is it?" Solomon asked.

"I just had a dream and the part I had forgotten when I was waking up was simply a voice stating. 'I am the Alpha and the Omega!' I believe it is the first time God ever visited me in a dream," he laughed.

From the frost of their breaths, Elijah noted that all had abruptly stopped speaking and looked at each other, then back at him, before resuming normal breathing.

"So did he," Solomon murmured in wonder. "That's what brings us to you!" but without words someone slipped Elijah a fully charged shotgun.

"Who is this he...and what's this for?" Elijah asked, confused.

"Come and find out," someone in the group said

then all turned and walked away in the direction of the main building, ghosts fading into the wintry mix. Elijah quickly slid the kettle back, put on his boots, adjusted his shirt tuck, grabbed his coat, and followed them.

The plot to indict Thankful Thomas Goodspeed and inflict the most pain was now in full swing. Dirty Abe saw this as an opportunity to redeem himself, Abraham and his trusted thugs and law marshal from Maryland. They traveled all the way up to Samuel's residence in Pawlet, Vermont. Their sources had told them that Thankful would be there, an easy target for apprehension, at Sam's funeral.

As Abe's carriage, his entourage, and the coroner pulled up to the deceased's estate, Thankful and the new widow Sylvia were not alone, nor unprotected.

In Abe's hand was the same document the Maryland Law Magistrate had issued: authorization to claim Samuel's body to perform an investigation.

However, he found himself facing a heavily armed contingent of Yankee veteran soldiers: Capt. Seth, 1812 War and Revolution vets; brothers, Isaac and Luther Goodspeed; Nathan's bodyguards Madagascar and another unidentified black armed bodyguard; two Law Marshals, one from the State of Connecticut, the other local from Vermont; and James Armistead Lafayette. To his chagrin there also stood before him Nathan of Goodspeed's landing and next to DeWitt Clinton, the newly elected Governor of the State of New York. Movement around the corner of the building caught Abe's attention, heavily armed men, including Elijah Good-

speed bearing a shotgun. Thankful and Sylvia were nowhere in sight, but busy preparing breakfast for guests
and other family members.

"What in blazes brings you to Vermont, Abe?" Nathan
barked, not even giving the befuddled eighty-year-old
time to get out of his carriage.

Abe looked anxiously at his Maryland Marshall whom
both Nathan and DeWitt knew well. This turn of events
made the Maryland Marshall and his deputies nervous,
realizing that their hosts had been tipped off, and worse
realizing they were out of their legal jurisdiction.

Reluctantly the Marshall handed the writ to Nathan,
who took out a large fighting knife and cut the envelope. Nathan quickly scanned it and handed the document back; but timed it so that just before the Marshall
could take it back it fell to the ground at his feet. The
Marshall, embarrassed, was forced to bend and pick it
up, saying, awkwardly, upon rising, "This was meant
to be delivered to the widow Sylvia to..."

Nathan cut him off, "So you want us to dig it up for
you?"

"Well, yes," the magistrate said hesitantly.

"What's the justification?" Nathan demanded, letting his anger show.

Long silence ensued before the Magistrate could bring
himself to answer.

"For the alleged poisoning of the deceased by defen-
dant, Thankful Thomas Goodspeed..."

Nathan embarrassed the official with a derisive laugh.

Then to everyone's surprise the front door opened

and Thankful Thomas, relaxed and calm, stepped out, her arms folded in defiance.

Abe's thugs started to raise their muskets, but Nathan's loyal troops quickly raised theirs. The Maryland Militia had the good sense not to do anything.

"I think they want the remains, Nathan," she calmly stated. "Sylvia requested me to give the authority to proceed, although she said she's not going to press charges. She wants you all to leave immediately."

Sylvia herself appeared, hugged Thankful, put a protective arm around her in a firm embrace and glared malevolently at Abe.

"Did you murder my husband or have the nurse do it?" she asked at point blank range. The Magistrate from Maryland glared at Abe. Nathan gave a more wicked laugh, enjoying Abe's stunned look.

"Why, right this way to the family cemetery plot!" Nathan announced mockingly, taking a step off the porch and turning to the Indian and Madagascar, both now bearing shovels as if knowing this had all been planned ahead of time.

Now Abe had all he could do to hide his fear and stop from retching.

"Come on, Abe!" Nathan said, calling him like a dog. Now even soft laughter could be heard from the relieved Maryland Militia, knowing that a dangerous confrontation was no longer necessary.

"Oh..." Nathan added casually, as if almost missing something significant. "Tell your men to remain here under my troop's protection!" The laughter from the estate became more general and more dangerous to Abe's personal health. He now reluctantly followed the remaining party to the grave site.

It didn't take long for the strong Indian and Madagascar to empty a shallow grave. Abe then did throw up, now shaking violently. Before him were three very long-dead, shrouded figures that he immediately recognized; his victims in their sea-burial shrouds complete with burial weights.

The Indian threw a rope over the branch of a large oak overhanging the macabre scene. The lamplight threw ominous shadows as the noose dangled just inches away from Abe's face. He looked like he was going to have a stroke. The lantern was swinging deliberately from Nathan's hand and threw ghastly moving shadows on the accusingly empty eye sockets. The dried and mummified faces were poking out of their deteriorating shroud fabric.

Even the Maryland magistrate had to laugh at the pathetic spectacle Lincoln made. Flecks of a pleasant dinner, now soured and clinging to his withered chin, made him appear pathetic. Nathan addressed the magistrate from Maryland.

"If you want more bodies, George, there are twenty-seven more waiting for you at Goodspeed's landing." Everyone burst out laughing on Nathan's side, including Sylvia in spite of her grief.

"Yes, we already examined Samuel, and can save you the time to investigate further," Nathan informed the magistrate. "The same levels of poisons were in both

John Goodspeed and Samuel which is about the same as the three bodies at your disposal here!"

Grinning, Nathan looked around theatrically as he gently put the noose around Abe's neck and then gave it a sudden tug to draw it tightly around his trembling guest's throat till he couldn't speak. Just to make sure he remained silent, he lifted him ever so slightly off the ground till his own weight cut off his rapid breathing and Abe started struggling.

The magistrate looked reproachfully at Nathan but didn't move to stop him, secretly enjoying the show himself.

With a grunt of satisfaction Nathan released his would-be victim who now fell to the ground, faintly gasping at their feet like a fish out of water. His glazed eyes gradually cleared as he became painfully aware of his embarrassing situation and the laughter of everyone, including his Maryland escorts who were standing over him.

His head was only inches away from where he had fallen and he stared into the sunken, dehydrated eye-sockets of one of his deceased victims. Quickly, he got up, covered in his own puke, spit, and fresh grave dirt. It took him a while to regain his ability to stand, and his formal pressed traveling suit now displayed puke-stained ruffles. He was a very laughable sight to behold. He was bathed in sweat and fresh guilt.

DeWitt, who up until now had been a silent witness, had only one thing to say.

"George, I think we can all profit from lessons learned

here today," he said, then winked at Nathan. Nathan forced a smile back at his friend but didn't feel at all civil. He turned to the Maryland Militia and barked.

"Now take him back home and hang him!"

"Hang him!" Sylvia also shouted. But in the deep state of slavery, justice would eventually be forgotten on either side of the Ohio River.

The Maryland magistrate saluted Nathan and stated upon parting.

"'It is not my desire nor interest to pursue this matter any further. Politics is not our business. I'll leave you rivals to your own devices, especially you, Abraham. There is nothing more to say except stay out of trouble!"

Abraham nodded, but surly, like a chastised school yard bully.

He would die sooner than Nathan and until that time Abe had learned his lesson. He knew that he had been outfoxed by a superior, more competent adversary. He would never personally trouble Nathan and his relations again, nor would he be allowed to by his gang overlords.

In this last desperate attempt to restore his status, Abe had gambled and lost. This time it would cost him his life. The overlords had had enough of his incompetence. It was the code of the gang; no longer useful the label, the kiss of death the cure!

There were cheers when Nathan entered Silvia's home, but they were short-lived. Thankful had gone back into the bedroom and Madagascar told Nathan that she was crying. Nathan motioned to Sylvia to go see her while the visitors now changed their tone, including Heman, one of Samuel and Sylvia's surviving sons. They waited silently until Sylvia and Thankful came back, then Nathan offered both widows brandy liquor that he had summoned Heman to get. Thankful accepted, belting it down in uncharacteristic fashion. Thankful looked at Mashpee.

"I want you, Madagascar, and Nathan to find Rebecca. Samuel was helping, but he's gone!"

The Indian solemnly nodded, then addressed the group.

"Children of Thankful. If you hold any information on Rebecca when you were bonded out, please share it now!"

Oldest son Solomon replied, "I was never bonded out but helped mom financially whenever possible during that horrific time."

"I'm afraid I know even less!" said Thomas, who rarely spoke.

"And I'm Jane," she stated simply, without adding anything else. That caught Mashpee's interest.

"I'm a shipwright working for Nathan to get even for how badly we were treated!" Jabez said. "Also, like you Mashpee, I will look into it. But today I want to thank Nathan for coming all the way here to stop a real family tragedy from taking place!"

"I would kill to know myself!" said Nathan. He was tight lipped, haunted by his exposure too early in life to separation and abuse.

"Well, I guess I'm the omega, if Solomon was the alpha!" Elijah said, nodding at both Nathans. "But why is my dream about Jesus, just like yours"

Nathan gave a start, feeling eerie knowing Elijah had just had a similar dream.

Old Nathan had planned on giving an Alpha and Omega speech from his vision of the family's origins, destiny, and spiritual parallels. In place of it, he simply placed his hands on Elijah's shoulders and spoke.

"You're all adults, no longer children. And you, Elijah, the youngest, are now master of your own ship crew, and your own destiny."

Thankful fought back another powerful wave of sadness and fear, looking over at Jane. She tried in vain not to think about Rebecca. But even the Indian scout's vow was of little comfort to blot out her own pain, when she had anticipated all afternoon that it might.

"We had it the worst of all!" Jane said, speaking in empathy of her sister, noticing her mother's silent distress. Jane looked as if she was going to add something else. Mashpee caught that the look that Thankful and everyone else had missed; Jane knew something about Rebecca that she wasn't going to share with anyone, especially her mother.

Silently, Mashpee stored that thought for future reference and gave Nathan a slight nod indicating that he had gotten what he needed, for the time being, and for Nathan to proceed with the meeting.

"The day Noname was rescued, he was only a boy. He tells me he was always determined to find his freedom after he was sold as a very young lad and transferred from Kentucky to Maryland. He saw men and women being beaten until they threw up blood; old and young girls also. It was a hellhole of drugs and poison experiments, and to the intimidated, submissive inmates a hellhole of human trafficking!"

Nathan paused just long enough to let the message sink in and allowed time for the protest response against such social evils to subside.

But now encouraged, Noname rose to speak.

"When I was only a boy, emaciated and starving, I saw my opportunity to make a break the night of the fight and death of Silver Nathan. I would rather die standing up than on my knees a slave. When I spotted your ship and made another break, I was shot for my efforts which was worth the price for freedom!"

Strong applause thundered in the room. Nathan spoke once more,

"My time grows short. My wife is gone and I'm tired. I believe shortly I will be joining her for eternity. Circumstances indicate that you all are at dangerous crossroads, for the enemy is not far behind and has a terrible blood lust for power, gain and vengeance!" He paused and looked each of them in the eye.

"So, make preparations for a new adventure, for life, and for your destiny. Let not your hearts be troubled! De-Witt here, with the Goodspeed's Landing Foundation and with federal assistance is going to build a canal. Heman will help early next year to break ground for what will be known as the Erie Canal. I only wish that I could see it!"

Nathan looked directly at Elijah whom he had just met a few weeks earlier. He liked what he saw. Elijah's positive attitude, focus, courage to never give up, and instinctive desire to stand up for what was right were each attributes that Cap. Seth had also observed and was as equally impressed with.

"Elijah, we need you. You will become not only a station keeper but a conductor on the Hudson, Ohio, and Mississippi Rivers. You will leave these dangerous grounds where you were born for good works out West in Athens Ohio. Heman will do works in the East. Now faith without works is 'death.'"

That truth resonated and looking around, he continued.

"When I die, Joseph will build Elijah's steamship. Congratulations, Elijah and Heman! You have earned the recognition. I have assigned Madagascar and Mashpee Chatham as your guides for out West. Mashpee especially is a good organizer, a gentleman in peace, a warrior if necessary: So good luck and Godspeed!"

Endless Winter and a Match Made in Heaven

"On June 6 and 7 another snowstorm hit northern New York and New England, with several localities recording six inches of snow. On June 7 snow flurries occurred in Boston, which was the latest instance of snowfall in Boston history. In July and August, the unprecedented cold weather continued, with temperatures dropping to forty degrees Fahrenheit as far south as Connecticut."

The following August, Nathan introduced Elijah to Olive Goodspeed, a distant kissing cousin, from the line of Roger and Alice's second son, John (Author's line).

At age eighteen, the Olive in the above picture looked much like her future granddaughter, Florence, pictured on the right. The youthful Olive had that same fire in her eyes.

Elijah knew that if he were to relocate to the frontier, he was going to need someone to partner with him; a strong wife with the courage and conviction to stand.

Old Nathan was blunt on that issue when he intro-

duced her to Elijah. That summer Olive was interning with Nathan to learn of his network. Nathan had Elijah for a conductor, as he had also selected Olive based on what he knew about Elijah's formative background.

Olive knew the details of Elijah's life, that he been separated from his mother and his siblings since he was five and had never known his father. Olive sensed that void upon meeting Elijah, but she was up to the challenge. Olive's penetrating, fiery glance and warm smile immediately filled him with confidence that he need not look further for such a competent mate.

"Will you show Elijah the schoolhouse?" Nathan suggested.

"Sure, Gramps!" Olive irreverently responded, much to the man's amusement.

"What schoolhouse?" Elijah asked, smiling and intrigued by their relaxed relationship.

"You'll see!" Olive answered. She was already out the

door without waiting for Elijah. With one quick glance at Nathan Elijah saw the elder nod as if to say "You'd better get going!"

Elijah was out the door.

"This way to Elijah Attwood's estate," she said, as she started through a wooded shortcut. They passed a clearing overlooking the impressive Connecticut River.

"What?" Olive asked, seeing Elijah stop, then noticed rats in the lumber yard.

"Oh that!" Olive laughed, and with one smooth motion threw a large fighting knife that she found sticking in a nearby post and skillfully nailed one sluggish varmint in the cold no less than twenty paces from where they were.

"Wow!" Elijah breathed.[10]

"Hungry, Elijah?" she jested, as she retrieved the knife.

"Where'd you learn to throw?" Elijah asked. "You almost cut him in half!"

"That was my plan," Olive commented dryly. "I learned from Mashpee Chatham." She looked at Elijah, "Do you know his history?"

Elijah took the knife out of the post again.

"No. But I have a feeling you are about to tell me."

She laughed. "Forgive me."

"No apology required as I'm waiting now to 'wow' you." He flipped the knife with practiced skill.

---

10 First-known usage of the word "wow" used to express strong feeling or wonder (as pleasure or surprise); root probably taken from Jehovah or YHWH (Yahweh) was first heard in William Shakespeare's time circa 1513 A.D.

"Well, as long as we're waiting for you to 'wow' me, do you want me to proceed?" Noticing his wry look, she hastened to clarify. "I mean, proceed with our Indian friends' history?"

"Oh, by all means!" Elijah said with just a little too much enthusiasm.

"Sorry, dear. You'll have to marry me first," Olive responded to match his mettle.

"Mash's ancestors..." she begins but is stopped as Elijah nails a rat at no less than thirty paces.

"Wow," she added with mild sarcasm, to hide her irritation.

Elijah could not resist pointing the knife in the kill's direction, then triumphantly stated "Cut in half," just to rub it in, then he cleaned the knife and avoided Olive's stare, and her arms defiantly crossed.

"Funny man!

As they neared the Attwood estate, Olive resumed her history of the schoolhouse.

"The building you see before you is the schoolhouse Nathan Hale taught at months before he left. He became a soldier, one who didn't like the violence of war and so became a spy instead. Ironically, a Loyalist relative turned him in and he was tragically martyred. This schoolhouse was purchased and moved north on Main in 1800 by Captain Elijah Attwood, my cousin Ann's husband. It was a joint historic venture with Captain Abner Comstock married to Ann's older sister Eunice."

"What's the connection to Mash?" Elijah asked.

"Well, we have to go back one hundred forty years to

an Indian attack in September of 1677, to understand what that event has in common with another attack during the Revolutionary War."

Olive looked at the beautiful Connecticut River then turned back to Elijah.

"When people judge individuals not as individuals but as a collective entity it will always, and I mean always, cause conflict and bad blood. Not all Indians are good and not all Indians are bad. Not all patriots are good and not all bad," she spoke, then as an afterthought added, "The same for the British."

"What about Negros?" Elijah asked, lost with strange pangs of emptiness and sadness.

Olive unexpectedly stepped up to Elijah, embraced and then gave him a sweet kiss that caused him to tear. Then she took his face in her hands and tenderly kissed his tears. "And yes, all men are created equal, even you Elijah Goodspeed!"

She broke away from his involuntary embrace giggling at his dazed reaction.

"Did I fill that void today?"

"Not quite," he remarked, breaking into a cheerful whole-hearted laugh, "but it came pretty close!"

Olive was pleased that the challenge was easier than she had anticipated.

"Huh, you better say filled and leave the qualifiers with your purity!" She returned to focus again on the history.

"The Indians, that terrible day, wanted revenge on white settlers, and then less than a hundred years later, the patriots wanted revenge, that terrible day, on British soldiers.

"An Indian war party converged on the great-grandfather of Nathan's wife Mary when the grandfather Samuel Kellogg was a young lad. He witnessed Sarah, his father's wife and his only brother brutally killed. They searched for Samuel to kill him as well, but one Indian started arguing with the other braves to stop. Then he pulled a flint hawk out against the principal leader of the attack! This cooled down these red brothers so that upon finding Samuel they spared his life and instead took him captive to Canada. A year later they released the boy back to his father.

"The boy grew up had a son, also named Samuel, who had a daughter Mary Kellogg, who married Corporal Nathan Goodspeed, whom I lovingly refer to as 'Gramps,'" she took a breath before finishing.

"That brave Indian, who stood up for peace, had a son, and two generations later the son named Mashpee Chatham! A kindred spirit not only to his tribe but to the white man as well."

Elijah was thunderstruck. After a reflective pause he stated, "Now I understand what you mean 'judging individuals as individuals and not as a group.'"

Olive continued into more current events.

"Lt. Nathan Hale, along with Corporal Nathan, joined the Connecticut militia. Hale was well-liked until he got caught spying. He was treated terribly before they hung him, which really set off those that loved him. He requested a Bible the night before his execution but that request was denied! He asked to see a minister and that request also denied!

"So, when our soldiers later found a small, separated team of British soldiers, no prisoners were taken! Our corporal confronted his angry troops; even the officers among them were sympathetic young officers. As were Elijah Attwood and Abner Comstock who knew that killing unarmed and surrendering soldiers was wrong.

"Abner and Elijah stood up for him. Nathan repeated over and over both on the field and in his defense, 'If Nathan Hale was alive he would not seek vengeance. So honor him! We make ourselves out to be no better than our image of the British as brutes when we ourselves behave and carry on as brutes!'"

Comstock and Attwood escorted Nathan to East Haddam to help him establish Goodspeed's landing, both as a military necessity and to establish funds to restore this schoolhouse as a memorial to Nathan the martyr. Thus, it brought us to the abolitionist cause that our old soldier, Nathan, took with increased devotion as a visionary. That led our troops away from slaughter, rejecting the unruly passions of errant collectiveness thinking!" Then Olive turned, pointing to the schoolhouse.

"Less than fifty years after Elijah had married Cousin Ann, he became the principal caretaker, moving that building to his estate in 1800 and completely restoring it before he died. He administered its maintenance and established a binding trust for permanent preservation, for future generations."

To Elijah, Olive Goodspeed was poetry in motion. Her quiet rapid-fire voice and deliberate well-planned movements, and her ladylike bearing was as soothing a song as a nearby fountain, running its stream of living waters. She was filled with future promises of seasons yet to come and gardens yet to be planted.

She brought light to dispel darkness and gave meaning to life that had no meaning or purpose. With her gentle inspiration, bad dreams and visions were displaced by stronger purpose and transformed Elijah's belief in a cause eventually into a magnificent obsession. The thought of her ever leaving, be it circumstances or death, was the only thing in life that would trouble him from there until the end of his days. This was indeed a match made in Heaven.

Second Generation Builders

Slippery Sam

There was a Negro in Bridgeport Connecticut, a free man named Slippery Sam.

Nobody really knew how he got that name. Some say it was because he could talk his way in or out of any situation, which was true. Or he cheated slavery when his master died, the man who had bonded him out to the Pacific Foundry in Bridgeport which was also true.

They say later in life, while working for P.T. Barnum, that he talked the man out of beating his slaves, black or white. Rumor had it that he gave the man *Uncle Tom's Cabin* which changed the man's attitude.

Either way, Slippery Sam was a free and freedom loving man.

It was said he could break a devout preacher and hard-working engineer to drink and sin faster than anyone; but more often than not, he could be found in the bar rather than in the boudoir. Sam loved debate, sharing profound engineering ideas and equally profound religious beliefs. Slippery Sam bought his freedom when the owner of the foundry took a shine to Sam's brilliant wit and promoted Sam to foreman after his master's death. Sam's mind worked like no other man's mind could fathom, he was a genius and libertine joker.

Sam came up with the idea that first got the owner's attention by adding manganese to steel to keep metal from cracking when hardened by quenching. That's when the name "Slippery Sam" stuck over the issue of hardening and lubrication. Some of his co-worker drinking buddies took credit for that, no doubt! But Sam didn't mind drunken barbs as long as he "gat paid" at the end of the day!

Sam quickly worked his way up to superintendent where he was given an office staff of amusing, attractive, and witty female clerks to help keep log of his inventions and ideas.

It was at such a time that Nathan and Joseph, showed up at his office.

The time was April 1818. Joseph was thirty and Nathan would die within a month of the meeting.

Sam put an iron pig on the balance and tipped the scale to its base on his desk. He then put a similar size ingot of grayer color on the opposing pan. The scale dial didn't move the heavier darker ingot though it was much denser. He put a second grey ingot on and the scale's dial moved slightly. It took four more to level the balance.

"Gentlemen?"

"My God, you did it!" Joseph exclaimed, while old Nathan laughed at his son's excitement. He winked at Sam.

"Ductility tests prove out that this alloy will withstand unequal heat distribution of boilers better than the heavier material, giving a ship less displacement in water. The ship will glide faster with less energy wasted and be three times more durable under such stress! It can withstand stress causing deadly fireship explosions, and from here on we, in this office, refuse to call 'fireships' and shall only refer to them as 'steamships'".

"My engineers are now drafting different brick baffle designs that will distribute the temperatures more evenly. We'll also put heating tubes within the boiler itself which will eliminate the need for elaborate fire boxes and baffle systems and free up space for fugitive slaves," he explained, leaning forward.

Nathan spoke up.

"The only drawback, Sam, is that the Fulton Patent bars us from production."

"But that doesn't mean we can't make prototypes! Joseph responded. As their patents get old, we can modify, change, and improve. And get around their building monopoly, right?"

"They've won so far," Sam commented. "But yes, we can conduct our experiments in secrecy and so far, we have until that day comes that we can challenge them openly in court. You can borrow my legal team." Sam said, with a wink in Joseph's direction.

Nathan laughed a generous laugh in the age of great laughs.

"Slippery Sam is a fireman who procured my son's wife!" he proclaimed, then coughed.

"Watch it, white man!" he retorted.

"Yes, about your legal team. I fell in love and married one of them," Joseph said and smiled with reference to his wife Laura Tyler. "Married her seven years ago after a very brief courtship when the Fulton Livingston Suit first came out."

Despite weighty issues, Sam broke out brandy and cigars for them all.

Nathan made a rare toast to his son for taking over the business but refused the cigar, then requested time alone with Sam. Joseph excused himself and went out in the lobby.

"Sam, I want to ask you a personal question, if I could?"

"Yessir!"

Nathan hesitated, so Sam helped him.

"Why I never settled down instead of hanging out with whores?" he suggested. Embarrassed, Nathan nodded.

Sam knew Nathan was dying and he loved him like a father. For once, Sam became deadly serious and responded without smiling.

"Because I never wanted someone that bad if I thought I might lose them."

He could see Nathan understood.

"That cruel separation of families and wives... The Negro wedding vow, till death or distance part..." Sam continued.

"I'm sorry I asked."

"Oh, please. Don't be, I'm just curious you didn't ask before now. But I think I know why," Sam answered and tilted his head toward the closed door and the spacious lobby beyond. "Does he know?"

Again, Nathan nodded and thought back to his college days when he almost killed himself. Now, like then, he had never feared death although this made him sad but not depressed. He thought about Nathan Hale and Marston and smiled; then about Silver Nathan and his wife, his secret weapon in life! Now they were gone and missed the most.

"I have no regrets," he offered. "I've had a good life."

"I wish I could say the same," Sam confessed.

Other men or women would have been driven to tears of despair. Sam got up and walked over to the window and looked out at the beautiful tree lined avenue leading up to the foundry. No, not Sam for he was far beyond that emotional loss. It had been driven out of him a long time ago. He too reminisced.

In one instance, he had been shackled to a deck helpless as he watched his mother commit suicide by jumping overboard in the night. After his new master had separated them in a cold-hearted on-board business deal, the cruel master looked on without doing anything as she jumped in view of her son. He called her "a worthless investment and pathetic consort for the new owner" and even laughed about it in front of the child.

Then he gagged the boy before he could cry out for help. It was a brutal contrast and strain of different cultures under that same heavenly beautiful cloudless sky and starry nights, breathing the same air. Free for many, but costly for slaves!

Personal thoughts of guilt and suffering had tortured him but he wouldn't, or couldn't, share them. Nor would he explain or burden anyone else with his torment, not even Nathan in his final days.

Samuel turned around toward Nathan, his focus now back in the room.

"I replaced all that bonding and love with only transients, hoping to finally find that contradictory Judeo-Christian spirit of courage and wherewithal to end this peculiar and pestilent trade of slavery forever someday. And to hold to that amazing grace, that yearning and instinctive desire for truth, justice and what is right ... and everything to do with God and brotherly love!"

Then changing the subject, he briskly walked over to the door with a new inspiration and invited Joseph back inside in order to displace those tragic memories.

Out in the lobby Joseph had walked by all the display cases and read some of the newer legends and admired the hall of mirrors on Samuel's side of the hall opposite the wall of windows. It was a clear and beautiful sunny day he noted as he looked at himself in one of those mirrors, then turned and faced the hall of beautiful tall windows. From there he observed the activity below and watched delivery carriages at the building's base.

He noticed many men were wearing those familiar Yale short top hats, cone-shaped but flat on top. Also, that the carriage welcome attendants, but not the carriage drivers, were still wearing the three-cornered hats.

In the lobby waiting area he saw the same thing concerning men's fashions, especially the hats which most of those waiting now had on their laps or on the arms of their chairs.

It was at this point in his musing that the door of Samuel's office opened. It caught Joseph's attention with Sam motioning him to come back into the meeting.

"Gentlemen, since aluminum is part of the mix and British pig iron is prohibitively expensive, I've decided to do you both a favor! On behalf of Pacific, I will give you a future development discount. I have a growing fondness for Goodspeed's landing that refuses to do business with the Deep South. We'll work together with DeWitt Clinton to look into developing an investment firm in New England to make this venture pay."

Coming off the Line

"Sam, go talk to her!" Sheryl Lee the Chownings proprietor whispered so not to attract attention from her girls and clients.

He looked at the black woman with a bruised face. Before another man could, Sam took another glass of champagne from the server's tray, walked over, and offered it to her.

"Good job of covering up that bruise, Bess. Keep smiling. We're being watched."

Nathan had returned home and Joseph was still with Sam in Bridgeport. They were in the upstairs parlor, resplendent in tapestry and lace curtains, with soft violin

music from a slow serenade creating an impeccably relaxed atmosphere.

With no other intentions but an occasional cigar and
single tumbler of brandy, Joseph watched Sam. They
were on a rescue mission like many times before.

"I'm in trouble Sam, I can't go back!" Bess kissed him
and whispered in his ear.

Sam could see the desperation, reminding him of the
look of his mom bore just hours before her death.

Sam laughed, "You could fool even me Bess, keep it
up." He pulled her head back and looked into her forlorn
eyes and soul, her desperation was hidden, barely skin
deep. His mouth came close to her ear and he whispered.

"Fourth room on the right at the end of the hall." Joseph was behind him now as put his cigar out, placed it
on a silver platter, and walked out into the hallway for
the next phase.

Sheryl Lee saw that signal as the "love struck" couple
took their cue. Sam winked at Sheryl Lee on the way out.

Twenty paces from the door, Joseph lit another cigar as
if waiting in the hallway, as Sam and Bess proceeded into
the bedroom. After Sam closed the door, she broke down.

"I can't go back, Sam. He'll whip me till I threw up blood,
and I'll never be able to leave here for a while, if ever!"

"Hush," he said and hugged her to console her. "How
would you like to go to Canada tonight for something
different?"

She drew a breath and pulled back to make sure she'd
understood him. She was about to ask a question, but
Sam placed his finger on her lips.

"Your child is in the carriage waiting for you!" he informed her. Then an instant later, "Stop it.... don't strangle me!" He laughed.

"Hush, mama, here, I brought you a new dress."

"That ain't no dress. That's men's clothes!" she exclaimed.

"You're a fast learner. Let's see how quickly you can put them on!" But like a gentleman he didn't turn around as she rushed by to quickly change.

He drew her hair into a tight coil and secured it with a blue ribbon. He wiped off the rouge with a handkerchief, and took a man's straw market hat from the ornate nightstand. He adjusted it to look casual yet cover the telltale compact bun, then drew its brim down to shadow her face and inspected it all with satisfaction.

"This way to the window!" he instructed.

They exited onto the flat slightly tilted roof to a waiting ladder and down to an enclosed coup carriage below. There waited Conductor Elijah Goodspeed, the driver, and Madagascar riding shotgun. In the dark of night in the alleyway was Mashpee Chatham on a spotted pinto, who was their heavily armed escort for a long trip.

CHAPTER FIFTEEN

Fly, Little Bird Fly!

With the window still open, Samuel listened to the sounds of the departing party till lost, like a bad dream, to time and memory.

"Fly, little bird, fly!" he said, then he closed the door and for the first time in many years, he wept freely.

Perhaps it was the business deal he had closed today, or perhaps it was for some other reason that he wept... he didn't know. It just felt good to be alive pursuing a cause that was near and dear to his heart.

"Dear Lord, let this mission continue till the day I die," he prayed, which was another thing he rarely did.

Meanwhile, Joseph puzzled at how long Samuel had been in the room and there patiently stood vigil. Sheryl Lee appeared from the parlor and looked quizzically at Joseph. He shook his head and shrugged. Sheryl Lee stood out from other owners, despising pimps and rescuing her girls from their wicked bullying ways. She shrugged herself and smiled, then walked past Joseph and knocked softly on the door. After a moment she went in and closed the door behind her without looking back.

She took good care of her girls. She watched the Black women carefully, especially those whom she knew were bonded out. She was diligently watchful to those who needed extra protection or rescue.

In the hall Joe waited. He realized that perhaps he shouldn't be caught standing there and decided it best to go downstairs to the restaurant and wait there for Sam. Joseph turned and walked past the parlor down the sumptuous spiral staircase.

1818 – Westward Bound

Late in April it took our party and the fugitive Bess and her young daughter a month to reach Madison County, New York, where the deceased Samuel's son Heman[11], had moved to work for Zebulon Douglass on the Erie Canal. A year earlier on July 4, 1817, at Rome New York, in the adjoining county he saw De-Witt Clinton "throw the first shovel full in that enterprise."

About the same time they arrived, Nathan died on May 26, at age 87 years "of gradual decay." The news of his death mailed by Joseph actually arrived in less time than it took them to get there, but by the time of its arrival, they were already headed further West to Niaga-

---

11 Author's Great-Great-Grandfather

ra County and beyond to Toronto and freedom for Bess and her young daughter.

Thanks to Mashpee, their expert guide and scout, the "package" was delivered safely to her brother who surprised her in Toronto. It only took a week there and a week back to Madison County. It was in mid-June that they learned of Nathan's death.

Since half the country was out gunning for them, the mandate was set for all those that had anything to do with Nymphas, Samuel or Thankful's surviving family to make a mass migration west in 1818, way beyond New England in the East or bust!

Madagascar took it the hardest that he couldn't have been there to be with his close friend and master in his final days. But now he was concerned about Joseph's and Thankful's future and safety.

Search and Departure

"What's wrong, white man?" Mashpee asked.

They were on their way back to Bridgeport with Madagascar to have a meeting with the surviving proprietors, Joseph and Sam.

"I'm thinking about our youngest long-lost sister."

"Rebecca?"

"Yes."

"She'd be about twenty-six now."

Elijah nodded.

"We will find her. We're going to have to find her now!" Mashpee vowed.

"Hopefully, we will. She was six but I never saw her because when she was bonded out, I was just a baby," Elijah recollected.

Bridgeport, Connecticut - Late June

The Chownings parlor was normally empty in the afternoon, but for the cleaning maid who made a brief entry and quicker exit on seeing that the room was now entertaining a small gathering. Her mistress Sheryl Lee, Samuel, Joseph, Madagascar, Noname, Elijah and Mashpee had gathered in the ornate room.

"What was this girl's name?" Sheryl Lee asked, eyes narrowing.

"Rebecca," Elijah repeated. "What?" Elijah asked a moment later, noticing her reaction.

The Indian turned and studied her reaction. Then Joseph looked up at her and back at Elijah.

"Excuse me... I'll go get one of my business journals!" Sheryl Lee said, stepping out of the room.

She returned with a log and journal which was numbered and dated.

"For legal purposes I keep journals and logs of events," she began to explain. "Now let's see."

She opened the journal and started thumbing through its yellowed pages.

"I have someone here who matches that description. Rebecca—ah , here it is. Rebecca Goodspeed."

Joseph sat bolt upright in his chair, as Mashpee and Elijah got up and looked over her shoulder. She read aloud.

"Nineteen, thin; in halfway house. Alone, single. Thanked us for putting her up. She had an old gingham blue dress that had to be laundered, and mended, but no other possessions." Sheryl paused and looked up at her guests.

"At the time I thought she was joking. She saw Nathan downtown once and said that was her name, too. Several times I asked her for her real name but each time she'd only say 'Becky.' She didn't like to talk much," Sheryl sighed.

"But one particular night she started telling me about how her mother sold her to strangers when she was only six." Elijah shook his head.

"It wasn't my mother's fault. I know, because she talked about her quite often, and missed her terribly. She dreaded a time when they would eventually come for me!"

Mashpee probed, "When did you last see her? Where was she headed?"

"Now hold on. That was seven years ago and she was here only a week. They told me she had left the boarding house and wasn't seen again."

"Was she a drifter?" Joseph asked.

"Apparently so", Sheryl Lee responded, but not without compassion and interest; even frustrated and angry with herself.

"I'm sorry, Joseph. I should have brought it to Nathan's attention or Madagascar's. There must have been a reason, but it's not on record anywhere."

"I wished you had told me," Samuel spoke up, then added, "I would have contacted Nathan."

They were all upset, except Mashpee whose mind was already analyzing all the viable options for tracking her. "Who was the manager at the time over at your boarding house? Is he still working there?"

"Yes."

"Is he there today?"

"Yes."

"I'll be back; I'm boarding there too," Mashpee headed out at once. A quarter-hour later, he was getting some answers.

"She was leavin'...gettin' married," informed the manager.

"To whom?" Sheryl Lee asked. "Do you remember his name?"

"I think. I rec'lect that since she said she was a Goodspeed it stuck in my mind. I think it was William, if I recall correc'ly, but I know that the last name was Freeman."

"Did they say where they were going?" Sheryl pursued.

The manager said uncertainly, "Out East I guess, here or maybe further out?"

"Out West, you mean?" Joseph asked.

"No, sir. East of here.

Elijah was depressed. His sister had been a drifter looking for work as a prostitute, even though she was "gettin' married".

But one day Mashpee finally shocked Elijah.

"Elijah, I found her," he announced.

"Where is she?"

"She was with no man. It took every trick in the book to find her. In desperation I found a Woodlot Indian shaman who in a shamanic spiritual medicine trance. I consulted with him and he led me to her, but damned near killed me!" Mashpee paused to give Elijah a hard look.

"Now here's the deal, Elijah, but please hear me out first before we get there. She's safe with our council, however there are a few things you need to know. She doesn't want to have anything to do with the family. But please allow me to tell you some things first." With that, Mashpee began to describe what happened on that journey weeks before:

Mashpee woke up disorientated and sick. He rolled over and vomited at the banks of a river nearby. It felt so bad, like a terrible hangover, that he was "afraid that he was actually going to live."

The Woodlot shaman or the spirit's voice had given him instructions, but Mash was in no condition to move on, wherever he was, at early dawn. He vowed he would never take that "medicine" again and he struggled to hold on, wrestling with devils.

As he was convalescing, he regained some sanity and studied the surrounding flora and fauna to determine where that miserable shaman had dumped him. His directions included that he was to go to the North on the river. With the rising sun that was easy enough to determine. North was facing him when he eventually rolled over and sat up.

After a while from what he knew of flora and fauna, he figured out that he was still in Massachusetts, but much further in the western portion near Rhode Island. From other explorations he knew the river was either the Fall River or Taunton River, but since the Fall River ran more east and west and this river ran north and south, this was most likely the Taunton River, south of Shepherd's Cove.

Mashpee felt like an idiot as he dragged himself closer to the river to revive himself, a process that took quite a while. That wicked shaman looked down laughing at him. Mash broke the spell and in spite of his pain had to laugh at the stupid mess he had gotten himself into.

Towards noon he finally rose up. At least the shaman had left him armed with his knife, hunting bow and some tack, jerky, and flask of water for this adventure. He also found his shotgun wrapped in raw leather. He proceeded northward along the short Taunton River, using the raw soft leather as a sort of shawl.

He slowly shook his head for he was still very hung over. This was so stupid, he thought but at the same time felt guilty and ashamed for thinking that.

He nobly bore this low-grade depression until he spotted not just one, but three deer, when both clarity and vision returned as he remembered the shaman's instructions to move north with the deer.

Three deer, young without horns, like brothers, like the Trinity... he thought, reflecting. *The Trinity; the Father, the Son, and the Holy Ghost!*

Then Mash recalled other instructions that had

something to do with a vision. His last thoughts before blacking out were about deer.

That's right! he thought, but it wasn't Indian custom that helped him to recover mental clarity, but Christian concepts of faith! Those really guided him: moral principles and an instinctive desire to stand up for what is right, teachings from a higher Christian level from another mentor, Jedidiah Morse!

This made him feel better! It was then he knew he was where he needed to be. So even though he spotted other deer, he stubbornly focused just on following or tracking this trio. Also, they didn't seem to mind him following, and in his condition knew he had a strong musk scent although he had bathed to vainly try to refresh himself. And he was armed because he also had on him his hawk weapon strapped into his waist belt and his sling with the shotgun.

Up ahead along the bank, the deer now further up from him, Mash noticed they were coming up on a small shack, like a hunter's cabin with the roof starting to cave in.

Ominously, the deer stopped and watched him till he got too close then all three suddenly scattered and took off as spooked deer normally do. He knew he would not be able to keep up with them or track them further and he wondered what he would do next.

Then he heard it!

He heard noise of something moving inside the structure, then silence. He shifted his shotgun from his left to right hand slowly and deliberately in case he needed it, then politely stood his ground just in case the cabin's occupant was home.

Finally, Mash spoke up softly in case it was not an animal but a person.

"I don't mean to trouble you... but I'm looking for someone."

A door creaked and he stepped back, ready for anything. Slowly the door opened. Mash controlled a gasp at what he saw. The woman!

She was exactly as he had seen in his vision, but she also had a shot gun, elbow bent, forearm cradling the weapon in a defensive posture but not pointed at him. At least not yet, unless Mash did something stupid.

While she looked in command, she also looked lost just like him, although both knew that they were in the same state. But her expression, the one of someone lost emotionally and spiritually, revealed that they were indeed very different. He was calm and still slightly hung over, but the alpha male, nonetheless. She was a wary woman-child guarded and alert as she had trained herself to be!

"Rebecca?" he called softly.

She nodded, as the gentle wind blew through her long flowing hair.

Mash continued speaking with Elijah, finishing the story.

"After that change, after I rejected Woodlot shaman's ways, I was troubled until I saw three deer in the forest at the river's edge. This caused me to think about the

Trinity and I knew all was well with my soul." Chatham paused and looked at Elijah, then smiled.

"Immediately after that, on the very same day I found your lost and lovely little sister, Elijah!"

"Take me to her!" Elijah begged.

"Perhaps, but there is something I have to tell you first," Mashpee hesitated.

"What does that mean, Mash?" Elijah was stymied.

Mashpee looked away, thinking, then slowly turned back to him.

"She's a servant in one of our councils but she doesn't want to have anything to do with you, Thankful, or the family," he delivered the news as gently as he could.

Elijah was trying to understand.

"Elijah! Listen. She doesn't want anything to do with members of her own race!"

Elijah was surprised but upon reflection laughed, then with further reflection, laughed louder. Mashpee smiled.

"She'll be just fine. They're taking good care of her. She works and she has her own life now and can do mostly whatever she wants."

"Oh my God: I'll have to break this to mom!" Elijah said with stressed recognition.

"I wouldn't do that, Elijah. She's allright, and occasionally visits Jabez and Thomas."

Elijah nodded, then asked, "Does Jane also know?"

Mashpee bit his lip but nodded.

"Good God!" Elijah exclaimed incredulously.

"But not Solomon or Nathan. Elijah, please just remember this. I'm taking Solomon, your mom, and Nathan out to Athens first. Then I'll be coming back for Jane next, then you and Olive," Mashpee reminded him, as he leaned forward grabbed his arm.

"If anyone is eventually going to talk straight to your mom about this, let Jane be the one. You know how close they are!"

One Loose Cannon

1821

That December the week of Christmas started with a new moon and was the darkest of nights. The son of deceased Abe, killed by members of his own gang, was also found dead. The Maryland gang members made it look like Abe had actually done it. But for once in his life of killing, Abe was actually not involved with his son's death. Someone else, closer to home was! His son had been tied down in a chair with his throat cut, and family credentials blown off, then abandoned in a hunter's cabin in Maryland.

That year Thomas Goodspeed, Thankful and Nathan's second son, had had enough. He was the family's weakest link in the chain that would break.

Closest to Jane who was born just after he was, he loved his older sister but even more so loved the younger sister born after Jane and Jabez.

Jabez was not as affected as Thomas was about Rebecca's visit to a whore house. Jabez never regarded Rebecca as cute as Thomas did. Being in between both sisters in age, he regarded Jane as the wise, older, bossy sister and Rebecca as the rival younger, spoiled sister, with nothing cute at all about her.

It was true that Jabez resented the treatment they had all received, as did Thomas and the rest, but the possibility that Rebecca may have been abused, only put him into denial.

When contact was made, Jabez and then Thomas had their first visit with Rebecca. Then rarer visits, with Rebecca only visiting Thomas and Jabez, no one else, since she didn't want to have anything to do with the rest of the family, especially her mother, who in the mind of a six-year-old had bonded her to be taken away. And she blamed her own father for just dying!

The Maryland Gang sought to destroy the family, did indeed!

Jabez was first to ask Rebecca about her life as an indentured servant. What she told upset him. Eventually he told Thomas in '21, which was the last time Jabez saw Thomas. Jabez wrongly thought Thomas took the news better than he, but Jabez was wrong. Dead wrong!

Thomas was silent and shy by nature even with wife Martha. The last person that had any contact with Thomas in the family was Rebecca.

When news of the murder reached Joseph, it didn't take long for him to figure out the motive and who was involved.

Joseph did know that the deceased was involved in sex trafficking of Negros and Whites. The solution to the motive came up his driveway in the early morning hours of Christmas day was a mud-spattered carriage driven by Noname. That carriage pulled up into Goodspeed's landing.

Earlier, Sunday, December 23rd, Joseph had been informed of the murder and feared the implications and retribution to come. He noticed only his bodyguard, Madagascar; Thomas, and Noname were absent.

Now, just before dawn on Christmas Day, Noname's travel-stained face told the story.

"Where's Thomas?" Joseph asked, dreading the worst.

"We got separated after fording a river in order to lose the scent dogs. That's the last time I saw Tom," was the reply

"Do they know who did it?" Joseph asked, more earnestly.

"No. But the scent dogs will eventually find his body."

Joseph whistled for Madagascar.

"Madagascar, we've got a problem. Get our best scent dogs and find him before they do!"

An hour later just as Madagascar was in the buckboard, ready to go, another buckboard pulled up. Mashpee, the driver, with a woman. This was the first time for Joseph and the rest to see Rebecca and be introduced by Mashpee.

"You would have been too late; they already had their hounds out!" Mashpee bluntly addressed Joseph.

Mashpee calmly got out, went around and gently assisted Rebecca. She was tired and worried by the long sleepless night and longer trip which included the search and recovery of the body. Joseph, Noname, and Madagascar went over to the cart as Joseph pulled the cover back from the still figure underneath the blanket. Rebecca stood by silently but tears were running freely down her face.

Mashpee reached into a compartment for the shotgun, covered with frozen mud, and showed it to Joseph then put it back in its compartment.

"We burned up the wood stock of Tom's gun." Mashpee added. "What's left of it you can have Slippery Sam at Pacific melt down, Joseph, in order to destroy what's left of any incriminating evidence."

Again, Joseph grimly nodded, then turned reverently to cover the frozen head.

"Thank you for finding it in time. Do you have the knife?"

"No, Becky tipped me off but by the time we got there they had found the knife."

Noname spoke up.

"Thomas took me by surprise, and I'm still not sure if the gun went off by accident or not. But the man was in great pain...I had to think fast in the confusion, cut his throat...I never killed before." Noname broke down, not being able to speak further.

Days later, Thankful, was now at the funeral of her first offspring to die. Joseph spoke.

"They tried to make it look like a suicide by cutting

the cords and leaving the knife. It would have made more sense, Noname, if you guys[12] had left the shotgun and taken the knife instead." Noname shook his head.

"Where Mashpee discovered your son, Thankful, I had walked right by in my frantic search for him, after that cold river we crossed to lose our scent, ma'am. I could have saved him,"his voice broke. "Oh, why didn't he sing out!"

"Because he was already in the advanced stages of cold exposure," Mashpee explained. "The mind plays tricks. The victim hides thinking that every living soul on earth is his enemy. It wasn't your fault."

Rebecca did not attend the funeral, but Jane told Thankful the good news that Rebecca had been found. However, Jane withheld the bad news about her ordeals and abuse and bitterness towards her mother and others of her own race.

Thankful had already figured it out, and said with greater pain, "So it drove my son to murder and destruction and destroyed my relationship with my youngest daughter."

Jane flinched but slowly nodded.

Thankful felt like she'd been punched in the stomach. Tears ran down Thankful's face. "I should have run off with her before anyone could take her away at that fragile age!"

---

12 Author's Note: The word "guys" has been around since 1606 AD. Gun Powder Plot to blow up the House Of Lords, the plot that failed November 5, 1605; perpetrator Guy Fawkes and his gang. By 1606 referred to as "the guys" but by the 1700s to 1800s took on a more collective but positive meaning for an assembly of two or more people.

Jane broke down crying.

"No mom, please don't blame yourself. It was Rebecca's own testimony that Thomas's last words were not directed at you but did seek redress for the defilement of his sisters."

Everyone present caught Jane's mention of "sisters" instead of "sister". Mashpee bit his lip and looked away. Before anyone could respond, Jane stormed out of the funeral.

Elijah had been away on sea duty. It was agreed to bury the whole affair. The potential was too great for opening up a deadly war between Goodspeed's landing and the Maryland gang. It would be hell to pay!

On Joseph's instructions, the massive cover up of Tom's actions and death began. The connections, though numerous, fortunately were easy enough to bury. Those would not be revealed for another two hundred years.

Rochester, Massachusetts

1824

In 1798, when it seemed the world was coming to an end, Jabez was nine and although vulnerable, he wasn't as vulnerable as his younger sister. The other two boys or rather, boy Nathan and baby Elijah, were not at the statutory age to be bonded out. Jabez at least understood that it wasn't his mother's fault what was about to happen.

But not so with Rebecca, who in her heart, at age six, blamed her dad for dying at sea and blamed her mom for "selling her to strangers".

Jabez, now thirty-five, was a successful and prosperous shipwright working for Goodspeed's landing. He lived and worked out of his home office in Rochester, making frequent visits to Nathan after the terms of his indentured servitude was over. Under Nathan and after Nathan's death, he was no longer bonded and was promoted to senior engineer under his new boss, Joseph.

"To get ahead in this business, patriot, you have to have an incredible sense of two things: first, a sense of self-worth, and second, an instinctive desire to stand up for what is right," Jabez would say.

Jabez was the middle of the pack of Thankful's children who were now all adults. As a shipbuilder he was also an incredibly expert material handler. He was the glue of both the family and Goodspeed's landing business. He was the "rudder, keel, and anchor" of the business.

As material handler ordering parts and supplies, one of his favorite statements was "one small bolt will sink a ship"! Which translated meant the critical difference between a "build" and "no build" in production and that could make or break a company overnight.

Never missing a production date, he became the "go to" guy of the nineteenth century, for not only Goodspeed's landing, but Pacific Machines and Iron Works as well. He was their secret weapon against competition and insurance and assurance of survival. Jabez, in demand by all, eventually became wealthy!

When he died in the very early years of the Civil War, he would be dearly missed by both the family and the business. Things would never be the same.

Fortunately, his vision would live on to produce the "90-day gunboats" that Lincoln and the war demanded, that they would set the record for ships sunk and confederate forts lost by the enemy. Eventually they would bring the South to its knees.

"Union First" and "Faith without works is dead," he would carry on and inspire others from Old Nathan on... to his own grave.

Jabez was doing quite well in 1824, when Elijah and Mashpee paid him and Malintha a visit, following a written invite from Jabez.

Mashpee opened the meeting.

"My parents taught us from a very young age, as is our custom, to remember our dreams. We use our dreams for spiritual guidance and healing," Mashpee continued. "But as my current mentor Jedidiah Morris often quoted, Colossians 2:8. 'See to it that no one takes you captive by philosophy and empty deceit, according to human tradition, according to the elemental spirits of the world, and not according to Christ.'" he ended.

"My former mentor, the shaman, was wrong! Did he predict to his people the correct side to be on in the years of our last war? When the leaders of the Indian nation sided with Great Britain, gambled, and lost? A man who is held up to be a prophet! He was wrong and he cost our Indian nations a price we will never be able to pay!" Mashpee spoke adamantly.

"No! Nathan was right! I came back with Rebecca a new changed man. That faith without works is dead... That faith without works is death!"

Elijah by this time had learned that his sister Rebecca had been raped but didn't suspect how badly mistreated she was or that Jane herself had let it slip that she too had been sexually abused. Folding his hands in his lap, he caught Elijah eyes in a mesmerizing friendly gaze.

"Elijah. Pay attention. This is to introduce you to the reality of your sister's tragedy but not start a civil war between good and evil spirits."

With a nod from Mashpee, Jabez stood up.

"What?!" Elijah's attention now focused.

"There's no easy way to say this so I'm just going to say it."

"What?" Elijah repeated, as Mashpee smiled briefly behind his back.

"I think I already know." Mashpee stated, remembering Jane's behavior at Tom's funeral, now leading the script cooked up between him and Jabez.

"It's about Jane, isn't it?" but that remark seemed too staged.

"Yes." Jabez then confessed the truth he had long withheld from Elijah, but now was the chosen time to reveal it to Elijah.

"Jane, your other sister, was also raped one time, abused also." There was dead silence for a moment as it slowly registered on Elijah, still in a fog of confusion but more or less under Mashpee's spell.

He raised his hands in fists and fell on his knees.

"Oh my God!" he cried out.

Mashpee gently laid his hands on Elijah with tremendous empathy as both he and Jabez, and then Jabez's wife Malintha, now came into the room and helped him get up. This had also been orchestrated for Elijah's health and well-being. But what's this? A visitor from the West to overload Elijah's senses further in order to dissipate his anger upon getting up from low estates? A new guest followed Malintha and entered the room.

"Fool!" Jane proclaimed, which further surprised and shocked Elijah out of his confusion. "True, you finally face reality, my young brother Elijah, but there is little you know of women who have been deflowered. You men that know so little about us so called tender creatures!"

"I thought you were out West!" Elijah stammered.

"No! I'm their guest!" Jane went on.

"But this would destroy you too, Jane, even..."

"Stop!" she warned Elijah. "Don't treat me like a victim!"

She grabbed Elijah's arm.

"Listen to me Elijah, your mom forgave that monster on his death bed. Do you care to know my state of mind after the attack?"

"If there's something to be gained, yes," Elijah responded.

"Did you ever tell mom?"

"Yes, she told me everything even about Becky," came the reply from an unexpected voice.

Elijah spun around as his mother now entered the room. Surprised to be greeted by his mother, from the West, he looked as if he were going to pass out. Thankful, Jane, Jabez and Mashpee all rushed to prevent this from happening. Then they all laughed, but Elijah's eyes narrowed in concentration, and he started looking at all of them. His eyes narrowed further, then slowly he raised his hands.

"Wait! I was slow to catch on, but I think I'm getting

this," he spoke calmly, then started laughing. "So, this is what family life is really all about."

He pointed at Jane.

"You and Becky were both raped, right?" Jane nodded smiling, fascinated to see his wheels turning.

Elijah now pointed at Jabez and Mash, "You both set this up, right?" They grinned like boys getting caught by a wise teacher in a prank. Elijah's eyes, now just narrow slits, gave Mash a sidelong glance.

"And Thomas wasn't killed in a mere hunting accident, was he?"

This shocked everyone present, which Elijah, man of the world made note of, and still laughed.

"So you think I'm going to turn killer on the gang and you are worried? Because if you are, then yes, I am capable of doing just that. But I won't and what's more, I never will, unless I set a trap for them just like Old Nathan used to do, correct?"

Awestruck, everyone in the room simply nodded.

Finally, Elijah turned and went directly to Jane and hugged her, lifting her off the ground and laughed.

"And you were about to teach me the lesson of forgiveness just then, or leading up to that, right?"

Jane could only laugh, shaking her head but Elijah only laughed back at her knowing she was lying.

All Jabez wanted to do before Elijah could turn on him, was to hastily conclude the meeting.

"Welcome home Skipper!"

The rest of the evening the homecoming turned into a happy reunion, celebrating family, and friendships.

Goodspeed's Landing

1825 - East Haddam Connecticut

At the time of this meeting, Jabez had a family, although he had started late for his age by those days' standards. His oldest, Sara D. was three going on four when they had Rebecca Jane (dedicated to *the offended sisters*), born July 28, 1825.

Later, Jabez would propose that name for Elijah's ship when it was launched. The *City of Rebecca Jane*, a steamship, destined to deliver scores upon scores of slaves to freedom in many a daring rescue.

Now it was Elijah's turn to serve America. He had finally married Olive in 1825, although they had been forced again and again to delay their wedding date.

One delay was the age old Fulton Livingston lawsuit, that strangled steamship building by their competitors.

The other family plans of migration also came ahead of Elijah and Olive wedding plans, complicated the situation further, courtesy of Joseph at Goodspeed's landing.

When the Supreme Court decision finally came down on March 2nd, 1824, Joseph's office was immediately contacted. Joseph was elated although he already knew as early as Christmas Eve, 1823, from DeWitt Clinton associates, that a favorable outcome was most likely to be that month. So, Joseph, with confirmation from his own legal staff, made the call to authorize the completion of Elijah's steamship. Jabez adjusted the production schedule for a March/April completion date, just in time for Elijah to report back from sea duty in Boston. Joseph winked at his staff, "Not a word, let's surprise him!"

Coyly adding, with a chuckle, to the message "not to make any future commitments."

"Well, glory be! Joseph just delivered the stripes!" Elijah declared with glee. This was a reference to Connecticut Harbor bass early spring runs. Quickly he turned to his first mate. (This notice came late the summer of 1825).

"Get my luggage off this ship, please!"

He was so excited he ran up the cobble stone raceway, slipped and bruised his knee but didn't care, even laughed as he wiped the mud and scented fish grease off his pants and jumped into a ferry horse drawn cart.

"To the nearest livery at once please!" he called.

There he hired a livery and carriage, and once loaded with his personal effects and inventory checked and secured, he was off to Barnstable in a flash. Vague instructions or not, Elijah knew exactly what this was about!

It was springtime and everything was in blossom, and heaven was filled with bird song. Olive read the news of the favorable Supreme Court decision and she rushed into Elijah's arms when he arrived. When Elijah shared the message with her, they cried, laughed, and in thanksgiving got down on their knees. Then they rushed over to where Mash, who had just returned the previous week, was lodging. Within the hour, all three were on their way to East Haddam in the very same livery that Elijah had rented in Boston.

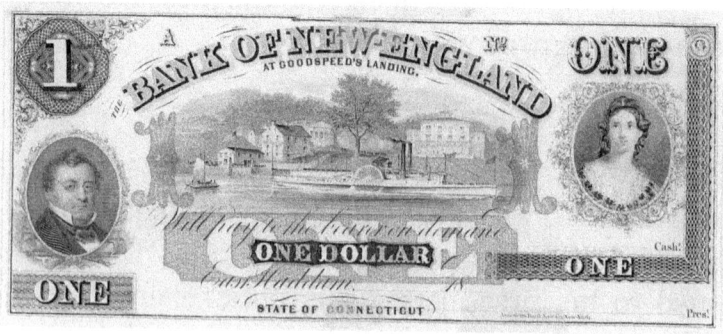

Joseph Goodspeed - and wife Laura Tyler Goodspeed

They were tired until they got to the magic of the mouth of the Connecticut River where they were re-energized when they saw the spring army of fishermen. As far as the eye could see, they were there by the thousands chasing a great feast of free-running striped bass in its fishing water basins. Commerce travel on the waterways was at a temporary standstill as the sports fishermen commanded the bay.

"Thank God we took the livery!" Mashpee Chatham shouted and laughed over the rushing waters.

As they arrived at Joseph's estate, Mashpee, Elijah, and Olive could smell the spring sweet-scented honeysuckle that was blooming all over the white pickets. They saw Joseph relaxed and casually seated on the steps, leaning back on one of the beautiful white balustrades. He cordially waved and when he saw them alight from their carriage, he stood up.

"Right this way!" Joseph yowled and greeted his travel-stained arrivals with enthusiasm. This assured them that nothing had changed with Nathan gone. Joseph was young and as energetic as ever, if not more so. His sons George Edward, age eleven, and William Henry, age ten, also looked precocious and enthusiastic about the business as well, and they were also introduced to Laura Tyler, Joseph's wife.

"Don't worry. You'll get plenty of refreshments and rest, but I want to show you something now."

They got into another bigger sumptuous carriage with an impressively uniformed driver in gray top hat, yellow breeches, and red coat. He delivered them to the small steam vessel docked to port the party across the Connecticut River to the large shipyard and larger joiner facilities. This would be the first time Elijah had ever been on a steamship. For a moment he entertained the notion that this was his new vessel and felt a twinge of sad disappointment on observing its lesser size to larger ships he had commanded.

Joseph read his mind but pretended not to notice. Joseph's ship steward was Noname, immaculate in a white coat, and he served lemonade refreshments and a light lunch to the guests. The atmosphere was formal but relaxed and Noname and Joseph put the guests at ease with humor and good stories.

On the drive over, Joseph produced a complete transcript of the U.S. Supreme Court decision, Gibbons v. Ogden. Then he began to read.

"The acts of the Legislature of the State of New-York, granting to Robert R Livingston and Robert Fulton the exclusive navigation of all the waters within the jurisdiction of that State, with boats moved by fire or steam, for a term of years, are repugnant to that clause of the constitution of the United States"...

"Repugnant!" Joseph howled gleefully, "Boy that must fry Livingston's onion!" The guests joined in his mirth, laughing heartily as well.

"We had to convince Governor DeWitt Clinton that it was in his best interests to not encourage Fulton to make it hard on smaller businesses, that would actually dramatically increase commerce and traffic revenue on his Erie Canal project. After that, it did not take long for Clinton to get an audience with Judge William Jay of Winchester County, who in turn got an audience with the Honorable Chief Justice John Marshall who himself was sympathetic to our cause. He swayed the case in our favor, as well as allowing free market trade and navigation to flourish. Adin Ballou[13] be damned." Then Joseph frowned.

"The only downside to all this is that it also makes it easier for the slave traders to navigate and conduct their evil enterprise on the Mississippi."

Joseph noticed that the Indian was slowly shaking his head and smiling as they approached dock.

"Why are you shaking your head, Mashpee?" he asked.

"Do you think slavery in America will ever end?" he responded by asking.

"Do I think slavery in America will end?" Joseph repeated then reflected. "No." Everyone turned to look at him. "No, I don't think so, not if it is left up to man. I can see no way that the system will change."

"Why were you also smiling, Mash?" he pursued.

"Because like all of you", Mash responded, "I believe in a greater spirit that will not rest until it is settled. But I shake my head at the pain the black man has endured and will continue to endure until it is."

The steamer was now rubbing gently against the dock bumpers as mooring lines were being cast to the waiting attendants. Joseph responded with a quiet "Amen!" as they walked onto the wharf.

"I'll take you on a tour of the shipyard," Joseph announced.

---

13 Author's note: Adin Ballou (1803-1890) was a famous Unitarian Universalist, and critic of the so-called injustices of capitalism and honest people like Joseph Goodspeed, whom he wrongfully accused of greed and corruption. Adin hated God, like Karl Marx, for creating free markets and interfering with their manifesto.

"Where're the rats?" Elijah said softly for Olive to hear and was rewarded by her firm squeeze on his arm.

"Quiet, dear!" she warned through clenched teeth only for Elijah to hear.

"Why? Did you bring your fighting knife?" Elijah teased, only to feel the grip tighten toward his funny bone.

Mash walking a few feet behind them smiled at Elijah's antics.

"Better watch it, white man. If she lets you win the first match, she will not be so generous the second time with you as the target."

"Oh, the pain!" Elijah laughed.

"That's right, dear!" Olive breathed with emphasis, giving him one last parting squeeze.

The cleanliness of the area was impressive. The organization of tools and workstations, the smell of turpentine, varnishes, and fresh caulk, bleach in one area, in another polish, waxes and lacquer sticks, all made for an immaculate workspace. Stock rooms with drums of different oils for various applications, and secure paint rooms had nothing out of place. The machinery stations were impressive and the hulls in various levels of completion made it obvious that this was an assembly line. There was a worker's holiday for Joseph's honored guests.

They went through a door into the larger adjoining amphitheater. Elijah gasped and Olive renewed her grip on him to kept from crying out.

A huge steamship spanned over half the entire length

of the Quonset building. It gleamed white, freshly painted, and boasted a red-brown flat hull, with stabilization runners accented with gold leaf relief at the water line. Fulton himself would have been envious.

Joseph looked at Elijah. "So, what do you think?"

Elijah in shock, as a color guard and six-piece military band struck up the "Star Spangled Banner." Elijah, Olive and Mash noticed a gathering of familiar faces in a reserved area and upon their entering, they all stood up to pay tribute and gave a hearty welcome to the visitors, and guest of honor, Elijah!

After the anthem a piano softly started and a familiar voice began to sing. Thankful sang of Christ's obedient ransom, and Louisa Albright joined her to end the song in a beautiful duet, extolling with joyful gratitude such a sacrifice.

The entire assembly applauded.

Elijah asked Mash, "Who's that woman?"

"That's Heman's wife Louisa Albright. They married this past season," Mash informed.

"Which reminds me," Elijah said as he turned to Olive, "Time to get married?"

"No," Olive started coyly, but then with emphasis squeezing the arm, "It's about time."

"I'll second that!" Thankful embraced her son and Olive. "When we're done here, let's leave for Barnstable, and then you two can get married."

"You be my best man, Mash?" Elijah asked, then Olive posed to the pretty blonde, "Louisa, be my best maid?"

"You bet, sweetheart!"

"We wouldn't miss it for the world!" Mash rejoined.

"Mom, that song!"

"This is my song. Now it's yours. It came to me the day you were taken from me. I could have given into fear and despair or turned to hate, but the joy of the Lord lifted me up!"

Joseph rushed over to Thankful.

"What was the name of that beautiful song!?"

Elijah responded instead, "Thankful's 'Song of Freedom'!"

"Well done, Thankful!" A new voice was heard and Elijah noticed Mash start, as if the voice had come from God.

"Yes, Mashpee, my dear friend. It is I, Jed."

Mash embraced the old man in black in obvious joy.

"My God, I thought you'd be with Mayor Strong in paradise!" he cried.

Elijah never saw Mash lose his composure.

"You know this man?" he asked to understand his past better.

"These men, and Governor Caleb Strong, were my childhood inspiration," he said, then to Jedidiah, "I'm so glad to see you again!"

Joseph laughed.

"You didn't think I'd forget about you, Mash?" Joseph continued. "Allow me to introduce you all to Reverend Jedidiah Morse, degree in divinity from Yale University, and D.D. from the University of Edinburgh, '95; well-worn from lifelong struggles with the Unitarian Church."

"Dear Olive, good to see you," the Reverend addressed her. "You're a true friend to Hale's memory!" Olive moved into the Reverend's open arms and embraced him warmly.

"Thank you!" Olive said. She looked at Elijah, then back at Reverend Morse. "We're to marry in Barnstable, early next year, can you attend?"

Jed looked at Elijah, "We would be deeply honored if you could."

The Reverend burst out in laughter.

"What you mean to ask if I will officiate, the answer is 'yes,' that is if I am still around. What date?"

"May 28th," Olive responded, obviously pleased.

Thankful laughed in joy. Another prayer answered. Her last child was getting married!

Fifteen Years After
Their Western Migration

1833

Elijah was the last to depart the Atlantic Seaboard.

"I'll be damned if I'll be the first to go! As God as my witness, I'll be the last! Family and America first!"

Elijah and Jabez decided to name the new ship the *City of Rebecca-Jane*. Elijah made sure that the Eastern survivors who were determined to stay, Rebecca and Jabez, were safe, as Mashpee could assure. Olive had already settled out west with her children Harriet, Henry and newborn Jane.

Solomon, the oldest brother in their family, had children Chloe, Nathan, Allen and Thomas who had just turned ten and all the boys were allowed to tag along for the great adventure on the giant Atlantic Ocean. It was the thrill of a lifetime for such young lads!

"Just the boys!" Solomon laughed.

Nathan, now age twenty in '33, had become best friends with Elijah and traveled back east with his two younger brothers to join Elijah to take *the City of Rebecca-Jane* on her last voyage down the Atlantic coast.

Elijah, who himself was only fifteen years older, was especially fond of Nathan who was named after a father he had never known.

The ship had already seen action during some shake down cruises on the Connecticut River, through the Hudson River through the Erie Canal and was already taking scores of runaways to freedom in Canada.

The Broad Atlantic

All were having the time of their lives, and Elijah beguiled them with adventure stories of Privateer Samuel and as well as his own accounts. He told of Samuel's last adventure along the coast of Maryland where Grandfather Nathan had died.

"Look what 'Uncle' Mash brought... fireworks!" Elijah laughed.

Mash grinned at Elijah and the boys pried open a crate containing a trip's worth of fireworks and one six-pound Spring Rocket.

"I also brought some clear glass rods for lobster catching," Mash informed as the boys carefully unpacked the rods secured in cloth bags. "Here Nathan, I'll put you in charge of these to keep them from breaking. Careful!"

"Thanks, Mash! You kids are going to love this when it's time!"

The boys danced.

"We can't wait!" Allen shouted.

Soon the tranquil rose twilight sky was set ablaze with fireworks and the rocket that soared two thousand yards up in the sky exploded was the grand finale. In fact, the *Rebecca-Jane* steamer was bearing south two miles off the New Jersey shore from Fort Henry's coast to give the beach strollers a patriotic treat as well. Large bangs and flashes in the sky could be seen and heard for miles.

"Full speed ahead, Fred!" Elijah yelled.

Mash, in charge of launching the rockets already knew the drill. He concealed the stern iron grate launch platform, secured it in hinge down position, washed and covered.

Meanwhile Elijah sat down and told the boys the story.

"In 1813, before John and Samuel's death, we were all together with another inventor named Mr. Beath, the inventor of these Spring Rockets which were very similar but superior to the Congreve Rockets that the British were throwing at John the night of that dreadful shelling. Although in constant pain, John had briefly rallied and surprised us by saying that he wanted to go and see Mr. Beath's rocket demonstration, especially since he had heard that it could travel further than the twelve-pound Congreve Rocket. And it did! That rocket took off and flew two thousand yards! This was five hundred yards further that the *Congreve* but it only weighed six pounds."

It brought a tear to Elijah to recall that as it remained

one of his fonder memories of when he had just been liberated from forced slavery.

Traveling South, they loved the semi-tropical wild-life of Florida, and they fished and explored secondary reefs where they saw colorful fish and sea anemones. They took in the Spanish fort of St. Augustine, Castil-lo de San Marco, which since the War of 1812 had been surrendered during Jackson's Administration.

Another afternoon, as they got closer to where the city of Miami would one day tower but then it was merely an inland swamp with uninterrupted miles of unspoiled, uninhabited beaches, dotted with the ubiquitous sec-ondary reefs in full uninterrupted sun with their mag-nificent flora and fauna.

"Now for those glass rods!" Mash announced.

"It's about time!" they shouted delightedly.

The ship anchored some three hundred yards out. It was a calm day and they secured the lifeboat on the beach.

Mashpee, dressed in just his skivvies with a belt and sash, swam to a primary reef at low tide, explored it, paused, and then explored again, repeating his actions until he found what he was looking for. Then he mo-tioned to the oldest boy Allen, to get one of the sacks with the glass rods along with a hooped net and had him come join him.

The boy struggled in the chest-to-neck deep surf but carefully held one arm high with the bagged glass rod.

Mashpee took the clear glass rod and wrapped the empty bag around Allen's neck like a scarf.

"Now watch this," Mash said, as he dipped the clear rod into the clear salt water.

"It's gone!" Allen exclaimed. Mash smiled.

"No, it hasn't gone ...look!" he explained, raising his hand with the rod as its glass shaft grew as it came out of the water.

"Oh, I see!" the boy exclaimed, realizing the optical trick that Mashpee performed. "The lobsters won't see this either," Mash laughed.

"I get it!" the boy responded.

"Let's get the lobster's attention, shall we?" the Indian said with a gleam in his eye as Allen giggled.

Looking down, he pointed with the glass rod at something and waited for the boy to see what he was pointing at. Allen saw the lobster's antennas peeking out from under a dark underwater coral shelf.

The boy nodded. Then Mash slowly submerged the rod into the saltwater bringing his hand closer and closer to the lobster antennas till they could both see one of the antennas tweak.

With a shriek of surprise Allen jumped back as the angry lobster came to life and shot out of its dark shelter to strike the invisible intruder. Just as quickly, Chatham's free hand swooped in with one stroke of the net and bagged his prey.

The boy clapped with delight.

Without pausing, Mash moved quickly to the next burrow and the next, until he had successfully bagged three others then raised the net high out of the water.

Those on the beach cheered along with the boy. In

the distance the steamship horn blew four times to announce the score, echoing off all the lonely beaches as far as the eye could see.

Mash came around the reef and strode back up to the beach and its waiting customers. Allen trailed close behind, a shadow.

They roasted their clams, the brilliantly colored lobsters, and fresh catches on open beach fires and bathed till they were all quite swarthy-looking like the pirates of the previous ages and Privateer Samuel's adventures during the Revolution.

It had been five years since the new Conch Republic was named thus and was a jewel as they cruised along what would later be known as Key West, Florida.

Further out into the Gulf of Mexico, the Tortugas held the adventures of Samuel and his skipper-mentor to save their precious cargo for the colonies during the revolution.

Their last night before their entry into the Gulf of Mexico through the Bay of New Orleans they anchored off the Dry Tortugas. Mash had one last treat planned for them.

At twilight, with torches and lamps, they searched the stone shoals for Morays, with their teeth jutting back into their mouths with ciguatera poison coating on the roof and other dangerous microbes to cause infection and further pain. In their burrows the very muscular long eel is a menace and a trap for anyone who should get caught by these carnivores.

But Mash was up to the challenge.

It was well past dusk before Mash spotted the eels. A small fish on a hook dangled in front of its shelter enticed the eels out into the open where it had nothing to brace or coil back on. Mash lost a couple of fish, but finally got one massive seven- footer!

Ceremoniously, Mash cut the dragon in half with one swipe. Then the Indian took a collection bottle and poured its mysterious contents over the remains.

"Out with your lamps, gentlemen!" he commanded, and when they had complied, they gasped.

In the bioluminescent liquid the serpent glowed. On their last night it was a fitting farewell rite of sacrifice in tribute to their successful voyage.

The evening ended with an ominous blessing. Towards midnight it started raining, then came thunder and lightning until from their shelter many yards off, a massive bolt struck the dragon!

Everyone jumped except Mashpee, who got up and interpreted what it signified.

"That subtle serpent of old shall overextend and be cut off!" Then without another word Chatham took his leave till daybreak and walked off into the wilderness. The thunder and rain stopped and the winds picked up.

It was the presence of Ruach Elohim, the spirit or breath of God.

The following days, the festive mood was gone as they approached the city of festivals, the port of New Orleans they focused on their goal to buy slaves with gold!

Now it was time to get down to business as they sought out the slave markets. Their mission was to act on behalf of James Mott, Lucretia Mott, Robert Purvis, and John C. Bowers to buy slaves with gold from their abolitionist society/foundation back East, to purchase and rescue Negro slaves.

They would then transport them under pretense of being traders to get their "packages" safely to Ohio. Elijah was to make his first of many trips up to Athens and transfer the slaves to John Kleinhan's[14] Station, at Port Clinton on the Erie, then on to the final leg that took them to Canada and freedom!

14 Author's Note: John Kleinhans or John Klinhinz of Ottawa County, Ohio, Port Clinton on the Erie worked to transport fugitives in the West while in the East Heman and Louisa Goodspeed transported the fugitives to the same destination: Toronto to Freedom! Louisa Albright G. in the East and John K. in the West made the blankets that dotted the bondsman's Erie Canal/Ohio route from Ithaca N.Y. to New Fane, Niagara County, N.Y. These 'Liberty blankets' dotted the entire route both ways even past the Sherman families' General store! "277 blankets from Ithaca to the falls; path, stations, and distance to freedom!" The bondsman's guide along the way. They only had to know how to hide, count and subtract in order to survive the path to freedom.

Elijah contacted the procurement handlers who were actually undercover agents and paid them the gold. During these secret exchanges they gave Elijah insider advice.

"We've been hit hard by (yellow fever, know locally as) 'Yellow Jack'. Take care with your 'package'. Some may be sick even if they don't show signs of sickness. Watch for black vomit. The first signs won't last but the second bout is the bad one when you'll see the bronze or yellow skin color," the ominous instruction continued.

"Travel slowly for two reasons before you reach the Ohio (River). One, it will attract less suspicion of port authorities. Also, your ship may have to go into quarantine. But don't worry. You'll have handlers on board with the proper auction and quarantine papers. The inspectors will be less apt to search you if the ship is under quarantine. No one wants to mess with the sick and infected if they can avoid it."

The handler reviewed his notes, "We're new to this business too, but there are a couple of other things you'll need to know: You'll have two more stops on your way up so save some of your gold. Your next stop will be by Forks in The Road at the port of Natchez. Be careful. It's a rough town in the lower port... lots of bad fights, murders, prostitution, brawls, and duels. Forks in The Road on the upper ridge is where the slave markets are, and you'll want to head directly there. Stay on the ship at night and travel only during the day." There was more.

"If you have a bad breakdown, for God's sake avoid the Natchez Trail! That's how Wilkinson and the Gang out of Maryland got Meriwether Lewis, God rest his soul! That whole damned satanic trail is ruled by robber barons and cutthroats! Thank God Wilkinson is now gone." The good handler spat.

"Your last stop is north of Memphis where you can start picking up branded or whipped runaways where it won't be as dangerous. Understand? Good!"

Davy Crockett - Last Year of Jackson's Administration - 1836

The Indian Removal Act was signed into law on May 28, 1830, by President Andrew Jackson. The law authorized the president to negotiate with southern Native American tribes for their removal to federal territory west of the Mississippi River. The Indian Removal Act didn't impact the North as much as the South, but it did impact Mashpee and Rebecca's lives, in other ways, in the historic Mashpee Woodlot Revolt of 1833.

As he addressed the House on his election defeat, Davy Crockett was righteously offended and concerned over the wrong direction his country was headed. What he said was quite revealing of what would become a trend that would define America, both good and bad, in the future.

The following year Davy Crockett resumed his frontiersman life and died at the Alamo in Texas on March 6, 1836, along with Jim Bowie, a scrapper from the lower port of Natchez.

But Jackson was indeed the People's President. He was a popular war hero though he had made enemies with former House Speaker Henry Clay and former Secretary John Quincy Adams. They were friends of rich bankers, who as lawyers, protected these rich friends and their own interests at the expense of the people. Honorable people like Davy, Jim, and Elijah, were all from a diversity of laborers, farmers, sailors, folklore heroes, and builders.

Jackson did more or less leave the New England Native American tribes alone which included Mashpee Chatham's people, even though they protested and revolted successfully against their white founders of the Wood-lot Revolt of 1833, then successfully sued for their tribal rights. All this happened while Andrew Jackson was still President. He never interfered with their dispute with their white plantation owners even when Obed Good-speed, the Treasurer, willfully and graciously surrendered the bookkeeping records to the tribal council. He vacated his position in agreement with their terms.

Historians would do the devil's work, and judge Jackson by today's standards applied to yesterday's standards! But Jackson, on his deathbed in 1845, pointed to the Bible and said, "That is the only book that matters!"

Sherman, another general who in the last half of this story did, along with Grant and Halleck, save America and changed society for the better. In the ongoing battle between liberty and tyranny what they did was only relevant to their time, but remained amazing by what they accomplished as individuals called on by God!

Twenty-Three Years After the Goodspeed's Western Migration

Bronze John (local name given for yellow fever, at that point in time)

Kanawha County, Virginia, was no friend to slavery and eventually became the state of West Virginia during the war. It was still not a place Elijah would have wanted to go with his ship unless they were in trouble.

In 1841 they were forced to do so.

The Port of Kanawha County or Charleston would have also been a costly detour southward out of their way although it was the port-of-call they had filed with the southern port authorities so to not attract undue attention. It was still part of Virginia in Antebellum Times. Its entry point was the Kanawha River off the Ohio River at Point Pleasant, taking them south in an emergency. Point Pleasant was very close down river from their usual final destination, docking at Port Pomeroy on the

Ohio River, for all roads leading to Athens, Port Clinton to Toronto.

Also, that year Joseph's sons, George Edward and William Henry, twenty-eight and twenty-seven respectively, were very capable business partners who were trained to the business from childhood by Joseph. Long before they had attained their majorities, they had mastered all details and had become their father's chief assistants. They were steady counselors and had made themselves invaluable to the vast and varied interests of the business.

Tragic Year

That year started later than any other year for conductors Capt. Elijah Goodspeed and Pilot Nathan Goodspeed, Captain of the Ohio Militia. Nathan was married, with just one son they named Hiram M. who was almost three years old.

A heavy winter resulted in an extensive spring thaw and flood waters in the Mississippi delayed the season's start. Rescue missions started a couple months later than the usual April start date, going into June. Heavy snow melts caused massive flooding, and the mosquito population exploded in the deep south. Due to seasonal delay and flooding, an overstock of sugar inventory created a food source for a mosquito population explosion, They carried the deadly yellow fever virus and this now made for a perfect storm for local epidemics from New Orleans to Natchez. Emergency health boards in Natchez had to be organized.

When the Goodspeeds arrived at the Port of New Orleans it was a bright sunny day that second week of June. The usual sad gathering of slaves was loaded in chains aboard Goodspeed's vessel. It would be a couple miles further north before these slaves began to notice something different happening. The steamer would proceed further north, then further still without stopping. At some point the slaves would look around at each other, and after more non-stop miles, they would dare to look up inquiringly at their unusually quiet masters and busy crew members.

Finally, Captain Elijah would come down the ladder to cordially greet them. The "masters" would then do something else very strange. Without a word they began unlocking and removing their leg shackles. Then they would stand by just long enough for the most agitated to settle down. Next, gently without speaking, they removed the painful wrist manacles as well, usually from the surprised rebellious looking captives first. Next came murmurs of surprise, hope, and puzzlement from former destitute mouths. Lastly, Elijah would address them.

"We're here to rescue you," he announced, then smiled broadly. All the "traders" also smiled reassuringly. Negros and Caucasians, at that point on that cruse, were called, on by Captain Elijah and his crew as simply 'patriotic Americans'!

As the miles peacefully rolled along, support teams were assigned for every individual. They were given baths, some for the first time in their lives! Their rags would be mended, washed, and transformed to clothes.

"At times we will have to chain you up again at each stop, but don't worry. No one's going to take you away! So be patient so that we can get you out of here safely to freedom!"

Usually, simple messages like that were all it took to sooth the most anxious or righteously rebellious heart. They were expected to work with the crews but were promised that they all would get paid for their service.

Elijah and Nathan couldn't help but marvel over the fact that to many former slaves the concept of getting paid for working was totally foreign.

Family members were reassured they could stay together, while the ones permanently separated by circumstances were consoled as best they could.

The more savvy black men started the process of weapons training with pistols, rifles, and fighting knives. As the group matured and spent more time with their personally assigned trainers, and they became close friends by the time they were half-way up the Mississippi.

Everything was going as planned.

Then one night, about a quarter mile from Fort Vicksburg, one new wheelman got too close to the shore and hung up on a sand-muck bar. A sudden lurch and groan of the hull was heard, then horrible screeching, dragging sounds, and telegraph to "all stop" just moments before the dreaded dead stop occurred. Soft curses came from the crew and maintenance, but otherwise all became quiet and maintained a professional even strain. They knew that they were in trouble, all still in enemy territory. The black males were now called on to help out and became part of the team.

Dawn neared with the ruthless attacks of mosquitoes throughout the night upon desperate members who were half-naked in the Mississippi. They used shoring timbers or anything they could find to use for leverage. Even officers were involved and had an equal share in the process where there was temporarily no rank. Elijah was half-naked working alongside the black gangs with Nathan. When the task was completed, everyone was complimented in relief with a friendly, firm pat on the back but no talking was allowed to avoid attracting undue attention from shore patrols.

Elijah, Nathan, and everyone else began noticing the tell-tale symptoms of the fever. Complaints of chills, loss of appetite, nausea, and muscle pains were rampant, and in some cases, backaches, and headaches. Now both pale and drawn, Elijah had to take shifts with Nathan.

The next five days were hell until the first wave of fever broke. They did what they could to clean up and wait for the second dreaded wave. It broke Elijah's heart, due to this emergency, to not make their usual planned stop at Memphis, and forgo rescuing any poor suffering souls there, in that community!

They were one hundred miles from the Ohio River when the next wave hit. Unfortunately, Nathan who wasn't as big a man as Elijah, got all the same symptoms back. Several of the black team and a full third of crew members were similarly affected.

Nathan and the rest were at least relieved that their Captain's health had improved enough to regain full vigorous command. He kept the others spirits up. Elijah and Nathan decided to head south for Charleston and divert from the Port of Pomeroy on the Ohio to the Kanawha River. But now Nathan took a terrible turn for the worse and was no longer able to function. He was confined to quarters. Everyone hoped and prayed for him.

On the Ohio headed to Point Pleasant at the mouth of the Kanawha for the south detour Elijah was given the sad report that Nathan had turned color, and threw up the black crud. By the time they reached Charleston. Nathan was delirious.

July 8, 1841, Nathan died. His last words: "Thank God the rest made it! Say hello to dad and tell Sarah I love her."

The Athens Station

Late July, 1841

Nathan, born in 1813, had married Sarah Fonner. Elijah blamed himself for Nathan's death although everyone at the funeral, except Sarah Fonner, said that it wasn't his fault.

Nathan's widow openly blamed Capt. Elijah for her husband's death. But even Solomon, before his own death a year later in October, had defended younger brother Elijah at his own son's funeral.

Sarah Fonner Goodspeed wouldn't relent and announced in front of Thankful, Solomon, and Elijah that she wanted nothing further to do with the family and was going to take her son Hiram to start a new life further west, which eventually would be a farm in Indiana.

This totally devastated Elijah and everyone in Thankful's family could see it in Elijah's eyes. She openly told

Sarah to stop talking like that and wasn't welcome to stay!

As a result, a month later Elijah attempted to resign his commission as captain of the *City of Rebecca-Jane*. But rather than accepting his resignation, Goodspeed's landing put Elijah on temporary leave until he could pull himself together. Olive was especially incensed and sent Sarah a brief note to Indiana that it was over between them.

But Hiram, her three-year-old boy, grew up determined to rebel against her tears and enlisted twenty years later in 1861, to fight for the Union to avenge his dad's death. Once enlisted, he served three years in the armies of the Ohio and Cumberland, participating in all engagements in which his regiment fought and was later captured at Stone River (Murfreesboro) and sent to Libby prison. While there, he made friends with Francis W. Kelley till he was exchanged, rejoined his regiment until July 4, 1864 when he was permanently disabled in battle. Francis, a local of Michigan who my Grandfather, John Goodspeed also knew of, wasn't so fortunate, stayed and died in prison, February 1865, just before the end of that terrible conflict! Lucky Hiram M., was commissioned as Postmaster at Ligonier, Ind., by President Lincoln in December 1864, and served with credit as such for twenty-two years.

A year later...Solomon's Funeral at Solomon's farm

The news of his oldest son's death in July the previous year drove the spirit out of Minister Solomon. So, at age fifty-nine, a year later he died.

At Solomon's funeral Jabez cooked up a surprise with Thankful's help to cheer up Elijah. He tracked down a childhood friend of Elijah's who had befriended him during Elijah's sufferings while indentured to the cruel master from that neighborhood.

"Elijah, I have a surprise for you!" Jabez announced.

Then without another word the curtain opened from another room at Solomon's farm estate and Joseph C. Miller walked in. The boy, now a man, was received with much gladness and celebration! Jabez indeed was the spiritual glue of the family!

**Thankful Thomas Goodspeed's Funeral –
Family Reunion in Rochester at Mattapoisett**

Thankful had lost her grandson Nathan. Then her oldest son passed after her second son Thomas. Those losses were very hard for her, as she had now survived both of her oldest sons and even this one special grandson!

To Thankful, the birth of Solomon seemed just like yesterday and when she and Silver Nathan named him for her husband's older brother, how they had hugged and cried. Next Thomas was born and at his naming they again hugged and cried as a couple. But now her husband was gone and the shock of his death at sea still lingered. Just like yesterday!

The same oppressive system that abused her daughters and destroyed Rebecca, as well as their relationships, had no signs on the horizon of abating. It was too much. Too much!

Thankful lived less than three years after her oldest son's death and that shadow took its toll. Her death followed on June 9th, 1845, in Athens County, Ohio, at age eighty- four.

Even before shots were fired in the Civil War good people were dying.

"It's remarkable and wonderful, Elijah, how Thankful also was that spiritual glue that held your family together...so sorry for your loss, my friend," Joseph C. Miller said, tearing himself.

Joseph had come back for this funeral all the way from southern Pennsylvania. Elijah valued that and again appreciated his coming. They were now as close as brothers in their back-and-forth correspondence which was bonded by their mutual instinctive desire to stand up for what was right.

"It's remarkable how Jabez at fifty-six can keep up the energy he has," Elijah commented. "We look at life the same way, but we're not so old, or at least don't remind me," Elijah laughed.

Joseph smiled. "Yes, my friend. We that despise slavery and indentured servitude have all borne the same scars in the ongoing battle of liberty against tyranny."

"With courage and determination. Courage and determination against all odds! Eh?" Elijah responded in spite of his own deeper guilt for the death of Nathan.

"At least we still have ourselves for inspiration," Joseph Miller responded in praise.

Elijah and Joseph both looked around at Thankful's surviving sons and daughters.

"We are all getting old. Me at forty-seven, Nathan at fifty..."

Elijah was about to continue with "Becky at fifty-two..." when to everyone's surprise, in she walked with Mashpee Chatham!

Elijah was thrilled over her unexpected arrival.

Jane whooped with joy and shock upon seeing her sister Becky enter, and rushed into her arms and Mashpee's.

"I'm so sorry!" said Rebecca. She now broke down and sobbed. "Sorry in so many ways!"

Rebecca wore a beautiful white Indian wedding dress. With tears she spread her arms to welcome Jane with fringed wings of an angel. The rest of the white dress had blue small, beaded panels centered on each shoulder that ran vertically to just below the breast sections, girded on the front with a broader horizontal blue-beaded paneled belt.

"Oh, my God! You are beautiful!" Jane cried, as they both embraced and wept.

Mashpee winked, "Not bad for a fifty-year old woman, eh Elijah?"

Elijah was speechless.

Mashpee Chatham wore a hat that reminded both Elijah and Joseph of a Yale graduate, a short grey-coned shaped top hat with an eagle feather in the hat brim, that was balanced with a very proud mischievous grin that Chatham gave them.

"The spirit of our ancestors salutes your ancestors!" Mashpee intoned. The hosts could not for the life of them know if the Indian was dead serious or playing the deuce on them.

Joseph Goodspeed was the first to catch on, "You're married in accordance with tribal tradition!"

"Yes, Joseph, we bring honor to Thankful's memory."

"My God, this is serious. And an honor!" Jabez exclaimed, laughing in joy.

"Pray do tell us your story!" Joseph Goodspeed immediately requested. "Come sit!"

"The death of my eldest brother made me sad, as did Thomas' death when he died for me," Rebecca started.

"I soul-searched early childhood thoughts. I blamed my dad, but like all mankind and living creatures, people die I finally realized. My evil masters made me believe that mother had 'sold me into slavery". But with the healing influence of Mashpee's tribe, I realized that was a lie! My mother loved and missed me. Then after her death, I felt horrible and lonely. All those years of hate replaced by guilt drove me in my heart to at last forgive."

"She came late to the party," Mashpee added, after Becky started to weep in joy again. "But come, she did."

Elijah and his friend Joseph cried openly the whole time. Elijah identified with his first meeting of Olive whom he now lovingly hugged, remembering when they first met in that wintery New England 'summer'.

Elijah and Joseph C. Miller then finally said good-bye, sadly never to meet again.

Goodspeed's Landing

Abraham Lincoln Patent #6469 May, 22, 1849

Just a month after Thankful's memorial funeral

For Elijah's sake, Joseph had called him into East Haddam to meet Abraham Lincoln, a young lawyer and inventor from Illinois. Sam and Jabez were also in attendance.

"This is not the Abraham of the Maryland gang who killed your dad, thank God. He's dead along with that land grabber Wilkinson from the West, the murderer of General Wayne and explorer Meriwether Lewis," Joseph reassured, then paused and sighed.

"Anyway, long live their memory!" Joseph intoned in resignation.

"Lewis and Clark went out and made all the necessary connections and resources necessary to be able to accomplish Jackson's wildest dream from sea to shining sea!"

Joseph looked directly at Elijah.

"Best wishes for the dead heroes, Militia Capt. Nathan, Samuel, Thankful, and their surviving son Elijah who this meeting was called in honor of! All their memories too shall not be in vain!"

In Nathan's old office in East Haddam, sons George Edward, 33, and William Henry, 32, were also present and sat on either side of him. Sam sat off in the corner.

"This Abraham is a true abolitionist, and he is on our side," Joseph added, suddenly realizing his impropriety. Lincoln cleared his throat, embarrassed for Joseph.

"I'd prefer you not call me an abolitionist so freely," Lincoln quipped, to subtle laughter. Lincoln the diplomat, changed the subject, then leaned forward toward Elijah and addressed him directly.

"I have reviewed with interest your resignation letter to Joseph and wanted to meet you so that you could tell me first-hand what happened that led to your pilot's death," Lincoln spoke softly. Elijah stirred uncomfortably.

"Elijah, listen!" Joseph interrupted. "Stop blaming yourself, for God's sake! Captain of a vessel is a weighty responsibility and means that you must make decisions, both good and bad decisions without reservation. You know that!"

Elijah nodded, "I know that, but that's not why I resigned. I should have been more attentive to detail before we ran aground. I resigned because his death made me realize that I was getting too old for the job. I carry no regrets about that...No! I resigned to have more time to do studies and take soundings of the Mississippi River and to publish charts to avoid further tragedies!"

Abe nodded with respect.

"Anyway, I came here out of respect Elijah! Errors are experience, that makes us more valuable to a free society. Please, be at ease. How did Nathan die?" he pressed.

"Yellow fever sir."

Abe rephrased the question.

"Where does that come from, yellow fever I mean?"

"Perhaps from bad water..."

"But you had fresh water and plenty of it to drink, correct?"

"Yes."

"So, it couldn't have been the water."

"The mosquitoes were bad when we got grounded and labored to get free."

"So, you think mosquitoes?"

"Correct."

"How long did it take your team to get free?"

"Most of the night, sir."

Abe got up and walked over to a table that had a simplified platform model of a boat hull. Elijah recognized it as a facsimile of the *Rebecca Jane*. A second level platform had pins representing vertical shafts running through both levels to four flotation pads, two on either side, fore and aft. A space between both pads on either side showed where the paddle wheels would operate, if the model was more detailed.

"According to your notes, you used shoring timbers, where I have here lift rods mounted on adjustable flotation pads to be raised or lowered."

Sam took his cue and stood up. Sam took up sixteen pins and pressed each pin into the top of each broader shaft.

"Are you familiar with Pascal's principle?"

William and Elijah indicated yes and William grinned comically at his older brother, giving Elijah a thumbs-up. There was laughter and George rolled his eyes.

"Don't worry, George," Elijah said. " Lincoln gave me the answers yesterday!" Abe slapped his knee and joined in the laughter. Nonplussed, Sam continued:

"Water can behave as both a gas that assumes the shape of its container, and as a solid it is incompressible."

Sam picked up a filled syringe and aimed it at Elijah. George smiled, vindicated.

"Take water in a syringe," Sam said, squeezing carefully not to hit Elijah, since it was the goal of illustration not distraction. "It takes much force to push it but the stream coming out of a smaller diameter needle has high velocity," Sam continued.

"Water in a tube..." Sam tapped the pins. "In a small diameter tube filled with water or oil then pushed with a plunger a short distance into a larger cylinder filled with water or oil will have considerably more force and can then do more work."

"So, with lever handles, one man's arm could raise a boat to power out!" Elijah interjected.

"Right!" Abe nodded.

"Dumb enough to be a leader!" Elijah humorously read Lincoln's mind. Lincoln laughed.

"Bravo!" Joseph laughed. "That's the general idea!"

Oh crap... Elijah thought and cringed... *a trap!*

"We want you to help us with these prototypes since you've had so much experience with running aground," Abe added, to howls of laughter. Elijah sighed.

"That sounds like an order to me."

Joseph got up and pumped Elijah's hand. "Congratulations Skipper. Welcome back to the fight!"

William H. (435)

George E. (434)

Elijah was too polite to say anything but he really didn't want his commission back. Also, he knew Lincoln's design wasn't going to work. After the meeting he waited until he was alone with Sam. Samuel agreed.

"Why did you support him then?"

"Two reasons, Elijah. One, he will do business with us over any other Connecticut firm. Also, we want to keep him on our side and help him get a patent for this. It's a good enough theory to actually work with more research! Two, he loves our lighter, faster ships and fire prevention systems, and he's getting back into politics in another year in his state. So, as he supports us, we'll support him!"

"Does Joseph know this?"

"Nope, but the boys do. You have time for lunch?"

In a windowless dirt-poor log cabin in Tennessee Nathan Bedford Forrest was self-taught to read and write proper English correspondence. He was extremely intelligent and resourceful and grew to be a six-foot-two-inch giant like Lincoln.

One evening in Horatio, Mississippi, time and history found twenty-three-year-old Nathan gambling in a saloon. He rarely drank and seldom smoked. Later that same year he became a Mississippi and Tennessee business, plantation, and stagecoach owner. He was a slave trader who, for economic reasons, later became a States' Rights advocate.

"I'm two jacks high!" he laughed amiably as he claimed the jackpot. He mused that he could have bid higher when his thoughts were interrupted by a gunshot that came from just outside the saloon. They were further interrupted by an excited customer who rushed in and spoke directly to Forrest.

"Your Uncle Jonathan has been shot!"

No stranger to danger, even when angered, he calmly stepped out on the porch and summed up the situation. He drew his two-shot pistol and mortally tagged the most obvious suspects, two of the four Matlock brothers who were involved in a street fight with his uncle. The surviving two rushed him in anger but the same customer who warned him of the event threw Forrest a fighting knife which he used to disable the closest charging brother. He then slashed the other man and subdued the last fighter by breaking his collarbone, striking him with his empty pistol; the man collapsed with a shriek of pain and fear, then passed out.

Nathan and his friend then quelled their own anger and got the suffering men medical attention. One of the men who recovered would serve under him when Forrest became a general during the Civil War some sixteen years later.

Days Later Back in Joseph's Office

"Samuel tells me you're still sad and won't accept the commission."

"Actually, I had time to think about it. Plus, Samuel shared how he lost his mother."

"Oh?" Joseph leaned forward. Elijah looked out Nathan's old office window as Joseph gave him time to collect his thoughts.

"At lunch with Sam, my brother Jabez was also there and they introduced me to Benjamin's grandson, my cousin Calvin."

Joseph's chair creaked, "Your deceased grand uncle?"

"That's right," Elijah responded. "Another mysterious death."

"You mean murder!"

"More likely than not," Elijah dryly responded. "But I'm not at liberty to discuss either death, Sam's mother, or Calvin's grandfather. However, their stories galvanized me!"

Joseph leaned forward and put his elbows on Old Nathan's desk in rapt attention. The flies buzzing on the windowsill didn't distract him. A gentle wind brought the fragrance of sweet-scented honeysuckle enticing the flies to the garden.

"That meeting brought me back to earth, so I'll cut to the chase here, Nathan. I mean, Joseph," the retired man began. "Dying is part of living. I have changed my mind. I will accept the commission, but only under one condition."

"You name it!"

"I'll captain only when there's an outbreak of yellow fever in New Orleans, otherwise, no." Elijah laughed seeing the puzzled look on Joseph's face:

"They say once you've had the fever you won't ever get it again. This means I want to protect your captains that have never had it, to spell them. I'll also serve as navigator and do double duty."

"What can I say, Elijah? That must have been hard for you," Joseph responded with sincere gratitude.

"Not really. It was good to see Becky again more frequently. She was there with that new husband of hers." Elijah winked.

"I bet!" They both laughed.

"She regretted at last that she never saw mom. Do you remember that at the funeral, Joseph?" Elijah couldn't say this without tearing.

"That was indeed a memory to keep," Joseph affirmed.

The wind picked up and the curtain weights tapped gently on the ancient open windowsill. Both men now gazed out at early evening and remembered.

"Once you go to sea you never can leave," he spoke pensively, then laughing, turned back to Joseph.

"I was never cut out to be only a farmer and Underground Station Keeper!"

Both men had a laugh, then shared a toast from Nathan's old brandy decanter. It would be the last time that Joseph and Elijah would meet.

Calvin Goodspeed

Calvin was one of Elijah's cousins with a curious story to tell Elijah about his grand uncle, who actually was Calvin's Grandfather.

Elijah already knew Calvin from early childhood before he was bonded out and vaguely knew about Calvin's father, John. But Elijah was surprised to hear from Calvin the history of Grandfather Benjamin.

Calvin took out his family Bible that he brought to the meeting.

"Here's the official account recorded in our Bible, which is bunk":

"In 1772, Benjamin went back to Barnstable from Nottingham in New Hampshire, where less that a year earlier he married and supposedly settled!

He determined to return to Barnstable to visit his relatives and accordingly started out on foot. Bidding his wife Hannah Hills, good-bye, he promised to return in a few weeks at most. Nothing was ever heard of him after he left. He disappeared completely, and his fate was unknown. A week or two after his departure, the body of an unknown man answering his description was discovered in a mud hole on the road from Boston to Barnstable. The body is supposed to have been him, though this was purely conjectural."

Calvin looked at Elijah, who could only whistle and roll his eyes.

"But the official account is wrong!"

Slippery Sam resumed explaining to Elijah the purpose of their lunch meeting since he knew that Elijah would not be familiar with Calvin due to his infrequent visits from New Hampshire, although the grandfather had originally come from Barnstable. John, Calvin's dad, had kept closer contact with Elijah's father whom Elijah never knew because of his own dad's untimely death off the Maryland coast.

What was Sam's purpose? It was to introduce Elijah to Calvin who was deemed to replace Capt. Seth as an undercover agent for Goodspeed's landing. Capt. Seth was retiring. Calvin was eight years younger than Elijah and wasn't physically strong like Seth, but because of his peculiar background he was known for his mental toughness, extreme intelligence, and discretion. At a very young age he had figured out on his own how his grandfather had died and even tracked down the gang responsible for his death. Again, like in Marston's case, there was nothing anyone could do about justice but this caught the attention of Goodspeed's landing. So, he hired on as an 'unofficial' intelligence officer. Samuel realized it was time for the two to get to know each other. Because of similar family mysteries, and the need to teach Elijah the business. Elijah would have naturally wanted to do that had he himself not been bonded out at an early age, unlike Calvin, who had a normal family life in that one respect.

Twenty-six-year-old Sherman

In the spring of 1846, first-lieutenant William Sherman was stationed at Fort Moultrie, South Carolina. The company was commanded by Captain Robert Anderson who eventually was the Union commander in the first battle of the American Civil War at Fort Sumter. In 1814, Ft. Sumter was a joke since it was just a sand bar and rock ballast from Northern ships unloading for Southern cotton. It wasn't even above water as late as 1834 when finally, they had enough rock to start the timber foundation. But even in that year it was still several feet underwater.

Sherman mused about his military future as he looked out from Fort Moultrie toward this artificial island just now starting to "brick up" barely above the water line. The entire Fort Charleston harbor system, including this emerging fort, Fort Moultrie, Fort Wagner and Fort Gregg, quite frankly left Sherman wondering if he actually had any real future in the Army after his West Point graduation and commission. Thank God he was still single on a salary which wouldn't even begin to support a single man, and a commissioned one at that, let alone a family.

This young red-headed man looked out at the harbor. The country now known as Texas had been recently acquired, and war with Mexico was threatening. One of their military companies had gone there the previous year and was with General Taylor's army at Corpus Christi, Texas.

Fortunately, that same year Sherman received the regular detail for recruiting service, with orders to report to the general superintendent at Governor's Island, New York, and left Fort Moultrie in the latter part of April.

1847–1848

"Joseph opened a store at Haddam, Conn., about 1804. With characteristic energy and ambition, he pushed every department of his business. About 1815 he moved across the river and opened a store in a building which is yet standing and is used as a joiner's shop in the shipyard. All of his business plans were wisely designed and resulted in rapidly accumulating wealth. It finally became necessary to enlarge his facilities, and he formed a partnership with Horace Hayden and built a large store. He amassed a handsome fortune and won great fame. At the height of his prosperity, on Christmas Day of 1847, while sitting at his desk in his counting-room, apparently in good health, his earthly career was closed without word, warning, or struggle." -Goodspeed Genealogy, page 482-

1847, Christmas Day

Heman and Louisa Albright Goodspeed's eldest child Marshall "took a very keen interest in the progress of humanity". At age 22, he started a life-long subscription to the New York Tribune edited by Horace Greeley and was an avid follower. He dreamed of Greeley's utopian society that promoted socialism, vegetarianism, agrarianism, temperance, and feminism. Greeley contributed great articles and hired the best talent he could find.

But Marshall was no dummy. He knew the difference between how to think and what to think! He knew the proud legacy of the Nathan Hale School and was proud of what Goodspeed's landing was able to do in such a short period of time with their family investments in their generations, enterprise, and society at large. Marshall keenly followed it all very closely. He was shocked that Christmas day when the terrible news of Joseph's death reached him. Coincidentally, Marshall was on Christmas break from Yates College in New York, where he had read an English translation of the Manifesto by the notorious agitator Karl Marx. It scared the hell out of him. Nonetheless, he was still a firm believer in the benefits of socialism, however, he wasn't so sure about the agitator's goals.

Marshall was greatly influenced, also by something else, scrapper, novelist, and poet James Fenimore Cooper wrote eleven years earlier, in a rare serious book The American Democrat, about the American Press that always stuck in Goodspeed's mind and guided him, as follows:

"Whenever the papers unite to commend, without qualification...; and whenever censure is general and sweeping, one may be almost certain it is exaggerated and false."

Just as true now in the twenty-first century as it was then in the early nineteenth century!

PART THREE

Last Generation Builders

Another Mysterious Death

1848-1849

Another mysterious death! It wasn't until the last of the old guard from Goodspeed's landing was gone that Elijah finally woke up. He missed the tales of Samuel and Capt. Seth. Those days were gone forever, and Elijah knew and dreaded that soon the memories of Old Nathan and Joseph would all fade. His mother whose love had supported him, was gone now as well, although for most of those formative years he was really always on his own.

Now he burdened poor Mash, the last and only person he knew and trusted. Mash knew and respected that although words were never spoken on that very subject. Olive also knew that Elijah had changed. Since young Nathan's death, Elijah had to deal with a real transition in life, from skipper to simply navigator and, like Samuel of old, to transition into a landlocked privateer and spy.

In late 1847 Slippery Sam took care of unfinished business after Joseph's death. Abraham Lincoln was in his final year as U.S. Representative from the 7th District for the State of Illinois and in 1848 he helped Lincoln to finally secure his patent with his steamboat prototype invention by 1849.

Samuel and his staff of zany but creative, professional, and attractive women and young men for Victorian times, did their research and found that in England Joseph Bramah had in 1795, started the contest when he patented his hydraulic press. His co-successor, William George Armstrong went on to successfully build three hydraulic cranes in 1845 and to do work on the Quayside. So, the technology was proven and Lincoln's patent was then easily secured. Lincoln's undying gratitude with Pacific Ironworks and Connecticut Steam Ship Builders were permanently established. Then Lincoln returned the favor and Goodspeed's Landing (landing finally officially spelled with a capital

"L") had at last become recognized as an official geographic location on the map. The Bank of New England, now established by the surviving brothers William and George after Joseph's passing was another long-time family goal attained.

"Well, what do you think about Joseph's death?" Mashpee asked Elijah.

"Strange, but I'll reserve comment, only to say we have much to do, my friend. No one was expecting this but we all should have. To change the subject, what did you think about former President Jackson and the outcome of the Woodlot revolt? I'm sorry I never asked before this."

On the buckboard Mashpee put his free arm around Rebecca then looked back at Elijah.

"No need to apologize Elijah, please! From '33 to '44, you were distracted by Yellow Jack, and blamed yourself over his loss and had to face your family over it! But you, General Jackson, and Becky have one thing in common."

"What's that?"

"You were indentured servants that were mistreated," he remarked quietly. Then after a brief pause Mashpee ventured to ask.

"Tell me, white man, what made you turn out so much more charitable toward Indians than Jackson?"

Elijah laughed and said simply, "A young pup has a choice when it is beaten by a cruel master. It either grows up to be kind or has to be shot!"

Both men laughed as Rebecca cradled affectionately against Mashpee.

"Getting back to your original question. I have no thoughts about our tribal uprising against your family, more specifically, Obed Goodspeed. I liked your cousin. He graciously and voluntarily surrendered his position as treasurer of the Board of Overseers later that month in '33'. Then Obed turned the plantation's books over to us," he continued.

"Reverend Fish, who also resided over us, at that plantation, unlike Obed, was despised, and he was told by us to 'be on the lookout for another home.' That we 'Indians' that Fish presumptuously claimed were converted under him from ages 8 to 12, only had been his constant attendees! We were for peace rather than anything else but we would never be satisfied until we had our rights, which that time and for the present eventually got."

Then Mashpee looked affectionately over at Rebecca then back at Elijah and concluded.

"So, Becky and I decided after that to move on anyway. For you see, Elijah, I, like you, and unlike the settlers, never put much stock in owning property or slaves. Nor as a freedom-loving individual really cared about tribal identity other than to push back. Like your wife Olive says, 'There are good settlers and bad settlers, good Indians and bad Indians.' Amen?"

Elijah nodded.

"Elijah," Mashpee added. "You, Becky and I all love liberty and believe in the Constitution and the rule of law for which Nymphas Marston, your father Nathan, Samuel, and Joseph most likely died or were killed. I hold no white man who is innocent to owe us anything other than we get along and mind our business."

Then he smiled grimly. "Whenever I find myself alone with a slave trader or slaver that can't mind his business and no one's looking, well, that might be a different story! I'm Christian, but only by degrees."

Elijah's smile matched Mashpee's.

As Mashpee and Rebecca were leaving Elijah rushed after their carriage in a wave of sadness and gratitude.

"What is it?" Mashpee asked.

"I just wanted to thank you," Elijah said with tears.

"For what?" Mashpee asked, genuinely intrigued.

"For taking care of Becky."

Mashpee put his free arm tenderly around Rebecca.

"Well, I also fell in love with your little big sister, little brother, so it was easier than expected." He laughed as did Rebecca and Elijah as they waved and turned their attention back to other mundane duties.

When Joseph died at Christmas of '47, it was Louisa and Heman's silver wedding anniversary. In Joseph's memory she saved one production blanket, from among other "liberty blankets" that dotted  the Ithaca N.Y. route to Toronto and freedom for the runaway. She also wanted to end that period of mourning and celebrate life, liberty and law, and pass those principles on to our generation, which this author seeks to preserve. She prompted the author to write this book to capture that which would otherwise be forgotten and lost.

Early 1849, The Grease

Calvin, an infrequent visitor from New Hampshire, now came into Joseph's former office to be greeted by its new occupants.

"We've been expecting that you'd come back from your father John's country, God rest his soul, but from the Natchez Trail too with news!"

"Indeed, I have. As you already know the commission opened his grave and in their final report wrote, 'It seems to be more probable that he died at the hands of an assassin.'"

"Did they give the reason or details?" George asked, with raised eyebrows and a frown.

"No," Calvin answered, then beamed. "But I was there and when I had the examiner alone, he allowed me to examine the body of Lewis for myself. I must have spent a full hour, but now I know the reason for their summary and could not agree more," Calvin said, then paused.

"Look as we might, the remains were still in good enough shape to determine that there was absolutely no evidence of powder burns, though the wounds to the head and abdomen were still very obvious!"

Dapper William Goodspeed, the brother was not surprised, not so much by Calvin's report but was surprised at the attitude of the officials. He shook his head and scoffed, "Of course, they will never give the reason for their findings and we all know why. To this day, it's still too political and sensitive to the Natchez and Maryland Gangs."

George added, "We are lucky at least to know more about our enemy, even though it's no surprise."

Then both brothers looked up to the messenger.

"Thank you, Calvin, please give Elijah our regards. And do stay a day or two if you want. The kitchens are always open to you and your guest, as well as the facilities. And your check is waiting in the lobby. So please, go fishing and hunting and use our guides. They are the finest and most knowledgeable we could hire."

"That's alright. Mashpee is with me," he retorted. They all laughed in agreement.

"What do you make of that guy?" George said to William.

"I don't know, George, but he's magic and a great asset to our enterprise!"

"Mashpee says he's quiet and blends into a crowd and would be the last person you would notice or pay any attention to. That might also explain how he got away with what he just accomplished. Befriending and charming the autopsy officials like he did!"

"Instead of calling him magic," William started, "I think I'll call him 'The Grease.'" They both broke out into a roar of laughter.

"Doesn't make sense, but that does strike me funny".

George then grew serious "Anyway, that's why whenever he's on vacation from the shoe factory or job as a railroad stock handler we have him go down to the Cajun Quarters and stay in New Orleans. We even rented him a nice apartment to stay near Baton Rouge just over the border in Mississippi."

William nodded "Great undercover man. They say he has an eight-year-old son now."

"John C.!" George interrupted.

"Yes, that's right, John C. Goodspeed... 'C' for Calvin, like the old man."

"In more ways than one, the perfect spy family!"

"They got that way because of the Grandfather Benjamin who disappeared. Another unsolved mystery."

George "Same history of sudden deaths!"

"Same history indeed!" William nodded with a slight frown.

George concluded, "Calvin may be genteel, but he has guts, determination and a history. Our undercover agent and America first man is tailor made for the job!"

The Missouri Compromise of 1850

Sherman had returned from California in January with dispatches for the War Department, afterward to the Secretary of War Crawford in Washington City. Sherman applied for and received a leave of absence for six months.

"I ran into him then," Elijah recalled and related to Olive. "He was at Mr. Ewing's house, getting married on leave I believe."

"He recognized me from the Ohio general store on the trail up to Port Clinton and asked me what I was doing in the City of Washington. I told him that I was there to get an appointment to change my status from a conductor to a signal man and to secure some navigation maps from the war department. He knew about Nathan and his death from yellow fever."

"Very much missed, a great militia man," Lt. Sherman said, then added. "I understand that you know

Lincoln. Sorry he failed to be appointed commissioner of the General Land Office and had to return to Springfield."

"I walked with him to the Capitol as we were headed the same direction to see Senator Webster's last speech."

"Did you get a chance to see that great man?" Olive asked.

"Yes, and thanks to Sherman, here's how it happened. We both wanted to hear it and went up to the Capitol an hour or so early. The speech was to be delivered in the old Senate chamber, used by the Supreme Court. The galleries were small, however we found them overflowing and feared we would lose our only possible opportunity to hear Mr. Webster."

Elijah rolled his eyes.

"Unfortunately, that speech on the floor was fashioned by Webster's fellow Whig, Sen. Henry Clay of Kentucky. Sherman was still in Washington that day and managed to get us in to hear Webster's last speech because he knew a Senator, a Mr. Corwin who was close friends with Sherman's dad. Once we got inside the Capitol, Sherman ventured to send him his card, 'W. T. S., First-Lieutenant Third Artillery.' I managed to read. Then to our surprise, the man promptly came out of his office! Sherman said, 'Mr. Corwin, I believe Mr. Webster is to speak today.'"

"Yes, he has the floor at one o'clock," Corwin responded. Then Elijah said to Olive, added

"Sherman told him he was extremely anxious".

"Well," he said, "what do you want from me?'

"William explained that he would like him to take us on the floor of the Senate. He had often seen persons on the floor from the gallery that were no better entitled to it than himself."

"Are you a foreign ambassador? Are you the Governor of a State?" Olive started to laugh. "Are you a member of the other house?"

"'No. Certainly not,'" we both responded and laughed."

"Have you ever had a vote of thanks by name? Well, these are the only privileged members."

"Well Olive, we thought we had lost until Sherman spoke up and said to the man, 'You know well enough who I am if you chose to take us in!'"

Olive gasped held her hands to her mouth "Do you think you all were being a little bit too bold?" She laughed.

Elijah gave a broad smile.

"Well, that's exactly what the man said next!" He laughed.

"He responded with 'Have you any impudence?' And of course he was looking at Sherman who had said it, not me, although Corwin did look at me too, like he knew me as well, perhaps from the hardware store!"

Olive giggled like a schoolgirl.

"'A reasonable amount if the occasion called for it.' Sherman shot back at him!"

"No!" Olive threw herself off the parlor sofa, rolled and held her sides in laughter.

"Do you think you could become as interested in my conversation as not to notice the door-keeper?' he said, pointing to him."

"Oh stop... I can't breathe!" Olive moaned.

"Sherman then told him that there was not the least doubt of it if he would tell us one of his funny stories. Corwin took Sherman's arm and I was bold enough to follow, dazed by the whole experience.

We found seats close behind Mr. Webster, near General Scott, and heard the whole of the speech. It was heavy in the extreme, and I confess that I was disappointed and tired long before it was finished. No doubt the speech was full of fact and argument, but it had none of the fire of oratory, or intensity of feeling, that marked all of Mr. Clay's efforts."

"Mr. President," Webster, proclaimed. "I wish to speak today, not as a Massachusetts man, nor as a Northern man, but as an American and a member of the Senate of the United States. I speak for the preservation of the Union. Hear me for my cause."

But it was pointless to argue about the continuation of slavery where it already existed for it was not going away.

"Newspapers throughout the nation and nearly everywhere but for us abolition-minded New Englanders," Elijah added. "He was lauded for his moral courage. But there, it was widely believed that he had cut a deal with Southerners to gain their support for the presidency."

Olive wiping tears away finally got up off the floor.

"I know and I agree." Olive picked up a paper and read "Ralph Waldo Emerson 'Liberty! Liberty!' Phoo! Let Mr. Webster, for decency's sake shut your lips. In the mouth of Mr. Webster, it sounds like the word 'love' in the mouth of a courtesan."

Elijah added, "Obviously Mr. Clay had a compromiser in support of special interests and not we the people. He prepared Webster's speech for Webster who was hoping to appease the Southern states and one day make his bid for the Presidency of the United States. "

Then Elijah went over to Olive and hugged her.

"But I've got good news for you, dear. Sherman is soon to become even more deeply aware of all this because after that, as we were leaving the Capitol, I invited him to see our operation, and he accepted!"

Again, Olive gasped. "And not just ours, but Heman and Louisa's operation as well!"

"Oh wow!"

"He already has us on his marriage and honeymoon travels itinerary list to see us all!"

Mr. Sherman paid the Goodspeed underground ancestors, like Heman and Louisa in the East and Elijah and Olive in the West, the honor of reviewing their operations in Niagara and Ohio, from intelligence he received from Goodspeed's Landing about the Natchez, New England, and Maryland triangle. It was about this time that Elijah unofficially received his commission in the Government Secret Service Signal Corp.

For Mr. Sherman the tour was an eye-opener to the plight of the Negro. Sherman himself shared experiences regarding the loyalty of the black community while stationed in California. One anecdotal story was about a black servant during the time of the California gold fervor. He was one of the few hard working and faithful survivors who stayed when soldiers, sailors, sea captains, and even officers were deserting to strike their fortunes in the mines. In many cases steamships out along the coasts were stranded and deserted, sitting idle due to lack of wood or coal fuel and labor and kept the ships from moving during the gold rush in the Monterey, Sacramento, San Francisco area, then called Yerba Buena.

Sherman wrote that it was good to be back in America from that wild country, although he enjoyed the good friendships and festive parties. Otherwise plagued and underpaid, the situation was so bad that even the officers were urged by their commanding officers to start their own businesses and take engineering jobs as governmental surveyors in order to survive financially, especially since commissioned officers were underpaid at that time.

Following his honeymoon tour, Sherman returned to Washington City by the 1st of July.

President Zachary Taylor participated in the celebration of the Fourth of July, a very hot day, by hearing a long speech from the Hon. Henry S. Foote, at the base of the incomplete Washington Monument. Returning from the celebration overheated and fatigued, he partook too freely of his favorite iced milk with cherries, and during that night was seized with a severe colic, which by morning had quite prostrated him.

"Mr. Ewing visited him several times," Sherman wrote, "and was manifestly uneasy and anxious, as was also his son-in-law, Major Bliss, then of the army, and his confidential secretary. He rapidly grew worse and died in about four days."

With his political base tattered, Webster soon resigned his Senate seat to accept the new President Millard Fillmore's offer to become Secretary of State. He denied the Whig Party's presidential nomination in 1852. He died later that year, despairing of the nation's future as he witnessed Fillmore's first term fall under fire when Fillmore sought the Whig nomination to a full term that same year but was passed over by the Whigs in favor of Winfield Scott. But by that time the Whig party was so badly damaged that Scott himself lost to Democrat Franklin Pierce. Millard Fillmore would be the last Whig President, but worst of all, the 1850 Missouri Compromise became law which would quickly lead to the nefarious passage of the Fugitive Slave Act. This would impact Goodspeed's Landing in their noble efforts for freedom and liberty, as well as negatively affect the bondsman's future causing death destruction and violence.

1850 - Slave Hunting Tragedy in Lancaster County-Goodspeed's Landing

"Congratulations, Elijah. Now your new first assignment!" said William.

Seated to Elijah's right was Calvin Goodspeed. Elijah had been just awarded his "official" commission as a Signal Secret Service man along with Calvin.

"I believe you already know each other and we're sending you both on a mission, you might say jury duty," the dapper executive informed them.

"Where are we going now? Expenses paid, I presume," Calvin said. William nodded.

"Lancaster Court House and Jail, Lancaster County, Pennsylvania."

"This ought to be interesting," Elijah said, "the "treason trial.""

"No. Actually for you, Elijah, your first assignment will be pretty boring, but Calvin there will provide you with some comic relief." Old Nathan's chair creaked as William leaned forward.

"He's going to be a juror and you're going to be an observer."

Confused, Elijah looked over at Calvin who was smiling as if he was in on a secret with William, which of course he was.

"I don't get it... How can he be assigned to jury duty when he doesn't even live in Pennsylvania?" Elijah queried. William smiled.

"We have ways."

George Goodspeed walked in and started to talk before he sat down in an old chair that James Armistead Lafayette, Capt. Seth, and Madagascar had each sat in.

"The word is out. It's about the Maryland Gang again." George paused to light his cigar. "They never forgave us for foiling their plot to frame us when Nathan was alive."

"You mean when they tried to set up my mother and Samuel?"

George winced like he had a sharp pain in his side and adjusted his position, not accustomed to sitting in that old chair. He nodded at Elijah.

"That's why they set up the fugitives to another state, in Lancaster, as payback. Not to mention that they saw an opportunity to test the new Fugitive Slave Act just recently passed." he continued.

"We also found out the hard way how sophisticated the Gang had become. They had the Newspapers and Whig rags in on it as well and got folks stirred up, not to mention more government officials on the take in no less than two states, Pennsylvania and Maryland."

The deepest feelings of loathing, contempt and opposition were manifested by the opponents of Slavery on every hand. Antislavery papers, lecturers, preachers, and others arrayed themselves boldly against it on the grounds of its inhumanity and violation of the laws of God.

On the other hand, the slaveholders in the South, and their pro-slavery adherents in the North, demanded the most abject obedience from all parties, regardless of conscience or obligation to God.

One year after the passage of the nefarious Fugitive Slave Act, a party of slave-hunters arranged set a president. During the time when alarm and excitement were running high, the most decided stand to defeat the law, and defend freedom was taken at Christiana, in the State of Pennsylvania,

Fortunately for the fugitives the plans of the slave-hunters and officials with Goodspeed's Landing leaked out while arrangements were made in Philadelphia for their capture and the information was sent to the Anti-slavery office.

"At once a messenger was dispatched to Christiana to put all persons supposed to be in danger on their guard," Calvin informed Elijah.

"Yes, I know," Elijah concurred, "among those notified were brave hearts, who did not believe in running away from slave-catchers. They resolved to stand up for what was right."

"Self-defense, and not afraid to shoot back," Calvin interjected. "Brave hearts they are. I'm glad we're going!"

"So am I!"

"They loved liberty and hated Slavery, and when the slave-catchers arrived, they were prepared for them."

"Amen."

The two signal secret service men agreed. "There were many heroes like the Negro woman, who blew the warning horn, and William Parker, and Quakers like Castner Hanaway and Elijah Lewis".

Elijah's job was to listen in court by day and help to

keep up the morale of the Negros and incarcerated Amish farmers inmates who had been unfairly seized at night. Then sent to the Lancaster and Moyamensing prison systems.

"There were so many of whom had been improperly detained for over three months," Elijah noted indignantly.

"William Parker's brave brothers had made slavers 'bite the dust,' and the press and public tried to get Thaddeus Stevens to cower! I remember that he responded, 'Give me liberty, or give me death,' not only for the white man but for all men. Heroic!" Elijah exclaimed back in their room.

Calvin's job was to screen the jurors and then eventually "report in sick" and disappear when his job was done. Sneaky refined Calvin![15]

"Good job, Calvin. Does this mean we have to take separate trains back before someone notices?"

Both laughed in anticipation of events that eventually unfolded, as planned.

In the aftermath, the biggest looser was Horace Greeley of the New York Tribune, a Whig rag when, in order to save a rather embarrassing publicity disaster when all defendants were acquitted, promptly switched his paper to hire a Karl Marx to do a special twelve-page fold as a German foreign correspondent. It was a col-

---

15 Author's Note: Hanaway was acquitted by the jury after fifteen minutes of deliberation. The prosecutor then withdrew the other charges, as it was apparent that the charge of treason could hardly be satisfied. The defense pointed out the absurdity of trying a group of poorly armed Quaker farmers for somehow levying war against the United States.

umn that Marshall Goodspeed enjoyed and followed, although he didn't always agree with the editors.

But the biggest loser of all was the Maryland Gang when they lost not only the trial but were killed as a result the Fugitive Slave Law. It was a minor miracle known only to God and all the prayer warriors of America who prayed and fasted for such a miracle. The friends of slavery learned that even with the law they were not safe!

1851-1852, Another Tragedy

The anger of the friends of slavery and the gang was fierce.

Prior to the new year Mr. McCreary took Elizabeth Parker from the house of one Mr. Donally in the township of East Nottingham, where she was living. Little was said about it by Donally, or anyone else.

Elijah and Calvin were once again summoned to Goodspeed's Landing.

"Our men are on the move again. At Donally's they kidnapped a black servant named Elizabeth Parker."

When George and William told them where in Pennsylvania, Elijah's eyes narrowed, teeth clenched.

"My friend Joseph's neighborhood!"

"Yes, we know!" William responded more serious even tense.

"Well guys," George announced. "Here are your train tickets to Lancaster, only this time head south toward Rising Sun, Maryland. Your friend, Elijah, lives two miles north of there over the border in Pennsylvania."

"Yes," Elijah responded. "Been there a couple of times."

"God speed and be careful. It's a hot bed of hatred from there all the way to Baltimore and only gets worse. We'll telegraph Mashpee to join you in Perryville, Maryland, on the estuary just south of where Joseph lives so I'm afraid you'll be bound!"

"Yes, I know. Two hundred twenty miles north of where my father died!" Elijah replied, with dread of what he was to find.

It didn't take long to find Donally at home, but the man acted nervous and when they started asking questions about Elizabeth Parker, he closed the door.

"I've got a bad feeling about this. Just get back in the buckboard. I'll take the reins!" Elijah told Calvin.

Calvin knew what was on Elijah's mind. Sure enough, in less than an hour they were in Joseph Miller's neighborhood cutting diagonally through his woods. Calvin, knuckles white-gripped the iron of his carriage chair arm but he was angry and determined to die with Elijah if necessary.

It was funny, Calvin thought, but in the twilight, he could hear a robin song and thought that the bird sounded stationary even though they were going at a very fast clip.

Mrs. Miller looked through the screen door at the strangers till she recognized Elijah.

"Elijah, I'm glad you're here!"

"What happened?"

"They took our maid Rachael, our..."

"Yes, I know your servant. Where's Joseph?"

"He took off after them, down that road." She pointed. "But he had to come back and take a detour."

Elijah swung back up into the buckboard, slapped the reins, then took off down that dirt road. A wagon blocked the road and Calvin marveled at Elijah's raw instincts as he grabbed an axe bracketed to his sideboard jumped out and started smashing the wagon to get the owner's attention.

"Hey! What do you think you're doing? That's my wagon!"

Elijah and Calvin instinctively knew the strange neighbor was more hostile than angry.

"Then move it and be quick about it!"

The stranger didn't know Elijah made the blunder of his life.

"Move it yourself," the snarky stranger replied.

"All right, Elijah said, slowly approaching the man. "God can move mountains." He was upon the man. "But prayer can move God!"

With a single blow of his fist he struck so hard he could hear the man's tooth break.

The man grabbed his face, "You son of a...." the stranger started to yell.

Elijah hit harder. More teeth were broken and now sharp pain radiated out. The man bled profusely from his nose and stumbled backwards.

"I'm not going to tell you again... Move that wagon!"

The man's son saw the whole thing and hurried down with a horse. Both son and injured man got the horse harnessed, then in total fear and pain, took the obstruction quickly off the road and into a ditch.

Elijah wasn't done with the ugly stranger. He grabbed his collar and jerked his forehead hard into his own, then threw him roughly into his son's arms.

"If my friend's dead, old man, I'll be coming back for you!"

The son spoke up, ashamed of his father's hatred, then pointed down the road. "They're on the way to Perryville to catch a train to Baltimore. Hurry, but be careful!"

"Thanks, son!" The buckboard sped off!

In Perryville, Mashpee with his sawed off shot gun strapped over his shoulder, waiting for them.

"M'Creary got Parker. There was another group that got Rachel's sister! This was a coordinated effort to make us angry, Elijah!" Mashpee told Elijah and Calvin.

"Well, it worked!" Elijah growled.

"I saw your friend Miller," Mashpee said to him, "but also another friend of Miller's, Abner Richardson, who was in pursuit of Rachel and McCreary. My instructions from Goodspeed's Landing was to wait for you, then proceed to Baltimore."

"You should've gone ahead," Elijah said quietly.

"I know and had it been up to me, I would have."

Elijah's heart sank. He knew his friend was dead, and in front of both men he started to cry. For sure, Joseph C. Miller was gone, and it had all been a set up from the get-go.

When they got to Baltimore, they met Abner and two others they didn't know but had to be introduced to by Abner.

"I'd like you to meet Eli Haines and this young man, Wiley from Rising Sun, who not only knew Miller but recognized Rachel," said Abner Richardson. But before he could continue, he too, began to cry. Elijah's heart was gone.

His thoughts were interrupted by the young man Wiley who filled in the details while Abner pulled himself together:

"Eli and I got up early this morning and just before we saw Miller and his party, we saw the girl and McCreary come through."

Eli Haines interrupted the boy.

"I knew Rachel and seeing McCreary there, and her so overwhelmed in sorrow, at once we guessed the situation, and Wiley and I changed our intention of going to Philadelphia. We went in the same car with McCreary and the victim to Baltimore, and quietly watched what disposition would be made. We felt certain you folks would be coming and were on lookout when Richardson, Morris, Miller and the party showed up in hot pursuit. And now you folks."

Elijah saw that Abner could finally speak. He asked him softly, "Where's Miller?"

Abner ran his fingers through his disheveled hair. It was obvious he had a sleepless night. He hesitated, then spoke.

"At first everything was going all right when we got

here. We met these two and they told us what they told you just now, but they also added that they were successful at locating Rachel who had been deposited in Campbell's slave pen. Then, that they were directed by an acquaintance of Francis S. Cochran, a prominent member of the Quaker Society of Friends who was well acquainted with Campbell...."

Before he could finish, Abner looked up at Mash and Elijah.

"Miller was still with us at this time, so we all went there with Joseph. Campbell turned out to be nice enough and assured Friend Cochran that whilst he approved of slavery and catching runaway slaves, he despised kidnapping and kidnappers.

When Joseph Miller heard all this, he ordered him to remove Rachel forthwith, which he proceeded to do. Then Friend Cochran insisted on going with them, and saw to it that the girl was deposited in jail to await a legal investigation." Abner started to weep again but continued.

"So, Miller and the rest of us went home with Cochran where we had our supper. However, Friend Cochran advised us that with the excitement being so great, he did not consider it safe for us to go to the depot directly. He procured our tickets and had us driven by another route. When we got to the train, he charged us to stay together and take our car seats immediately!" Abner shook his head.

"Soon after we were seated, Miller stepped out on the platform to smoke, against our protests, so we followed him, but he was gone."

"We called everywhere," Abner added. "We even had Wiley, who was least known, pass through the train but he came back and told us that Miller was not there."

At this juncture Mashpee, looking piqued, took up the conversation.

"I'll stay with you, and Jesse here and Miller's other friend and help search. If we don't find Miller right away, you two head back home tonight. Since no one here knows me, I'll continue searching until I find him!"

Mash paused and looked kindly at Elijah who was also crying, "You go back with them, sir, and that is an order! Don't get yourself killed. I can take care of myself."

"No," Elijah shook his head, "I've been through a lot my whole life, and this is just another day to me my friend!"

"I'm staying too," Calvin announced.

A Week later East Haddam

Mashpee returned and gave the summary to George and William.

"The party went back. We found him hanging from a tree. We cut him down but no caretaker was willing to work on the remains. We buried him in a shallow grave in a rough box with a narrow lid and then piled plenty of dirt over it. We went back to Miller's home and informed his family of the terrible news. I had personally looked at his body and saw things that made me suspicious. The gang was trying to spread malicious lies, saying that he committed suicide, supposedly to hide his disgrace as a slave trafficker. But direct testimony from Francis Cochran himself said that on its face it was not true! He was respected as a prominent member of the Society of Friends and the proprietor of Campbell's slave pen. He spoke the truth."

"What were the final autopsy results?" asked William, dead serious. "My understanding is that there were several."

"The results were terrible. Miller's body underwent an examination in Baltimore County, where a great number of rowdies attended and occupied their time drinking and cursing the Pennsylvania Abolitionists. The body reached its distressed home for interment. Drs. Hutchinson and Dickey were called upon to make an examination, which I attended. All were clearly of the opinion that he had been murdered. Wrists and ankles bore the marks of manacles; across the abdomen there was a black mark as if made by a cord; the end of his nose bore marks held by some instrument of torture. His funeral took place, followed to the grave by an immense concourse of sympathizing friends and neighbors."

Mashpee paused then continued, "The theory was that he had been suddenly snatched from the platform of the car in the Baltimore Depot, gagged, stripped, and lashed down by the ankles and wrists, with a rope across his abdomen, and that his nose had been held by some instrument. He was drenched with arsenic, and puked and purged till death. McCreary, or someone for him, had heard Wiley repeat that he was not on the train at Stemen's Run Station. They conceived the idea of taking his body there and hanging it to a tree to convey the idea that he had committed suicide at that place. Such was the statement published by some of the Maryland newspapers. His companions said he ate a very hearty supper that evening at Francis S. Cochran's which, with the facts that his clothing was not soiled, and his stomach and bowels were empty, goes strongly to substantiate the theory that he had been stripped and foully murdered." The room was now silent.

"We're so sorry, Elijah," Mashpee offered earnestly.

Elijah shrugged.

"All these years and I'm actually getting used to it. That's the scary part".

The Grand Jury of Chester County found a true bill against McCreary for kidnapping. A requisition was obtained, and B. Darlington, Esq., then High Sheriff, proceeded with it to Annapolis; but the Governor of Maryland refused to allow McCreary[16] to be arrested in that State." Elijah sighed.

It was a very aggressive violent act of the South against the North. That got little or no play in the Whig rags. Like the Christiana Lancaster hype did. They kidnapped his female servants that he was trying to rescue and cruelly murdered him in the process: The tragedy

---

16 Author's Note: McCreary died in 1870. Vilified by many and loved by none: a stranger to God most likely.

to which Elijah Goodspeed upon a visit was a witness. Joseph was a boyhood friend of Elijah for Elijah's sake.

After that event was over, Elijah despondent, returned home to Olive and his family.

But the compilation of events from Goodspeed's history in the Underground Railroad bears out the disturbing parallels with today's America. Decadent governments are capable of backsliding, and decadent they did become in America just prior to the Civil War.

Last Routine Excursions on the Mississippi

1852

Elijah and Olive read Uncle Tom's Cabin to see what would make Queen Victoria cry. They found out, as did the rest of the nation and world at that time, that even some in the South realized that all was madness! Christians were being misled by politicians, corrupt clergy, journalistic malpractice, and deep state elites such as Rev. Joseph Ruggles Wilson, the late James Wilson's son.

At this point Elijah was ready for one last steamboat adventure down to New Orleans, although he was starting to become more interested in construction and farming. He built a well-fortified station for fugitive slaves as only Elijah, Mashpee, and Noname could build!

In 1853 the worst and last case of yellow fever of the

century hit New Orleans. It was referred to by Yankees as "Uncle Tom's Curse."

During that time Elijah spelled the captain to honor his contract with the late Joseph.

"My God, Fred, are you still with us?" Elijah exclaimed.

"Yep!" Fred smiled, "How could I forget our last trip?"

"I thought you retired."

"No." Fred winked, "The front office called me back when they found out you was signing on. I wouldn't miss serving with you again one more time for all the tea in China. Besides, Elijah," he laughed, "We all agreed you were getting too old to be both Skipper and Pilot so we figured you'd need a hand!"

After more laughter Fred grew serious and removed a sealed letter from his coat pocket.

"Elijah, I have a message for you and a letter which I've been instructed to give you."

Elijah read the message. *"Capt. E.G: This is an urgent message that shall explain in part the unexpected death of our dad Christmas Day '47. Since the Maryland gang leader's death, we have had our team compile a list of names of all those associated with him and what their new leadership looks like. In one name: McCreary. Unfortunately, after his arrest, and unbelievably, he was never indicted, but you already know that. The Grand Jury of Chester County found a true bill against McCreary for kidnapping, a requisition was obtained, and B. Darlington, Esq., then High Sheriff, proceeded with it to Annapolis; but the Governor* *of Maryland refused to allow McCreary to be arrested in that State. This terrible affair cost the State of Pennsylvania nearly $3,000, as well as a heavy expense to many citizens of Baltimore, and those of this county who took an active part. There are rumors of him now organizing gangs now in Missouri and Kansas and as well as you already know, in the New Jersey and Maryland areas. Please be certain to keep an eye out in your travels. –Best Regards, George Edward Goodspeed and William Henry Goodspeed"*

Elijah knew what to do with the letter. He struck a match and burned it.

"You know about this?"

Fred nodded solemnly. "It is why we fight, sir!

No more words were exchanged nor were necessary as they turned to their other duties casting off.

O how majestic it was for Elijah and Fred, who had dearly missed it as they traveled along the route south turning onto the Mississippi River. For a while that euphoria rendered a sweet illusion of peace, but as the miles swept by, both Elijah and Fred noticed an unsettling change. For somehow, the southern towns they passed, especially nearing the Missouri border coast, were different.

"Can you believe this?!" Elijah heard Fred sigh. "What happened?"

It was as if the air itself was poisoned. Idleness, drunkenness, and slave auction houses in dirty clapboard lanes were in every port town! They observed faded storefront planks and signs that once boasted prosperity now in various stages of disrepair and weather damage.

At night only half the streetlamps were lit in the smaller towns as if some misanthropic proprietor had extinguished them altogether out of spite.

But as the *Rebecca-Jane* approached New Orleans they spotted the once familiar slave markets. They would now unload the gold to the buyers. Then they noticed many wooden caskets, and news, and warning signs of fever posted in plain sight. Finally, the *Rebecca-Jane* shrugged into her appointed docks after sun-up, manned by only skeleton crews to assist their landing.

The slave traders were more skeptical of ships like this coming from too far up-river. Even their gold made the waiting allies nervous and Elijah started to wonder if maybe next time it would be better to trade in local currency instead, to avoid suspicion or getting thrown into a local jail, or worse yet, a state penitentiary if the Law ever caught up with them.

After the auction was over, the slaves discovered their new freedom on the way up the Mississippi to the more prosperous and fresh Ohio River. Fortunately, there was no need this time to turn into the dreaded detour to Charleston on the Kanawha. Even if they had been required to, it would have still been a lot cheerier than where they had just come from.

A Wink and a Nod

When in New Orleans, if eyes didn't deceive them, Elijah and Fred were standing on their quarterdeck when

Elijah saw Sherman. The red-haired man spotted him and gave him, he thought, a wink and a nod.

"What is it?" Fred asked from around a corner not seeing directly what Elijah had briefly spotted.

"Nothing," Elijah replied, "just someone I recognized."

But Elijah turned away thinking the object of his attention was now out of sight. It couldn't be him, since he would be somewhere either in St. Louis, New York City or California. But it was Sherman. Nor was he wrong sensing that someone was also watching from the crowd, studying both men as Elijah's ship pulled away from the dock.

1854 - Bleeding Kansas

A wagon pulled up to Elijah and Olive Goodspeed's station in Athens. Elijah was surprised to see both Slippery Sam and Mashpee with an unidentified ugly-looking man with a bullet-shaped head and a stocky build. Elijah and Olive imagined they saw Simon Legree as described in *Uncle Tom's Cabin*, but then the man smiled and extended his hand cordially in friendship which broke the spell.

"Hi, sir. Sorry for my rough appearance. I'm not Simon Legree but glad to meet you!" he said with an Irish accent, almost as if reading their minds.

Olive, the worldly type, knew a trick or two and challenged the visitor.

"Say the number thirty-three."

The stranger roared with laughter knowing exactly what she was up to and responded.

"Terti-tree." Smiling, Olive looked at Elijah.

"He's Irish and just off the boat, and about as Southern as a kumquat!" She laughed and went back in the house to tend to the potatoes boiling in the kettle. The man winked at Elijah and said something in a perfectly rough Alabama accent, so perfect it made his hosts marvel.

"What's this all about?" Elijah asked.

"We're going to New Orleans on business, and you're invited, Goodspeed," Slippery Sam said quietly, then added, "Courtesy of Goodspeed's Landing".

"Is there another outbreak in New Orleans?"

"Nope, we have a lead however on McCreary."

"Oh? Then why are Mashpee and the new guy here? And why am I being so honored with the invite, if there is no plague to worry about?"

Samuel's face tensed as he grew serious.

"I have two privateer cousins that we have to rescue who were stupid enough to get apprehended. Mashpee is here because we're going to make a supply drop in Indian Territory south of Kansas after the 'packages' are rescued."

"Oh." Elijah remarked, not knowing what else to say.

"You coming, or not, sir? Call me Simon," the stranger queried.

"I don't have a choice, do I?" Elijah shrugged.

"You are correct, sir!" The stranger saluted him. That made Elijah realize the man was a member of the Ohio

Militia, out of uniform. Perhaps this man was the captain that had replaced Nathan, his beloved late nephew. It made Elijah sad to think about but he was determined, in Nathan's memory, to join them.

He had a bigger surprise when they got into the buckboard. He was proffered an uncomfortable seat on a crate. He examined it and discovered that it was a rifle crate. Next to it was another half size crate that was an ammo box.

"What the hell? We going to war?" No one answered him.

When the wagon pulled up to the pier of *the City of Rebecca-Jane* it was surrounded by Militia.

"Wow!" Mashpee said, driving the buckboard. He glanced back at Elijah.

"Not civil war, but close," the answer now came. "But don't worry, outside of being our special captain there won't be much for you to do." Then Mashpee handed Elijah a parcel.

"Here are your civilian clothes, Captain. You'll be told when to change out of your skipper's uniform. And the less you know, the better for this to work!"

"What do you make of this, Captain?"

Elijah looked at Fred. Both leaned on the bridge rails as the *Rebecca-Jane* swept along the last of the Ohio. They had long since tacked south down the majestic Mississippi, past the last of the Illinois shoreline. Both had witnessed the Militia change to civilian clothes.

"I don't know. For once we'll be as much in the dark as our 'packages'."

"Like only two?" Fred corrected.

"That's right...What do you know?" Fred looked out at the river.

"They're closing in on something, perhaps the gang. In fact their contacts have talked about Kansas and the tension that the gang seems to be fermenting in that territory."

"I noticed that some of the packages are guns with plenty of ammo," Elijah observed.

Fred shrugged. "The settlers and lots of folks moving over from Missouri are pro slavery and the rest like us, aren't. Do you think there's going to be trouble or a war?" Now Elijah shrugged.

"Well, from the newspapers and what little they've told me, it sort of looks that way. Also, something about a rescue mission, a couple of Samuel's cousins."

Fred knocked his pipe out on the rail. He had no further light to shed on the situation and returned to his duties as the Missouri shores caught the last red-green rays of sunset.

"Act offended!" Mashpee whispered as they stood on the bridge and pulled into the docks of New Orleans.

It was the first time since they left Athens that morning that Mashpee approached Elijah. He was about to say something when Mashpee again broke away before he could say anything.

It won't be a damned act, I assure you! Elijah felt like

shouting. Then he recalled a time he and Mashpee were hunting. Elijah confided that he had buck fever. Buck fever is when a hunter freezes up, gets nervous. Then he can't shoot straight or isn't able to shoot at all. He remembered that the Indian looked at him with the same weird smile he had just given him, and then gave him a cryptic remark like now. Yet the same day, with the deer in his sights, he didn't miss and was spot on. As he was gutting his kill, he heard Mashpee softly laughing. He looked around but couldn't find him. Then he realized the trainer had successfully taught the student without words. So now, instead of Elijah being angry, he would be on the alert at the auction for situations where he would feel offended. He also remembered that Mashpee had said earlier, "The less you know the better for this to work."

*Wow! Elijah marveled. Thank you, Mashpee...*For he was a great teacher, the best!

This morning as instructed, Elijah was not in uniform and had unpacked the parcel and changed into a light brown tweed perfectly tailored business suit.

Elijah looked around for Mashpee who was nowhere to be seen since they had boarded separate carriages.

Hand bills that announced the day's transactions were distributed and plastered around New Orleans about three days before. These fliers were printed with a second page which included the statistics of those being auctioned that afternoon. Elijah didn't like the inspection platform that was set up, expertly prepared by the exhibitors. As many times as he had piloted, he had never actually been to an auction. This was a first for him!

There men were stripped naked, along with some women and gone over and inspected like horses, but in private rooms and waiting areas. Two very attractive black women in formal dresses fearfully clung to each other. Sisters, braced for similar treatment that fortunately didn't happen, because handlers escorted them back to those not naked. They had done this to raise bidding interest.

Samuel gently tapped Elijah on the shoulder. Elijah relived the day he had been put on the block, and vividly remembered the stricken look on his mother's face, the blood on Samuel's face and being led away. It was still fresh in his mind after fifty years.

Now a different Samuel, a black Samuel, spoke to him.

"Allow me to introduce you to P.T. Barnum, Elijah!"

The whole experience struck Elijah as surreal, and only the presence of Samuel, and P.T. Barnum's kind and sympathetic look, kept him from walking out. They exchanged their mutual disgust at the proceedings. Some attending guests looked askance at the black free man and P.T. Barnum. This famous visitor's grand entrance even caught and threw the traders, slavers, handlers, and auctioneers off balance, as intended.

"Hear! Hear!" P.T. shouted in protest, as a big man stepped up out of nowhere and roughly handled one of the terrified formally dressed women. He left dirt on her white linen ruffled bodice. She broke down in tears. One of the handlers quickly approached the rude man and pointed at other naked black females to touch only them.

Before Elijah could cry out at the bullet-headed man whom he was shocked to recognize, he felt the cold barrel of a sawed-off shotgun in his face. He stumbled back then recognized the malevolent stare of an Indian warning him to shut up and behave. It was none other than Chatham!

"How could you!?" Elijah protested as Mashpee raised his eyebrows in warning to remain silent. Both P.T. Barnum and Samuel leaned in to protect Elijah and get him to calm down before things got any uglier. Mashpee holstered the gun, turned around and joined the bullet-headed slaver at the platform's edge, eyeing the two women.

Even some of the southerners looked in disgust at the man, while others looked at P.T. Barnum, Elijah, and Sam. Elijah had all he could do to stay calm.

Fred, at the ship's bridge, waited for the "packages." The same white enclosed town cab carriage that had left earlier now pulled up, Mashpee riding shotgun. The faux 'southern aristocrats' on deck casually strolled, laughed and made merry. The packages this time were the women with the apologetic, tender hearted bullet-headed man who debriefed the confused but rescued women. He offered the one with the smeared blouse a warm soap towel and drying towel. By the time they pulled up, the slightly older but attractive 'sister', caught on early, hugged the other younger one and helped her clean up and dry off.

"Don't worry, honey, this man was only getting us out of there to safety! And I see our men!" The same black carriage that had left earlier had pulled up, now unloading.

"Oh my God! It's P.T. Barnum himself!" Fred, surprised, now mused as P.T. emerged from the black enclosed carriage. Next Elijah and Samuel stepped down, waving up at Fred. Elijah, however, still looked tense. Then followed two black men in chains whom Sam had barely time to debrief. Hastily the captain came from below, now in uniform, summoned four of the male "aristocrats" to rush down before trouble started. The black men braced themselves for a fight as the four big men approached them.

"Don't worry and look! Your wives are here. We'll take the chains off you once you get inside and out of sight and before you get to see them, so we don't attract attention!"

P.T. also assisted by motioning them to proceed.

"Like the man says, you're going to Kansas and freedom with your uncle and wives as soon as we get you out of here."

This time the Black men nodded and understood, quicker than their wives. Soon they realized that their wives weren't separated from them after all, rescued from a life of sex trafficking and abuse.

Behind them, Elijah added, "Act like you're still angry. We're all being watched by the dock crowd and authorities!" he whispered.

Now Elijah understood how fooled he had been by this

morning's process. He smiled gratefully at P.T. Barnum, the showman. Elijah turned and pumped Mashpee's hand.

"Can I still sleep with my wife?" Mashpee grinned. Then he whispered, "Better say 'yes' because she's aboard and I haven't touched her in days!"

Elijah burst out laughing in surprise. "Of course, bastard!" Elijah now fully realized that Mashpee's shotgun trick had discouraged other bidders until the perceived "ruthless ruffian" competing with P.T. Barnum's team had their bidding duel without interference from any other bidders.

"Welcome to freedom, ladies and gentlemen!" P.T. added.

That evening in the private lounge of the *City of Rebecca-Jane* they had a meeting of concern for President Franklin Pierce and the Kansas-Nebraska Act he signed into law in May to counter California, a new free state with the possibility of new slave states to compete.

At the meeting Sam was concerned for Aaron, whose depression was obvious. The close call with family separation and slavery now made both Aaron and Robert reluctant to be privateers.

"Until today Robert and I had hearts filled with fire, but for the sake of our wives that we almost lost, we now feel differently!" Robert explained. "You don't have any idea how depressed both Robert and I are. The cynical way it was accomplished, fills us with utter dread and loathing," Robert spoke for the two of them.

"A merchant named Smith owned one of our cousins.

Months before escaping, our cousin had seen Smith selling, flogging, cobbing, paddling, and all other kinds of torture and outrage, by which he could inflict punishment in order to make the slaves feel his power. He tyrannized 'over about twenty-five head.' In a brutal mood, he made his slaves suffer unmercifully, he told us. On one occasion, about two months before our cousin was rescued, he saw the cruel master had five of the slaves, including some women, tied across a barrel, lashed with the cowhide and then cobbed. This was a common practice!"

All were shocked and silenced for a time. Finally, P.T. Barnum spoke.

"I owned slaves and allowed my staff to whip them when frustrated with black and white indentured servants. I should have known better since I was born poor myself. I was a Democrat until the outrageous Kansas-Nebraska Act was proposed. I had to walk away from my party!"

Now Sam spoke up. "No, we shouldn't feel joy about how life is for us, Aaron. But we did dodge a bullet today? Amen?"

All gave a very soft "amen."

Samuel continued, "Robert and Aaron on behalf of your wives it's settled, change of plans! Neither of you are going to Kansas! Not even to the new-found Indian Territory south of there. It would be too risky and jeopardize you to further exposure.

Become freemen first. Then decide what you want to do."

P.T. spoke again. "Samuel and I, along with Mashpee and Rebecca, will be headed to Pacific Ironworks and the Volcanic Arms remote western base, in the newly established Indian Territory. For two reasons. One, to keep Nebraska and Kansas free as originally intended! And two, to establish research, development, and testing of repeating arms. That is what Mash, Sam, and I are up to in the Indian Territory of Kansas."

Sam now turned and looked at Rebecca, waiting for her to nod if she was ready to speak. She nodded. Samuel cleared his throat knowing this would be difficult for her.

"Rebecca here has something to say to both of you, Aaron and Robert. You too, Elijah! Hopefully, that will provide some comfort in whatever you ultimately decide to do. And hang on Elijah, she's going to have something special to say to you as well." Sam and Mashpee exchanged tense, concerned glances.

"I was raped from when I was a child till I was a young adult. I was so badly abused and beaten that I lost a child and it doesn't appear likely that I'll be able to ever have children. I know what the humiliation of 'cobbing' is all about and witnessed it first-hand. And yes, it is exactly what you think it means!!" she hissed.

Elijah was shocked to hear it all for the first time. He was moved by her story. He had only suspected but never heard her say, let alone publicly share. He also started crying openly as did the others, including the wives of Robert and Aaron.

Rebecca continued.

"When they finally had no more use for me, they threw me out. At first, I was going to go out west, but the whores out west were too ugly, and dirty and sick with disease and infections. Suicide was common, beatings and killings in dirtier small portable tents or shacks were rampant. I didn't want to become like one of them, or die, although I thought about it often enough. So I went east instead and settled with the Mashpee tribe and ..." she paused then started laughing through tears."...met Mashpee!"

Elijah looked up to catch her looking at him radiantly through tears.

"Elijah, I'm changing my name to Thankful."

Elijah, realizing that he was the only Goodspeed present, and was honored beyond words. He rushed over and hugged her. Mashpee was beaming, knowing the emotional and spiritual transition in the meaning of names and self-acceptance. A milestone had been reached.

"Well done!" Sam applauded. Sam now picked up where he had left off.

"Here's the deal, Robert and Aaron. You earn your status as freedmen, then eventually you may come back to Kansas and help us. Not as soldiers as originally planned, but businessmen. I will train you to replace me. I have already seen what you two can do! Once you're established in New Haven making arms for whatever cause we find ourselves, I have no doubt you two will do just fine and be able to take over for me as the sons I never had!"

That day they all discovered they had this in common: They fought for a good cause and knew they were all part of something very special and pleasing to God in the ongoing battle between tyranny and liberty.

P.T. Barnum is famously quoted: "My only goal in life is to make others happy! A human soul, 'that God has created, and Christ died for,' is not to be trifled with. It may tenant the body of a Chinaman, a Turk, an Arab or a Hottentot – it is still an immortal spirit."

Ballot Box Stuffing, Corruption, Riots, and Bank Collapse[17]

1855-1857

Sherman now age thirty-five had many business and social connections and had temporarily resigned from the army for a proven business opportunity.

"That evening in San Francisco I hunted up Major Turner, whom I found boarding, in company with General E. A. Hitchcock, at a Mrs. Ross's, on Clay Street, near Powell. I took quarters with them, and began to make my studies, with a view to a decision whether it was best to undertake this new and untried scheme of banking, or to return to New Orleans.

"We soon secured a small share of business and be-

---

17 We the People are the Kings of this country, and if we don't get a say in our goals and desire for Liberty for what God have blessed us with, then bad things happen.

came satisfied there was room for profit. Everybody seemed to be making money fast; people paid their three percent a month interest without deeming it excessive. Turner, Nisbet, and I, daily discussed the prospects. With two hundred thousand dollars capital, and a credit of fifty thousand dollars in New York, we could build up a business that would help the St. Louis house, and at the same time pay expenses in California, with a profit".

"During the summer of 1856, in San Francisco, occurred one of those unhappy events, too common to new countries, in which I became involved in spite of myself.' W. Tecumseh wrote.

"William Neely Johnson was Governor of California and resided at Sacramento City; General John E. Wool commanded the Department of California. Politics had become a regular and profitable business, and politicians were more than suspected of being corrupt. In the election all sorts of dishonesty was charged and believed, especially of 'ballot-box stuffing'. Generally the better classes avoided the elections and dodged jury duty, so that the affairs of the city government necessarily passed into the hands of a low set of professional politicians." (Sound familiar dear reader? National Election Seasons 2020 and Midterm 2022 Michigan, Pennsylvania, Georgia and Arizona? Remember?)

Sherman went on: "Among them was a man named James Casey who edited a small paper, the printing office of which was in a room on the third floor of our banking-office. I hardly knew him by sight, and rarely if ever saw his paper; but one day Mr. Sather, of the excellent banking firm of Drexel, Sather & Church, came to me, and called my attention to an article in Casey's paper so full of falsehood and malice, that we construed it as an effort to blackmail the banks generally. I went up-stairs, found Casey, and pointed out to him the objectionable nature of his article, told him plainly that I could not tolerate his attempt to print and circulate slanders in our building, and if he repeated it, I would cause him and his press to be thrown out the window it led to Casey, having a fight with a rival newspaper editor. Casey in the heat of an argument that escalated into Casey, a former inmate to the State penitentiary at Sing Sing that James King his rival editor in a back and forth news editorial war led to violence on the part of Casey when he murdered King with a pistol after an earlier threat in the day," the article read.

Elijah and Olive had read about all this.

"More shootings in California and unrest where people get disenfranchised, and the natural results is more, not less corruption!" Olive recalled. She continued.

"It says here our Sherman, half businessman and half soldier, now had to address a Vigilance Committee, that was formed; its chairman in the midst of all the political corruption and frustration with crime rampant on the streets!" Olive read on.

"This corrupt appointed (not elected) governor said,

'I agree with you perfectly, and have come down from Sacramento to assist.' You bet!" Olive added sarcastically. "Poor Sherman!"

Meanwhile in Ohio, Olive with Elijah continued their discussion of the events.

"'Sherman and Johnson, the Governor of California who unfortunately was just corrupt enough to not be trusted by any other party!' Tut!" she added, then continued reading.

"'He sincerely tried to gain everyone's confidence but failed!' Here we go again!" Olive interjected. "The only competent administrator with true integrity in this whole affair was Sherman... but no! For lack of political strength they make our Sherman the fall guy!" Olive threw down the paper in disgust.

The next day's banner line read: "Johnson turns over Casey to the mob!!!"

"Elijah, listen to this... 'with another inmate named Cora, a man who had once been tried for killing Richardson, the United States Marshal along with Casey without a trial, were both hung by the neck-dead-suspended from beams projecting from the windows of the committee's rooms in a building the mob took over with the wrath of the media also stirring things up resulting in their brutal execution.' Oh my stars!" Olive exclaimed. "Terrible!"

Elijah read on, "But even with the media now turned to other issues, the Vigilance Committee of Benicia was not about to give up their new-found power and continued rioting. Hanging other perceived enemies and their prisoners some of whom also committed suicide" the article informed.

"It certainly is terrible!" Elijah said in agreement.

"This all after the fact when Commodore Farragut of the navy, would not intervene in local brawls."

"Wow!" Olive added. "Now this next, 'The Benicia Vigilance Committee as a permanent fixture of the community, that defied the public trust of law-abiding citizens throughout the country of California...' These people have gone crazy!" she read on.

"'Who in turn gave the Vigilance Committee free license to write their own history.' These people have gone insane!"

Now Heman Goodspeed and Louisa Goodspeed read:

"During the winter of 1855-1856 and indeed throughout the year 1856, all kinds of businesses became unsettled in California. The mines continued to yield about fifty million of gold a year, but little attention was paid to agriculture or to any business other than that of 'mining' and, as the placer-gold was becoming worked out, the miners were restless and uneasy, and were shifting about from place to place, impelled by rumors put afloat for speculative purposes. A great many extensive enterprises by joint-stock companies had been begun, in the way of water-ditches, to bring water from the head of the mountain-streams down to the richer alluvial deposits, and nearly all of these companies became embarrassed or bankrupt," at last the article concluded.

So ends the lesson of how corruption in politics can

have a devastating effect on the economy, and the bigger and more widespread the corruption in bigger cities as Thomas Jefferson predicted, the bigger the negative long-term effects to a free society!

(Flash forward to contemporary times, 2025 LA, California fires, due to corruption and bad policies regarding long overdue water irrigation issues. Sound familiar dear reader?)

CHAPTER TWENTY-EIGHT

Secessionitis and War Drums

1857

Sherman writes: "On the 30th of January I published a notice of the dissolution of the partnership and called on all who were still indebted to the firm of Lucas, Turner & Co. to pay up, or the notes would be sold at auction. I also advertised that all the real property was for sale and took passage on the good steamer Golden Gate, Captain Whiting, for Panama and home. In July 1859, I received notice from Governor Wickliffe that I had been elected superintendent of the proposed college and invited me to come down to Louisiana as early as possible. They were anxious to put the college into operation by the 1st of January, following. For this honorable position I was indebted to Major D. C. Buell and General G. Mason Graham, to whom I have made full and due acknowledgment."

1859 - Life in General During This Time in America

The net effect on public opinion was all the friends of slavery both north and south of the Ohio River were starting to talk about how Darwin had proven that blacks, though spiritual creatures, were indeed inferior to the white man. And Huxley, Darwin's bulldog, with Greeley's encouragement, was challenging the notion that Carl Marx was praising that religious truth had nothing in common with science and started the subtle game of straw-man arguments. Marx was against slavery for political reasons and used it to his advantage but rejected religion as anathema to the religious mores that both he and Huxley despised. Marx even corresponded very briefly with Darwin. But everyone was still reading the counter to Huxley's drivel in a book Edward Hitchcock published a year later after the Huxley-Wilberforce debates were over. Lincoln and Herndon liked that Darwin's friends dismissed it out of hand as nonsense. Blacks would have to be condemned to stay inferior for quite some time until the age of Intelligent Design would come and threaten the neo-Darwinians monopoly on the issue.

In New Haven, as "Bleeding Kansas" as Horace Greeley called that conflict, continued to bleed, Winchester forced the insolvency of the Volcanic Arms Company in late 1856. They took over ownership and moved the plant to New Haven, Connecticut. They reorganized it as the New Haven Arms Company in April 1857. B. Tyler Henry was hired as plant superintendent when Robbins

& Lawrence suffered financial difficulties and Henry left their employ. While continuing to make the Volcanic rifle and pistol, Henry began to experiment with the new rimfire ammunition, and modified the Volcanic lever action design to use it. The result was the Henry rifle.

The problem in 1854 was that the charge mounted inside the shell casing wasn't much for either hunting or warfare. But the idea that one could reload less often, and fire more often was gaining interest in investment and research.

In 1857 the firm of W.G. Armstrong & Company was now able to efficiently produce one hundred hydraulic cranes a year, but by this time Lincoln was more interested in politics and saving the country than religion, science, or inventions.

In 1857 Justice Robert Grier of the U.S. Supreme Court was siding with the majority in the Dred Scott Case and Representative Alexander H. Stevens that "blacks were inferior to whites and had no rights that a white man would be bound to respect". So Huxley was winning with the public opinion war, leaving politicians and scientists alike to find some other moral pathway to sanity and justice.

But there was one good thing. Elijah was doing well and at Olive's advice, caring less about politics in order to avoid depression. Mashpee too was becoming quite the businessman along with Aaron and Robert. Samuel in his involvement with the three made frequent westward trips. They were seeing the signs that a major split was inevitable and secessionism was in the wind.

Elijah encouraged his sons to never become soldiers if it ever came to a civil war but to become rich and live a long time. His sons took over the business and fugitive transports to Port Clinton, and on occasion dropped by to visit Heman and Louisa in Niagara County. Olive was aging faster than Elijah and it was starting to worry him.

October 17, 1859 - John Brown

By 1880, Frederick Douglass declared: "I could speak for the slave. John Brown could fight for the slave. I could live for the slave. John Brown could die for the slave."

"Damn that man! He was the reason that the press, politicians, and the rest maligned and marginalized us," Elijah ranted, and Olive agreed with her husband.

"It was bad enough when he and his sons hacked up those men in Kansas with broadswords. After that Justice Grier had nothing good to say about abolitionists in public and attacked the late Solomon Goodspeed's Presbyterians."

Olive and Elijah were just getting caught up with yesterday's news about John Brown's raid at Harper's Ferry. Elijah still wasn't done venting.

"Like this statement here from our friend Lincoln. 'It would have availed him nothing!' I couldn't have said it better!"

"Oh God!" Heman exclaimed, at his station in Lockport, N.Y.

"What?" Louisa looked up.

"We're not going to be buying any more wool or cotton from him any time soon! He just got arrested for murder in a shoot-out. Lee was called in to take him and his gang out. He survived, but it looks like two of his sons were killed. I'm surprised they didn't apprehend him earlier in Kansas. Now we're going to have a harder time winning hearts and minds to our cause!" Heman and his wife were sitting in the parlor reading. He was buried in the newspaper.

"Oh listen to this. How terrible! The first one to die was a freed black night watchman, and one of his gang, another black man was killed, and someone cut off his ears for souvenirs...Will it ever end?"

December 3, 1859 - Day and Early Evening after Brown's Execution

George Edward Goodspeed looked over at Lincoln.

"I think with your continued support, I will make a deal," Lincoln responded, then addressed William Henry. "I have watched Connecticut in particular. And I thank you William, Samuel. Mr. Henry, I thank you especially for working hard for almost three years now on the rifle. That was quite an impressive demonstration of that rifle you gave us earlier this afternoon. Very impressive, and I pray you continue with my blessing with its development. Please keep me updated, will you?" Abe now continued with the others.

"Your interest in building the might and muscle for the Union in ships and weaponry is unsurpassed! If I'm elected, Gideon Wells, a famous native of this state, will be appointed my Navy Secretary, but he already knows that!" Lincoln chuckled. "As of now I have yet to figure out who my running mate for vice president is going to be!"

The rest of them laughed and when that died down Lincoln continued.

"Do I expect war? I don't rightly know. I am on keeping the Union together! Nevertheless, I figure if it does come to that, it is always better to have a range of options, rather than no plan at all!" Then he turned to George.

"I also need to thank you for your intelligence network and you bringing it to my attention. I never knew John Brown was a traitor and apologize that I didn't believe your sources at first...until now!" Then Lincoln leaned back in Nathan's old chair and sighed, as he nodded at Samuel.

"I did believe in Fredric Douglas who Samuel here introduced me to recently, and I learned something very interesting! The night before Brown's raid on the Harper's Ferry Armory, Fredric was at Brown's campfire meeting, then just before the raid he fled to Canada." He paused briefly to assess the impact what this tidbit of information was going to have on the others at the meeting before he continued.

"Why did he do that? I'll tell you. He told me that he, John Brown, wanted Fredric to join him on that raid.

Of course, he courteously declined the invitation, and knowing he was publicly associated with Brown, made tracks to Canada!" Lincoln decisively slapped his knee, but this time maintained his gravity and didn't laugh. "Well! It was then that I knew George Edward that you and William and Samuel were right. John Brown was in fact no doubt a double agent, radical and traitor to the Constitution as you had foretold from your sources; Heman and Louisa. Brown's famous church pledge when he stood up...." Abe laughed. "Hell, he wasn't even a member of that church, but a Transcendentalist plant, where that pledge was staged to intentionally create maximum confusion and division! Just as your family warned me, they were running from the playbook of the other old Abe Lincoln!"

Lincoln now laughed, shaking his head. "At times I have wondered if I should change my name..." Now the others laughed along with Abe.

Lincoln, through talking, leaned back in the old chair, folded his arms, and looked to his right out of Nathan's office window. The curtains fluttered in the calm early evening breeze but a bitter chill was now in the air. Noname, the deceased Madagascar's replacement, went over and closed the window.

1861

Author's Note: War is a very terrible thing but with it came personal assistance for the bondsmen with the ultimate sacrifice of many a brave soldier's death.

Lincoln's primary goal if elected was to hold the Union at whatever cost. George, William, and Elijah realized the same thing knowing keeping a strong republic was vital to all for life, liberty, and law as an inalienable right from Almighty God. But where they disagreed with Lincoln was the second part of his statement which was: "If I could free the slave and save the Union I would do so...or if I could save slavery and preserve the Union...I would do so."

Elijah spoke. "Fred and I have been up and down the Mississippi so many times that we've lost track. I can't even remember when we did anything else in life. Every passing year cotton production kept demanding more slave trading and employment was no longer confined to the plantations. But now we find it is economic for city dwellers and store front keepers to own slaves and bond them out...decadence, idleness and misery is now everywhere," Elijah mused.

"With every passing year it spreads more and worsens at an alarming rate, not to mention that prostitution, the spread of disease, suicide and violence is everywhere."

Elijah exploded, bringing his fist down hard on the meeting table.

"I've seen its presence in our own family, so you can't even imagine how bad it is for slaves that suffer from cradle to grave. And Lincoln says he would save slavery if he could save the Union! What kind of a country would this be if we were at once united but then all starving to death? Nothing could be worse! We would all simply perish and there would be no Union!" Elijah had said all he could say, and was now struggling to get himself back under control. The specter of his own personal tragedy stared him straight in the face once again. A moment later, though, he was able to conclude in a much softer despaired tone.

"Thanking God I'm too old to get depressed for long over this anymore, or it would be the end of me." Then calmer, he managed to laugh. Everyone else sitting around the table couldn't help but reflect inward and acknowledge the drain it had been on their own lives. For quite a while no one spoke as each searched desperately for an alternative solution to put forward and struggled with their personal disappointment in Lincoln's comment. They adjourned for lunch still expecting Lincoln to arrive for the afternoon part of the meeting.

"Gentlemen, I only meant that without a Union there would be no possibility of ever working out a solution. I'm sorry if that deeply troubles you all...as it also does me!"

Elijah was thinking to himself that this was only so much political double talk. Lincoln interrupted Elijah's thought and surprised him by directly addressing him.

"Elijah and Samuel, if I was to become president and get the funds from the War Department, what would Pacific and Goodspeed's Landing name their first war ship should war break out?"

Elijah would have preferred for Samuel, George, or William to answer that question. He felt that it was not his place to make that decision, but noticed that "compassionate without pity" Lincoln was not about to break eye contact with him until he answered.

"Sir, I'm honored, but I have enough challenges with just piloting a slave rescue vessel, let alone captain a gunboat."

Lincoln nodded and waited encouragingly for Elijah's answer. Then he reminded Elijah about his own painful past, as a hint with just one simple observation. "Well, let's just call it good therapy, Elijah." Lincoln smiled and again waited for Elijah to ponder the ship's name.

Then it came to Elijah that a good inspirational answer would suffice, and that did his own pained heart good. "Well, if it was my ship, I would name it after the Kanawha River for my nephew Nathan, who with his dying breath, gave his wife love and wished us all the best in the beautiful Kanawha River Valley!"

Lincoln smiled but his eyes narrowed with interest in a new question for Elijah, one about Nathan's family.

"What ever happened to that boy Hiram M. who moved with Nathan's wife Sarah? If I remember correctly, they went to Indiana immediately after Nathan's death and settled when he was only two."

Elijah was shocked that Lincoln would have known about that whole saga and was suddenly very impressed with Lincoln's memory for intimate family details.

"I've seen him many times, sir. He works with me at our station in Athens on occasion. He grew to become a mature young man and in many ways has fared better than me." Lincoln laughed reading Elijah's look of marvel and admiration.

"Well, I've always had a mind for details, though slow to learn. Once learned it stays there. And that story was a touching one that was hard to forget." Then Lincoln became very serious and softly patted Elijah's knee in empathy.

"You folks have been through a lot, Elijah...a lot!"

USS Kanawha–built at Goodspeed's Landing–launch Oct. 21, 1861, commissioned Jan. 21, 1862, Pacific engine best blockade record of Unadilla Class Gunboats, rivaled only the USS Unadilla for which that ships class was named.

The goal in production planning was to complete the gunboat in ninety days. Regarding cost, it all hinged on Lincoln getting elected as the sixteenth President of the United States. By mid-to-late June of 1860, when three candidates had so far entered the presidential race, it was too close to call, although odds were good that Lincoln was going to win.

Goodspeed's Landing was in friendly competition with Gildersleeve & Sons in Portland. Between them and their engine suppliers, Pacific in Bridgeport, and Woodruff in Hartford just up the Connecticut River from them, they were all busy planning to build two of the twenty-three gunboats that Lincoln commissioned among twenty-three different, independent New England manufacturers.

Both local competitive firms were working with their

semi-retired shipwright Jabez Goodspeed, already going full throttle when the news broke that indeed a fourth candidate Bell just threw his hat in the ring. The Breckinridge's wing of the split was now in the throes of secession and Lincoln's chances of winning had suddenly dramatically improved! Passion would consume Jabez, goaded in memory of Thomas' and Rebecca's and now Thankful's trials. He devoted his dying breath to George and William on behalf of both firms which were to make the call on that one. They wrote Lincoln a letter outlying their production plans, as well as their partner's at Gildersleeve & Sons without comment, and waited on Lincoln's answer.

Finally, in mid-October, a month before the election, Lincoln responded that Gideon was definitely his choice for the Secretary of Navy position. He also added a comment that was rather cryptic, but George and William knew what it meant. Lincoln was not going to be the aggressor, he wrote back, but was expecting the south would eventually do something that would trigger war! In that cryptic response, Lincoln told them all they needed to know. After a brief meeting they voted to proceed. Not only did they commit to one ship with certain delivery dates for materials but knew that a second build was possible.

"Lincoln only requires us to build one ship, but we could build one or possibly two, possibly three sister ships, and commission one of those for our own fleet, George proposed. "What do you think William?"

"I commit to two sisters but not three, George. Don't

forget that rumor has it, that whatever treasurer Lincoln confirms, a personal income tax as proposed for a war, will drive markets down!" responded the dapper William Henry, uncharacteristically cautious. Toward the end of the day, it was finally voted to give Jabez the go-ahead for production of two ships, total. Those were exciting albeit challenging, days for Goodspeed's Landing!

Overall cost of the individual ships varied between $90,000 and $103,500, with cost of the hulls varying between $52,000 and $58,500. The largest price differential was for the machinery contracts, the first four of which, with the Novelty Works, were for only $31,500, as opposed to the $42,000–$46,500 for the later ships. (The differences were due primarily to the fact that the later vessels had 60% more boiler power than the original four, as well as lighter engines for Goodspeed's Landing and Gildersleeve & Sons). Total cost of all 23 vessels was $2,170,000 (Today's USD: $124,000,000). The two companies were in "friendly" competition with each other and able to lower their costs by working together on the project, with members on one company board often being members on the other. Wild times indeed!

For Jabez, starting in late 1860 through 1861, there was no time to think much about what was now gripping the nation. Jabez had made his last will and testament out on August 12, 1859, at age seventy. Knowing he was old, he wanted to make building the gunboats his last official business with his Shipwright firm in

1860. He pushed Goodspeed's Landing hard to make all timelines as scheduled. His last business on earth drew him out of retirement for the cause of freedom.

But for Elijah and Olive, it was a very significant personal transition. They both now had plenty of time to think a lot about the possibility of a production slowdown should a personal income tax go in effect to support an estimated cost of a million-dollars-a-day war effort! It was a lot to consider.

Lincoln had been elected president when seven southern states seceded from the Union as he had suspected they would. In April when Lincoln planned to resupply Fort Sumter, the fuse that had been lit by bleeding Kansas and the Brown raid finally exploded when rebel Charleston shelled Fort Sumter. Overnight, a full-fledged war had begun with both sides calling for more volunteers. Elijah and Olive watched in alarm as more states in the south threw in with the new confederacy. In a short a time, things changed quickly for them and for the nation. Gone forever were the days of steamboat rescues. There had been a brief pause between the Fugitive Slave Act and its resumption after the Christiana trial, and now this! Any Yankee ships like the *Rebecca-Jane* no doubt would be commandeered by the South anyway for the war effort.

The very remote possibility of emancipation some day in the future was more than anyone could wrap their arms around. Their slave rescue business was no longer possible now that the universal conflict of civil war had actually commenced.

PART FOUR

The Determined Generals

An Impactful Letter

August 1861

Captain Seth Goodspeed died Aug. 4, 1861, age eighty-one. His famous statement quoted in the obituary in the papers caught Lincoln's attention.

"He is said to have remarked a short time before death that he was born when his country was in trouble and would die when it was in trouble." Shortly thereafter, Abe sent a brief memorial recognition letter to Elijah. The President asked who else had enlisted from their immediate families that had migrated west to establish the underground efforts, but not to worry because they had already done enough! Elijah wrote back with the address Lincoln had personally given him and listed the following in his return letter.[18]

Dear Mr. President,

---

18 (Author's Note: *John's line **Ebenezer's line 1 KIA; 2 Disabled; 3 PTSD)

There are other Goodspeeds, but these are the sons or grandsons of who came West with us in 1818 that joined the Union Army.

Thank you for your interest in our family,

Elijah and Olive Goodspeed

August 18, 1861, Athens Ohio

* Theron Goodspeed, Heman Goodspeed's son, if his parents allow, will be going a year from now

* Arza Mathias Goodspeed, Joseph Goodspeed's grand son—May 1861

* Joseph M. Goodspeed, Joseph Goodspeed's grand son—going in October

** Allen Goodspeed, Solomon Goodspeed's son—going in December

** Hiram M. Goodspeed, Solomon Goodspeed's grand son—1861

** James Goodspeed, my brother Nathan's son—going in October-1861

At the end of the war three out of the six would be killed, two would be disabled, and one suffer from post-traumatic shock. This would be by far a much higher mortality rate then the rest of the Goodspeed men that had enlisted from other more distant lines. Elijah's two sons stayed out of it, as Lincoln said, they had all given enough already before the war. This only added more to their commitment which didn't go unnoticed by President Lincoln. As mentioned earlier, when Hiram was mustered out, he was awarded the postmaster position in Indiana and drew a handsome salary, since Abe had personally directed the War Department.

Marshall Goodspeed completed his education, moved to Illinois, and became a teacher after graduating in 1849. He engaged in the nursery business during the so-called Christiana tragedy that started September 11, 1851. The press Whig rags portrayed the lawmen as honest men and the blacks as armed Negros. The Quakers that defended the fugitives and restored civility were jailed, and framed by the same rags as ring leaders, murderers, and traitors to the US Congress. Yet oddly, before the end of that month they were all acquitted including the Negros. But what really got Marshall's attention happened October 25, 1851, when editor Horace Greeley, after an embarrassed silence, came out with a twelve-page edition rather than their usual eight-page paper. Not once was it mentioned anything about Christiana but featured a new foreign correspondent named Karl Marx. He was hired by golden whiskered Charles A. Danna, Greeley's young managing editor. Karl, up until the Civil War, was the world news small talk contributor. Marshall studied these installments with interest which seemed to have quite a literary style, until it was revealed that Marx, a German, could only write in German and had an English journalist named Frederic Engles as a ghost writer. Marx eventually would learn to write his own pieces but by that time was earning less and was finally let go by Greeley just before the Civil War started.

President Lincoln's Bold Decision - September 1861

The Constitution was intended to protect individual rights of the people by imposing negative liberties on the three branches of government. Maryland, which was a hornets' nest of death threats, kidnappings, aggression, hatred, and rumors of poison was always suspect in the business and nature of the Goodspeed's Landing underground enterprise. The more they did the more each personally risked in their effort to free others.

So, Lincoln shut down the Maryland council for even considering the notion of secession, for he believed military intervention was necessary for the sake of self-preservation. The City of Washington would have been totally surrounded by the enemy. So the president felt justified in stopping them. He put them in confinement, however couldn't charge them with treason, and jailed them indefinitely without a writ of habeas corpus which, as Commander-in-Chief during wartime, he felt obligated to do. For that, many senators and representatives, north and south, labeled Lincoln a dictator.

"Lincoln is our only rare chance, and if he fails, he will be killed or jailed and the friends of slavery will become all our masters and rule all of us as cruelly or worse, and we'll become an inferior race as well, subject to their bidding!" Elijah lamented, though at this time in his life rarely spoke out about anything.

Lincoln Plans for War

Kanawha "cutting out a blockade runner from under the guns of Fort Morgan"

1862

Between the various private intelligence establishments and Lincoln's genius they already knew what the war effort would require. The builder's questions were twofold. What kind of material, mechanism, and manpower would be needed to effectively blockade off the

Atlantic seaboard and Gulf of Mexico of the South from the rest of the world? How did they figure out that the war was to be a $1,000,000 per day war effort?

Lincoln and Gideon Wells, his Navy Secretary devised a plan to make ships that could be fabricated in approximately ninety-day cycles from start to finish. As early as 1850 they had determined that with Pacific Ironworks and Goodspeed's Landing single screw hull designs would be the most efficient steamship. Those would become the industrial standard of ship design and transportation over the next one hundred fifty years. It fell on twenty-three different northern manufacturing groups and eleven associated machine building facilities working day and night to bring the South to its knees.

Sam's design for lighter weight engines was frosting on the cake for a handful of these groups involved. They were built on time and on budget in the first year and a half of the war! Goodspeed's Landing and Gildersleeve & Sons were the lightest and fastest ships and they made out very well during the war, better that the twenty-one other Unadilla Class Ninety Day Gunboats!

Lincoln's Courage

As early as October of 1860, a little less than a month before election day, Lincoln, Wells, and twenty-three ship building firms along with eleven machine building facilities under Lincoln's direction and foresight, were making plans for the production of twenty-three ninety-day gunboats with projected costs being over $120,000,000 in today's USD.

Lincoln made several very bold decisions:

Based on his sources when he knew it was going to be a four-way race for the presidency they were confident that he was going to win.

They already knew what the south would need to wage an effective war against "northern aggression" and Lincoln had Salmon Chase looking into manpower, materials, and mass production strategies required to build an effective blockade fleet from scratch. Also to produce the modern warfare weapons that Lincoln was obsessed with.

For the first time in American history, a federal tax on income would have to be enacted.

For the first time in American history, war bonds would be issued.

For the first time in American history, banks agreed to cooperate by universally issuing such bonds, including the Bank of New England at Goodspeed's Landing and others, to help support a million dollar per day war expenditure. This was before a FED was created by yet another secret society that was based on self-centered reasoning, laziness, and greed that America never had any business getting involved with; nor was it constitutional. The banking industry would be forced to consolidate less than three quarters of a century later!

Nor was it intended to promote an IRS as the secret societies of that day had the good sense to agree that a sunset clause was necessary to implement and assure the public that "tax on personal income" would stop after the war was over. Had they seen what would eventually happen in 1913, they would have been as horrified at that time as they were about the John Brown uprising earlier!

Lincoln and the Bank of New England at Goodspeed's Landing knew that if they didn't get this all in place quickly it would turn into a longer bloodier affair that Americans would never be able to endure. And after four years, and was tragic enough. The one thing our forefathers had anticipated and dreaded was now happening with the escalating demand for cotton production and slave labor and political pressure.

Even sane businessmen in Baltimore, Maryland, in the face of violent protests, were willing to commit to building one of these ninety-day gunboats for the soon-to-be formed Union Army and Navy, and to keep it 'hush-hush' till the day of the ship's commission.

It was only a rumor up to that time that all politicians involved had agreed, in their diplomacy and polished edited speeches, to deny. After all it would be fantastic for business in Baltimore that a slave and morally bankrupt state was suffering from the same economic stagnation that the other states south of the Ohio River were experiencing. These were the same conditions that Elijah and Fred had personally witnessed over their years of piloting on the Mississippi before the war.

The Silent Pole Treaty: Lincoln's Secret, January 1862

Sometime in 1849, after Samuel's team had secured Lincoln's patent on his steamboat lift pad invention, Lincoln paid back the favor and revealed where the Yukon potential gold fields were. Samuel told Mashpee, who through his own network sent out word to the Indian Territory, south of Kansas, to go investigate and develop facilities for refining any raw material claims. Claims in those mapped zones were sold out at dirt cheap prices. By the late fifties there was enough profit from this venture to establish an Indian's office base in San Francisco, which Mashpee had never visited but was acting chairman of.

During the exact same period, both Samuel and Mashpee had invested in The New Haven Arms Company venture of establishing the arms interests. Mashpee awarded the tribal council chiefs in the Kansas territory the new and improved weapons so they could survive as a nation, and this particular shipment's final destination would be the Indian Council Office in San Francisco Elders Securities.

By this time, telegraph links had also been established through other contacts with Jedidiah Morse's son Samuel. The contacts were associated from the beginning with Nathan and son Joseph of Goodspeed's Landing. Lincoln was not a believer in treaties and had a "silent" or the Pole Treaty, as it was called, involving the New Haven Arms Company in 1862, which he gave directly to acting chairman Mashpee to carry out with his tribal council and bases south of Kansas and in San Francisco, California.

Mashpee knew exactly what was coming down from Samuel's two privateer cousins, Aaron and Robert, regarding the Henry Rifle on January 29th, 1862. When the truth of the Baltimore commissioning of the ninety-day gunboat *Pinola* was finally made public and riots started. This was the diversion to distract from a mysterious trip Mashpee, Fred, and Elijah made on the last tour of duty of the *Rebecca-Jane* going as far as their Ohio River route could safely take them without notice or risk of confiscation to final destination. A secret massive shipment of rifles and ammo was transported over old bumpy wagon trails all the way through Kansas back roads and finally delivered to the chiefs of the tribal council south of Kansas.

The Indian Council, initially was deeply offended after having been made to wait for this meeting through telegraph communications that were cryptic to say the least; especially when the massive crate delivered personally by Mashpee was labeled Volcanic Arms. They openly scoffed, till they were escorted to the Southern Clay Pits firing range of Kansas. A familiar and popular figure whom they liked awaited them: P.T. Barnum. It was then that the crate was broken open and to their astonishment a strange looking but massive rifle was pulled out from the first box.

At the firing range there were five gourds on a spiked post at one hundred yards and another five located at a thousand-yard range. They no longer laughed derisively when Mashpee produced the first rifle from the box, then became suspicious when they saw the massive .44 caliber bore.

"Is this a rimfire?!" an astonished chief asked incredulously, but impressed.

"You'll see," Mashpee said quietly as he took aim at the five gourds lined up at a hundred yards. Less than two seconds later each of the five gourds exploded without a single miss. Mashpee paused long enough to look back at the tribal council and grin.

Raising the level sight up and in less than five seconds he performed the same feat with the five gourds located at one thousand yards.

"How many rounds do you have left!?"

Smiling, Mashpee handed the rifle to the chief asking the question and responded. "Find out."

After emptying the rifle of six more rounds the chief was no longer scoffing.

"Love the action, Mashpee, what's the deal?"

The silent pole treaty referred to the Indian custom of putting their ear to a live telegraph pole and listened to the signal dispatches being transmitted. Specific lines would telegraph troop movements that might be particularly worrisome to the Indian Nations. Specific sites would relay any warning directly to the council and relay dispatches from the tribal council office of San Francisco. The shipment bound for San Francisco under secured Indian escort was never to be compromised unless a national emergency relay was transmitted to the council at those specific designated sites.

The rifles were available for sale to the public at $400 each, but the initial production of nine hundred rifles was reserved for the Union Army and beleaguered Indian Nations that fell under previous US protection treaties. Lincoln made it known through P.T. Barnum and Mashpee that both the US and the Cherokee and Sioux nations understood that Lincoln mistrusted these treaties just as much as they did and sought to make it right.

So, this one would never be in writing but held in confidentiality, and yet was honored by a gift of one hundred rifles from the summer's first production batch.

Nine hundred rifles were manufactured between summer and October of 1862, and by 1864, production had peaked at 290 rifles per month, bringing the total to 8,000. By the time production ended in 1866, approximately 14,000 units had been manufactured, 6,000 of which found their way directly into Union Army possession.

Underground Conductor, Harriet Tubman with a Henry Repeater

And one rifle was delivered to the famous Underground Railroad Conductor Harriett Tubman!

April 6-7, 1862 - Battle of Shiloh

Note to the reader: Within the inner circles of the elitist deep state media of the day and some of President Lincoln's Administrative cabinet some were there to embarrass Lincoln. The war was not popular but slavery was popular and profitable to even some northern politicians as well as the press.

In Kentucky before the Battle of Shiloh, the press wanted to create the impression that Sherman was insane and suicidal; neither case was true. Eventually the first Secretary of War Cameron was fired by Lincoln and replaced by Stanton.[19]

Grant was labeled by the media as a drunkard and their commanding officer General Halleck was put under pressure to fire or hold Grant back in favor of the Democrat General McClelland. He was more interested in suing for peace than fighting: Which played more popular with the establishment both North and South.

"Sherman I'm going to go for broke and gamble on a

---

19 Republican General Halleck—The 'pro slavery' Whig press influenced him against his own Republican Generals. The Democrat, press instead lied and promoted Democrat General McClellan, who was a politician who, they knew, didn't know how to fight. Republican General William T. Sherman and General U. S. Grant. were the target. The timeline below, clearly bears out. How the three Republican Generals, once united against the lies, became unstoppable to defeat slavery and tyranny!

Nashville incursion and breaking Confederate General Sydney's back!" Grant said.

Sherman, "What are you talking about Grant? Don't be a fool, my friend. The press are like cockroaches, worse than spies. You know they'll inflate the numbers of Union prisoners taken to look like men killed in action. The Rebs here in Tennessee might cut our communications that will put pressure on Halleck by the press thus blackmailing him, then the press labeling you a drunk and me crazy and suicidal!"

Grant, "I don't know but it's worth a try to make that move for me to head east with an exploratory detachment and try to cut Tennessee in half and cut off the Rebels, It's at least worth a try even if it does happen that Halleck gets concerned.... Let's try it's our only opportunity. Besides it will actually keep me sober!" Grant winked. The day started cool but would soon turn hot.

Halleck, way up in St. Louis, wasn't aware of the reality of rapidly advancing events down in Tennessee. In those days telegraph lines were the only means of military communications and with interdiction by the rebel enemy they were often cut down. Grant was progressing even further than Halleck could have imagined and wasn't sleeping or drunk on his watch, as the press claimed. He was down river exploring the possibilities of a Nashville incursion. Had that been feasible, it would have taken the entire state of Tennessee.

Albert Sydney Johnston, just prior to his tragic death that very same day, made a surprise raid of Grant's established camp headquarters.

Under Grant's directions General Buell's reinforcements turned the outcome around a couple days later and won the Shiloh Campaign. It was at this point, judging from the high mortality numbers in the Memphis Campaign, in First Lady Mary Todd Lincoln's opinion, that Grant got the reputation for being a butcher. That opinion was influenced by fake news who were intentionally inflating the mortality count with prisoners captured. In time this would catch up with the Whig rags but in the meantime the damage to Grant's reputation was done.

Grant could attest to his men's misery. His army had been pounded that day, and he had seen horrors that had almost made him sick; things that vastly overshadowed anything he had experienced during the Mexican War or earlier in this war. The abrupt death of one of his scouts, Capt. Irving Carson, who was decapitated by a Confederate cannonball while standing right next to Grant.

Though covered with blood and bothered by a throbbing ankle, Grant continued traveling his line that evening, joined by Buell, encouraging his men.

A lesser commander than Grant could have retreated during the night. Buell came to Grant while he was at the landing and asked what preparations he had made for withdrawing.

"I have not yet despaired of whipping them, General," Grant replied. "Retreat? No!" Grant responded, "I propose to attack at daylight, and whip them."

There would be a second day at Shiloh, to make sure

the troops were ready, he had ammunition wagons moving throughout the night. One of Lew Wallace's troops wrote, "No one talked of tomorrow. We knew we had to fight a victorious enemy who was expecting an easy ending to the battle, nothing less than an unconditional surrender. We knew in our hearts that we were going to lick them." If the first day put Grant in position to win the battle, the second day's fighting would determine the extent of that victory.

Now with the pressure of the ever-nagging press, General Halleck made the blunder of his career by being influenced for the one and only time and doubting Grant's capabilities. Halleck blamed Grant, from his remote St. Louis headquarters. He did not know just how rapidly things were changing in Southwestern Tennessee. He made the blunder of coming down and reorganizing the Tennessee Army after the battle of Shiloh was over. Halleck quickly learned to never trust the media again over Grant and didn't realize at the time how close Grant had come to resigning as a result. Sherman describes it below.

"Halleck issued an order, reorganized and rearranged the whole army. General Grant was substantially left out and was named "second in command. He still retained his old staff, composed of Rawlins, adjutant-general; Riggin, Lagow, and Hilyer, aides; and he had a small company of the Fourth Illinois Cavalry as an escort.

Sherman could see that Grant, although seldom complaining about his bad treatment, felt deeply the indignity, "if not insult, heaped upon him."

Early June 1862

After the battle Sherman wrote, "A short time before leaving I rode from my camp to General Halleck's
headquarters, and gossiped for some time, when he
mentioned to me that General Grant was going away
the next morning. I inquired the cause, and he said that
he did not know, but that Grant had applied for a thirty
days' leave, which had been given him. Of course, we
all knew that he was chafing under the slights of his
anomalous position, and I determined to see him on
my way back. I inquired for the general, and was shown
to his tent, where I found him seated on a camp-stool,
with papers on a rude camp-table; he seemed to be employed in assorting letters, and tying them up with red
tape into convenient bundles. After passing the usual
compliments, I inquired if it were true that he was going away. He said, "Yes." I then inquired the reason,
and he said "Sherman, you know. You know that I am
in the way here. I have stood it as long as I can and can
endure it no longer." I then begged him to stay, illus-
trating his case by my own.

Before the battle of Shiloh, I had been cast down by a
mere newspaper assertion of "crazy;" but that single
battle had given me new life, and now I was in high
feather; and I argued with him that, if he went away,
events would go right along, and he would be left out;
whereas, if he remained, some happy accident might
restore him to favor and his true place. Very soon
after this, I was ordered to Chewalla, where, on the

6th of June, 1862, I received a note from him, saying that he had reconsidered his intention, and would remain".

Master Spy

General Halleck saw the hand before he saw the man. "Thank you!" As his morning cup of coffee was set on his desk in front of him and General Halleck looked up. "Do I know you? Where's my other server?"

"Arrested sir!" Then the new servant said, then added, "Shortly there will be a knock on your door."

"Who are you?" You look very familiar to me," Halleck observed.

"May I?" said the man, pointing to a nearby chair.

"Certainly. Have a seat."

"I'm the man you met before when it was revealed that Meriwether Lewis didn't commit suicide but was assassinated," the man explained.

"Calvin!"

Calvin nodded. Then came the knock on the door and Calvin Goodspeed smiled knowingly.

"Come in!"

"Sir, your servant just got caught in a poison attempt... yours!" the messenger informed.

Halleck laughed then winked at Calvin. "Yes, we know!"

Now Calvin Goodspeed grew deathly serious and pointed ominously. "Look outside your window."

Before Halleck could stand up, one of his staff standing closest to the window exclaimed, "Oh my God!" putting her hands to her mouth.

Now Halleck bolted out of his chair and cautiously walked to the window. He froze for a moment, then calmly turned around and looked at Calvin.

"Who was he?"

"You mean the man hanging outside of your office window?"

Halleck nodded.

"Let us just say a drunken journalist and friend of the former disgraced and corrupt Secretary of War Cameron. I understand he couldn't pay his gambling debts," Calvin said with measured restraint and mock sadness.

Goodspeed added, "This time, unlike Lewis, it *was* suicide!"

With a gesture Halleck dismissed his staff. "Please close the door."

Once the staff left, Halleck calmly walked to his seat, sat down, then smiled broadly, and sipped his coffee

"All right. What would you advise us to do?" he asked.

"Please speak freely!" Henry urged.

Calvin, brave and bold like a professional negotiator, presented his plan.

"Reinstate Grant. You need him, and you know it." Then Calvin nodded toward the window. "That man hanging out there will no longer be able to blackmail you to make poor decisions!" he reminded him.

Based on what he knew and felt and reassured that Calvin understood and told him the truth, he nodded with respect. At this point he made the commitment to put his ego aside for the sake of the country. Nonchalantly, Halleck took another sip of his warm non-poisoned coffee in good faith.

"Thank you," he said humbly as the truly great general and warrior that he was. From that day forth Halleck would occasionally defer to Calvin Goodspeed for intelligence as an "unofficial" member of his staff, and later promoted his son John Calvin Goodspeed, a former shoe clerk, as Signal and Secret Service Officer. God does indeed work in mysterious ways.

Sherman writes, "After Shiloh, Grant hung in there and after his brilliant campaign in Memphis, General Halleck learned his lesson and reinstated Grant's authority. Later Grant won more victories at Arkansas Post, and then seasoned Sherman, Grant, and Halleck were totally on board with his two subordinate generals on July 4, 1863, when the Army of the Mississippi won the major victory over Vicksburg. That battle, along with Gettysburg, virtually ended the war, long before the South was smart enough to realize it."

The Courage and Faith of a Nation

In late 1862 and early 1863, Lincoln needed a spiritual as well as political boost. Withal only, by not the Constitution, but by blood, could the conflict be partially expunged but not erased. It could only be erased totally by faith in the blood of Jesus; and it would take courage to do that, greater courage than any other person running against him at the time of his election had; that courage he had then until after Lee's invasion of the North and the climactic battle of Gettysburg: The man Lincoln, like Washington before him, got down on his knees and prayed.

In 1862, Covenanters came from Scotland and Ireland as a delegation (Synod) to make a request to save the heart and soul of America. They had come previously to General Greene and the Army of Washington during the time of the American Revolution. Was it also to Lincoln? Was it God once again brooding over the face of the waters?

Religion Sanctions a Just War

"Religion supports valor by inspiring faith in the providence of God. Every Christian believes that the purposes and plans of God include, either directly or permissively, all the events of time, and that such are the resources of Divine power, wisdom, and goodness, that all things will be overruled to the final triumph of right. This is one of the reasons why those Christians whose theology lays great stress on the Divine purposes appear in history as such sturdy soldiers; in Switzerland, France, Scotland, England, and America. The Huguenots, the Covenanters, the Puritans—who have dared or sacrificed more than these? They felt that they were in God's hands, with the place of their lives and the hour and mode of their death marked out, and they had no other concern than to go forward under the guidance and protection of Divine Providence. The saint is bold in war because he has faith in God as pledged to sustain the right. He strikes hard; he takes aim coolly and accurately, because his strength has been summoned forth and his nerves steadied by fervent prayer and a conviction that God is with him. He kneels before he fires; he deals no blow without faith that God will make it effectual; he carries a rifle in his hand and a Bible in his pocket; and, like Cromwell's army, he 'trusts in God and keeps his powder dry.' Fighting in a good cause being part of his religion, he scruples not, but is zealous, rather, to do it well, that it may not need to be done again".[20]

"This trust in God as the defender of right is conspicuous in the conduct and words of the warriors mentioned in the Bible. The general of the forces of Israel, in the battle with the Ammonites, made this address to the troops —'Be of good courage, and let us play the men for our people and for the cities of our God; and the Lord do that which seemeth him right.'" (Christian Life and Character of the Civil Institutions of the United States, Benjamin Morris, p. 281, 1864, George W. Childs, 628 & 630 Chestnut St, Philadelphia)

July 4, 1863[21]

Sherman wrote, "The next day July 4, 1863, Vicksburg surrendered, and orders were given for at once attacking General (Joseph E.) Johnston.

---

20 Taken From the General Congress of America During the Revolution

21 Now the reader can see the results, (once the press was put in it's place) and once General Henry Halleck, Grant and Sherman were united and worked together became unstoppable had on the outcome against slavery and tyranny!.

"We closed our lines about Jackson. On the 11th, we pressed close in, and shelled the town from every direction. One of Ords brigades (Lauman's) got too close and was very roughly handled and driven back in disorder. He requested his relief, which I granted. The weather was fearfully hot, but we continued to press the siege day and night, using our artillery most freely; and on the morning of July 17th, the place was found evacuated. General Johnston had carried his army safely off, and pursuit in that hot weather would have been fatal to my command.

"Reporting the fact to General Grant, he ordered me to return, to send General Parkes's corps to Haines's Bluff, General Ord's back to Vicksburg, and he consented that I should encamp my whole corps near the Big Black, and with the prospect of a period of rest for the remainder of the summer.

"Port Hudson had surrendered to General Banks on the 8th of July. The most important enterprise of the Civil War. The recovery of the complete control of the Mississippi River, from its source to its mouth—or, in the language of Mr. Lincoln, the Mississippi went "unvexed to the sea."

July 3-4, 1863

Sherman writes about that time: *The value of the capture of Vicksburg, however, was not measured by the list of prisoners, guns, and small-arms, but by the fact that its possession secured the navigation of the great central river of the continent, bisected fatally the Southern Confederacy; and it so happened that the event coincided as to time with another great victory which crowned our arms far away, at Gettysburg, Pennsylvania. That was a defensive battle, whereas ours was offensive in the highest acceptation of the term, should have ended the war; but the rebel leaders were mad, seemed determined that their people should drink of the very lowest dregs of the cup of war, which they themselves had prepared. The campaign of Vicksburg, in its conception and execution, belonged exclusively to General Grant, not only in the great whole, but in the thousands of its details. No commanding general of an army ever gave more of his personal attention to details, or wrote so many of his own orders, reports, and letters, as General Grant. His success at Vicksburg justly gave him great fame at home and abroad. The President conferred on him the rank of major-general in the regular army, the highest grade then existing by law.*

God and Death: Lincoln's Private Office Late Summer 1863

"Herndon, I need to know: Is man God? Or is God God?" They both laughed or smiled rather.

"Mr. President, it would seem that God should be God, wouldn't it?"

"Huxley and Wilberforce had a debate where it seems Huxley got the better part of Wilberforce's son, it would appear." Herndon observed.

"I don't know," Lincoln dourly replied.

"Neither do I!" Herndon responded, more in empathy than wisdom.

"Christian privateer Elijah Goodspeed tells me that when he was younger living in Barnstable after he escaped bondage that Jewish privateers fought the Barbary pirates from time to time. The Jews hated the Spanish and influenced Cromwell against the Catholics in Ireland."

Lincoln now paused, deep in thought and Herndon, his close friend and business associate, knew better than to interrupt his constructive musings. Therefore, Herndon waited patiently for Abe to resume his thoughts verbally. Finally, Lincoln placed his hand on a letter from the Presbyterian Synod in Lancaster, and continued.

"I have here a document from Milligan and Sloane, Scotland Presbyterian Synod representatives, urging me to preach to the troops here among other things, even to put a resolution in the Constitution that God is God, so to say, 'for a recognition of the existence and the authority (of) God, but also of the mediatorial supremacy of Jesus Christ his son'. And I feel that I should for the sake of how slavery has torn this nation apart." (Christian Life and Character of the Civil Institutions of the United States, Benjamin Morris, p. 763, 1864, George W. Childs, Chestnut St, Philadelphia)

"But you won't!" Herndon said softly looking up.

Lincoln nodded in sad agreement.

Herndon saw that Lincoln looked very lonely, desperate, and sad and hoped that his dear friend was simply vexed at his wife's spending problems. Yet both men, dear friends, were disturbed by thoughts of recently mourning Lincoln's lost son, William Wallace Lincoln. Poor William died of yellow fever like Nathan. Purloined speeches were taken by Mary Todd and leaked to the press who found signs of "partial insanity" in his wife Mary Todd, as well. That didn't set well with either of them as the press despaired Lincoln greatly. Lincoln sighed.

"Once upon a time, during the American Revolution, the Irish and the Scottish Covenanters came united to Washington and met with Greene to discuss the spiritual well-being of the troops. Now all I hear is how bad Cromwell was to the Irish, but yet how much our former patriots beamed upon this monster. That's what is holding me back from doing it! Catholics have every bit a right to worship God as they please as much as the Protestants do, but without Cromwell we could have easily made the case for recognition and for the divine sovereignty of Jesus Christ in our Constitution. And we could have had the public support we needed to get it through, even among the Irish, and majority of Catholic voters!" Lincoln expounded.

"Like Sherman, they may think me insane, although we all know better." Lincoln paused, torn and in pain. A short while later he added.

"I will respond to the Synod as I usually do, with interest as a way of being diplomatically dismissive, but it won't please me or God either, for that matter. That my death may be the result and atonement for this bloody war."

Both men shrugged and then distracted, turned their attention to other matters.

Unlike then, today it wouldn't be about Protestant vs. Catholic but about Christian Nationalism, good or bad. Are Christians loving their heritage and national pride a good thing? Or is there instead going to be a war on Christians and national pride?

CHAPTER THIRTY-ONE

The Request

Early August, 1863

Elijah traveled to East Haddam to make a special request.

"Gentleman, I have a request. Please hear me out," he began. "I know that after the 8th of last month the Mississippi opened back up from its source to its mouth. Now I would like to resume my navigation mapping. Please, is it possible to contact the War Department or Lincoln himself on my behalf to initiate a dialogue as to when it might be safe enough and possible to resume activity? I have a written request regarding that which I would like to submit since I know it's going to take some time to fill that request."

William whistled, then George the elder spoke up.

"Thank you for this letter. Of course, we will tend to it and honor your request. But you might as well know that the way things are going it might not be until sometime next year. It is still quite risky to consider at this critical point in time. We are still at war, although technically we have conquered our enemy, but your ship is still in greater risk of being confiscated, George explained.

"In fact, William and I were just talking about having our two gunships registered as escorts for such a project, and even looked forward to an opening celebration of some sort. However, we shall contact you as soon as possible once we secure the proper safe clearance."

Years later Sherman describes what providence was then marking the path to follow against a hellish war, and a more hellish socialistic system of the Northern Whig rag (New York Tribune) and Southern "friends of slavery press." After the battle of Vicksburg was over, and after the successes in Gettysburg and Vicksburg, in reflection Sherman wrote: "In order to illustrate this peculiar phase of our civil war, I give at this place copies of certain letters which have not heretofore been published."

WASHINGTON
August 29, 1863
Major-General W. T. SHERMAN,
Vicksburg, Mississippi

My Dear General, the question of reconstruction in Louisiana, Mississippi, and Arkansas, will soon come up for decision of the Government, and not only the length of the war, but our ultimate and complete success, will depend upon its decision. It is a difficult matter, but I believe it can be successfully solved, if the President will consult opin-

ions of cool and discreet men, who are capable of looking at it in all its bearings and effects. I think he is disposed to receive the advice of our generals who have been in these States and know much more of their condition than gassy politicians in Congress. General Banks has written pretty fully, on the subject. I wrote to General Grant, immediately after the fall of Vicksburg, for his views in regard to Mississippi, but he has not yet answered. I wish you would consult with Grant, McPherson, and others of cool, good judgment, and write me your views fully, as I may wish to use them with the President. You had better write me unofficially, and then your letter will not be put on file and cannot hereafter be used against you. You have been in Washington enough to know how everything a man writes or says is picked up by his enemies and misconstrued. With kind wishes for your further success, I am yours truly, H. W. HALLECK [Private and Confidential]

The reply expected from Sherman was not delayed and was received less than three weeks later, a full explanation rendered in his own hand.

**HEADQUARTERS, FIFTEENTH ARMY CORPS,
Camp On Big Black, Mississippi,
September 17 1863
H. W. HALLECK, Commander-in-Chief,
Washington, D. C. [Private and Confidential]**

Dear General, I have received your letter of August 29th, and with pleasure confide to you fully my thoughts. That

part of the continent of North America known as Louisiana, Mississippi, and Arkansas, is in my judgment the
key to the whole interior. The valley of the Mississippi is
America, and, although railroads have changed the economy of intercommunication, yet the water-channels still
mark the lines of fertile land, and afford cheap carriage to
the heavy products of it. The inhabitants of the country on
the Monongahela, the Illinois, the Minnesota, the Yellow-
stone, and Osage, are as directly concerned in the security
of the Lower Mississippi as are those who dwell on its very
banks in Louisiana; and now that the nation has recovered
its possession, this generation of men will make a fearful
mistake if they again commit its charge to a people liable
to misuse their position, and assert, as was recently done.
I would deem it very unwise at this time, or for years to
come, to revive the State governments of Louisiana, etc., or
to institute in this quarter any civil government in which
the local people have much to say. They had a government
so mild and paternal that they gradually forgot they had
any at all, save what they themselves controlled; they as-
serted an absolute right to seize public moneys, forts, arms,
and even to shut up the natural avenues of travel and commerce. They chose war—and appealed to force. They begin
to realize that war is a two-edged sword, and it may be
that many of the inhabitants cry for peace. I know them
well, and we must recognize the classes into which they
have divided themselves:

First: The large planters, owning lands, slaves, and all
kinds of personal property. These are, on the whole, the
ruling class. They are educated, wealthy, and easily ap-

proached. *In some districts they are bitter as gall, and have given up slaves, plantations, and all, serving in the armies of the Confederacy, whereas, in others, they are conservative. None dare admit a friendship for us, though they say freely that they were at the outset opposed to war and disunion. I know we can manage this class, but only by action. Argument is exhausted, and words have lost their usual meaning. Nothing but the logic of events touches their understanding; but, of late, this has worked a wonderful change. If our country were like Europe, crowded with people, I would say it would be easier to replace this class than to reconstruct it, subordinate to the policy of the nation; but, as this is not the case, it is better to allow the planters, with individual exceptions, gradually to recover their plantations, to hire any species of labor, and to adapt themselves to the new order of things. We have two more battles to win before we should even bother our minds with the idea of restoring civil order—viz., one near Meridian, in November, and one near Shreveport, in February and March next, when Red River is navigable by our gunboats. When these are done, then, and not until then, will the planters of Louisiana, Arkansas, and Mississippi, submit. Slavery is already gone, and, to cultivate the land, Negro or other labor must be hired. This, of itself, is a vast revolution, and time must be afforded to allow men to adjust their minds and habits to this new order of things. A civil government of the representative type would suit this class far less than a pure military role, readily adapting itself to actual occurrences, and able to enforce its laws and orders promptly and emphatically.*

Second: The smaller farmers, mechanics, merchants, and laborers. This class will probably number three-quarters of the whole; have, in fact, no real interest in the establishment of a Southern Confederacy and have been led or driven into war on the false theory that they were to be benefited somehow—they knew not how. They are essentially tired of the war and would slink back home if they could. These are the real *tiers etat* of the South and are hardly worthy a thought; for they swerve to and fro according to events which they do not comprehend or attempt to shape.

Third: The Union men of the South. I must confess I have little respect for this class. They allowed a clamorous set of demagogues to muzzle and drive them as a pack of curs. Afraid of shadows, they submit tamely to squads of dragoons, and permit them, without a murmur, to burn their cotton, take their horses, corn, and everything; and, when we reach them, they are full of complaints if our men take a few fence-rails for fire, or corn to feed our horses. They give us no assistance or information and are loudest in their complaints at the smallest excesses of our soldiers. Their sons, horses, arms, and everything useful, are in the army against us, and they stay at home, claiming all the exemptions of peaceful citizens. I account them as nothing in this great game of war.

Fourth: The young bloods of the South: sons of planters, lawyers about towns, good billiard-players and sportsmen, men who never did work and never will. War suits them, and the rascals are brave, fine riders, bold to rashness, and dangerous subjects in every sense. They care not *a sou for niggers, land, or anything. They hate Yankees per se, and don't bother their brains about the past, present, or future. As long as they have good horses, plenty of forage, and an open country, they are happy. This is a larger class than most men suppose, and they are the most dangerous set of men that this war has turned loose upon the world. They are splendid riders, first-rate shots, and utterly reckless. Stewart, John Morgan, Forrest, and Jackson, are the types and leaders of this class. These men must all be killed or employed by us before we can hope for peace. Now that I have sketched the people who inhabit the district of country under consideration, I will proceed to discuss the future. A civil government now, for any part of it, would be simply ridiculous. The people would not regard it, and even the military commanders of the antagonistic parties would treat it lightly. Governors would be simply petitioners for military assistance, to protect supposed friendly interests, and military commanders would refuse to disperse and weaken their armies for military reasons. Jealousies would arise between the two conflicting powers, and, instead of contributing to the end of the war, would actually defer it. Therefore, I contend that we demand the continuance of the simple military role, till after all the organized armies of the South are dispersed, conquered, and subjugated.*

The people of all this region are represented in the Army of Virginia, at Charleston, Mobile, and Chattanooga. They have sons and relations in each of the rebel armies, and naturally are interested in their fate. Though we hold military possession of the key-points of their country, still they contend, and naturally, that should Lee succeed in Virgin-

ia, or Bragg at Chattanooga, a change will occur here also. We cannot for this reason attempt to reconstruct parts of the South as we conquer it, till all idea of the establishment of a Southern Confederacy is abandoned. We should treat the idea of civil government as one in which we as a nation have a minor or subordinate interest. The opportunity is good to impress on the population the truth that they are more interested in civil government than we are; and that, to enjoy the protection of laws, they must not be passive observers of events, but must aid and sustain the constituted authorities in enforcing the laws; they must not only submit themselves, but should pay their share of taxes, and render personal services when called on. It seems to me, in contemplating the history of the past two years, that all the people of our country, North, South, East, and West, have been undergoing a salutary political schooling, learning lessons which might have been acquired from the experience of other people; but we had all become so wise in our own conceit that we would only learn by actual experience of our own.

North as well as South had reasoned themselves into the belief that their opinions were superior to the aggregated interest of the whole nation. Half our territorial nation rebelled, on a doctrine of secession that they themselves now scout; and a real numerical majority actually believed that a little State was endowed with such sovereignty that it could defeat the policy of the great whole. I think the present war has exploded that notion, and were this war to cease now, the experience gained, though dear, would be worth the expense.

Another great and important natural truth is still in con-
test, and can only be solved by war. Numerical majorities
by vote have been our great arbiter. Heretofore all men
have cheerfully submitted to it in questions left open, but
numerical majorities are not necessarily physical majori-
ties. The South, though numerically inferior, contend they
can whip the Northern superiority of numbers, and there-
fore by natural law they contend that they are not bound
to submit. War alone can decide it, and it is the only ques-
tion now left for us as a people to decide. Can we whip the
South? If we can, our numerical majority has both the nat-
ural and constitutional right to govern them. Our armies
must prevail over theirs; our officers, marshals, and courts,
must penetrate into the innermost recesses of their land,
before we have the natural right to demand their submis-
sion.

I would banish all minor questions, assert the broad doc-
trine that as a nation the United States has the right, and
also the physical power, to penetrate to every part of our
national domain, and that we will do it—that it makes
no difference whether it be in one year, or two, or ten, or
twenty; that we will remove and destroy every obstacle,
take every life, every acre of land, every particle of proper-
ty, everything that seems proper; that we will not cease till
the end is attained; that all who do not aid us are enemies.
If the people of the South oppose, they do so at their peril;
and if they stand by, mere lookers- they have no right to
immunity, protection, or share in the final results.

I even believe and contend further that, in the North,
every member of the nation is bound by both natural and

constitutional law to "maintain and defend the Government against all its enemies and opposers whomsoever." If they fail to do it they are derelict, and can be punished, or deprived of all advantages arising from the labors of those who do. If any man, North or South, withholds his share of taxes, or his physical assistance in this, the crisis of our history, he should be deprived of all voice in the future elections of this country, and might be reduced to the condition of a mere denizen of the land.

War is upon us, none can deny it. It is not the choice of the Government of the United States, but of a faction; the Government was forced to accept the issue, or to submit to degradation fatal and disgraceful to all. In accepting war, it should be applied to the belligerents, till all traces of the war are effaced; till those who appealed to it are sick and tired of it, and come to the emblem of our nation, and sue for peace. Not coax them, or meet them half-way, but make them so sick of war that generations would pass away before they would again appeal to it.

The insurgents of the South sneer at all overtures looking to their interests. They scorn the alliance with the Copperheads; they tell me to my face that they respect Grant, McPherson, and our brave associates who fight manfully for a principle, but despise the Copperheads and sneaks at the North, who profess friendship for the South and opposition to the war, as mere covers for their knavery.

God knows that I deplore this fratricidal war as much as any man living, and there is only one honorable issue from it. We must fight it out, army against army, and man against man; and I know, and you know, and civilians begin to realize the fact, that reconciliation and reconstruction will be easier through means of strong, well-equipped, and organized armies that can be framed. The issues are made, and all discussion is ridiculous. The section of thirty-pounder Parrott rifles now drilling before my tent is a more convincing argument than the largest Democratic meeting the State of New York can possibly assemble at Albany; and a simple order of the War Department to draft enough men would be more convincing as to our national perpetuity than a humble pardon to Davis and all his misled host. The only government needed or deserved by the States of Louisiana, Arkansas, and Mississippi, now exists in Grant's army. All else will follow in due season. This army has its well-defined code of laws and practice and can adapt itself to the wants and necessities of a city, the country, to all parts of this land. It better sub serves the interest of the General Government, and the people here prefer it to any weak or servile combination that would at once, revive sad perpetuate local prejudices and passions. The people of this country have forfeited all right to a voice in the councils of the nation. They know it and feel it, and in after-years they will be the better citizens from the dear bought experience of the present crisis. Let them learn now, learn it well, that good citizens must obey as well as command. Obedience to law, absolute—is the lesson that this war, under Providence, will teach the free and enlightened American citizen. As a nation, we shall be the better for it.

I never have apprehended foreign interference in our family quarrel. I do not profess to understand Napoleon's design in Mexico, and I do not, see that his taking military

*possession of Mexico concerns us. We have as much terri-
tory now as we want, and I don't see that we are damaged.
We have the finest part of the North American Continent,
all we can people and can take care of; and, if we can sup-
press rebellion in our own land, and compose the strife
generated by it, we shall have enough people, resources,
and wealth, if well combined, to defy interference from any
and every quarter.*

*We must conquer them, or ourselves be conquered. There
is no middle course. They ask, and will have, nothing else,
and talk of compromise is bosh; for we know they would
even scorn the offer. I wish the war could have been de-
ferred for twenty years, till the superabundant population
of the North could flow in and replace the losses sustained
by war; but this could not be, and we are forced to take
things as they are.*

*The cost of the war is, of course, to be considered, but
finances will adjust themselves to the actual state of affairs; and, even if we would, we could not change the
cost. Indeed, the larger the cost now, the less will it be in
the end; for the end must be attained somehow, regardless of loss of life and treasure, and is merely a question
of time. Excuse so long a letter. With great respect, etc.,
W. T. SHERMAN, Major-General.*

Sherman writes, "General Halleck, on receipt of this
letter, telegraphed me that Mr. Lincoln had read it
carefully, and had instructed him to obtain my consent

to have it published. At the time, I preferred not to be drawn into any newspaper controversy, and so wrote to General Halleck; and the above letter has never been, to my knowledge, published; though Mr. Lincoln more than once referred to it with marks of approval."

"What do you think John, should I publish this treatise?" General Sherman had approached his trusted scout.

John C. Goodspeed quietly laughed. "No sir, I think you're right... Don't do it."

The General laughed too, "Hope you don't think I'm bullying you but your thoughts on this are important to me."

"Deeply honored sir. No, you are not bullying me. I one time had a bully who I was physically afraid of, but later we became best friends.

On your treatise", Goodspeed smiled, "I think the Union plays second fiddle to God given choice and liberty to chose."

The great general was amazed at the common mans wisdom and, indeed common sense.

A Partner's Final Farewell

Athens: 1863

"Elijah, I'm dying."

Elijah already had been crying. It was something no longer too obvious to hide. Harriet, their eldest daughter and caretaker of family memories and the history of the Underground movement had forced them to go out and get a daguerreotype which they were now both studying for inclusion in her journal. Olive felt that this was the appropriate time to break it to Elijah since he was cry-

ing, and get it over with, "and get it out in the open."

"I'm dying," she said, softly smiling, then went on, "It is good that when we both finally close our eyes forever that I, for one, have lived long enough to see the providential end of this terrible war and the terrible institution of slavery. Who would have thought?!"

With advanced age and consumption her vitality was gone. They hugged for a moment as if it were eternity. There were now less than two years to go before they would meet again in paradise, yet through tears they each smiled as affectionately as if they were still young and impish.

Elijah smiled and responded affectionately, mocking her, "Yes... Who would have thunk?" He was remembering Olive's usual way of deliberately mispronouncing the word "thought" that drove their children and grandchildren crazy. Now each smiled and wiped away each other's tears, then kissed.

Goodspeed's Landing made two ships but employed only one of them in the war effort, the USS Kanawha in memory of Nathan and William Todd Lincoln, both of whom died of yellow fever, and the Sherman's Willie who died of typhoid fever in '63. The Kanawha was the closest river to the second to the last stopping point of the SS Rebecca-Jane's home port.

But it gets better to know how effective that gunboat fared in this war. There was a good Lt. Commander named William K. Mayo, promoted from lieutenant and executive officer. He was transferred from the USS Housatonic before it was sunk by the submarine H. L. Hunley in Charleston Harbor toward the end of the war.

Mayo, with three other top-notch captains, held the record of sixteen ships sunk or captured during that war rivaling the *USS Unadilla*. The *Unadilla* also had the same number of blockade-running ships sunk or captured, being the first ship commissioned and the one for which the Unadilla Class was named, representing that production series of twenty-three Ninety-Day Gunboats.

The next closest ships were the *USS Sagamore* and the *USS Penobscot* that each had twelve Confederate blockade-running ships sunk or captured. The rest were in the single digits, so the Goodspeed's Landing Team did pretty well, to say the least! (Not to mention the contribution that Goodspeed's Landing made to education at the Nathan Hale Memorial School House and the Antebellum Underground Railroad effort in general.)

The Unadilla Class brought the south to its knees, depleting cotton revenue and starving the money supply in cotton exchange for precious weapons, food, clothing and medical supplies. But the richest find was the January 29, 1863, capture by the *USS Unadilla* of the single screw steamer *Princess Royal*. Found in its hold were not just one but two powerful steam engines intended for ironclads!

They starved the south with Lincoln's blockades, stayed on budget, and as Abe and the War Department projected, shortened the war to four years independent of a series of incompetent Union Democrat War Generals. That was, until Republican U. S. Grant replaced the showy but reticent George B. McClelland and made the difference in stopping by winning the bloody and costly war sooner.

It was also in this year that Juror Robert Cooper Grier in 1863 wrote the majority opinion in the Prize Case, upholding Abraham Lincoln's presidential power to institute Union blockades of Confederate ports and giving the Union strategic advantage in the war. Grier's reputation had been permanently marred by rumors and accusations of accepting bribes and leaking his decisions.

Perhaps, Grier reasoned, this would spare him personally from God's wrath and restore his honorable reputation.

Withal, Goodspeed's Landing was relieved and Elijah and Olive rejoiced his decision, while the Confederate state, Whigs, Marxists, and Democrats wailed a gnashed their teeth at Grier's perceived betrayal.

Olive died February 4, 1864 at age sixty-six, barely missing the end of that terrible war a year later. Elijah lived to see the passage of the Thirteenth Amendment, freeing slaves forever, Lincoln's assassination, and passage of voting rights for blacks, Reconstruction and growth of socialism. Elijah lived another three years after her passing, then died January 12, 1867, just shy of sixty-nine years. When he died, he was respected and lamented by the Athens community.

Sadly, George Edward had died unexpectedly just previous to Olive on Nov. 16, 1863. Once again, another mysterious death.

Early 1864

Olive did not live to see the end of the war, however she died with hope. She had witnessed the Gettysburg address after Lee's repulsed invasion on the North on July 4, 1863. Six and a half months later President Abraham Lincoln gave that address on November 19th of the same year. Both she and Elijah were there taking their last major outing together.

"...that we here highly resolve that these dead shall not have died in vain—that this nation, under God, shall have a new birth of freedom—and that government of the people, by the people, for the people, shall not perish from the earth."

The Battle of Fort Pillow in Tennessee, April 1864 – One year before Lincoln's Assassination

The history from April of 1864 found Lieutenant General Nathan Bedford Forrest on his horse on an observations crest overseeing the battle for Fort Pillow.

As a witness with his scope in hand, he saw a hard fight and the closing of the action going on before him. He was proud of his men who had come against 200 troops of Union soldiers, mostly black. It reminded him that both sides had fought hard. He reflected on the last lines of Lincoln's speech, those in which Olive found such hope, and respected the courageous efforts of the blacks on the opposing force, though they were now getting beaten badly.

Then unexpectedly, he spotted something that alarmed him as he witnessed one Black man being forced by his men to hold a horse and get down on his knees in surrender. They shot him! Nathan blinked. Then he quickly scanned the area and witnessed other Blacks and Whites both surrendering and being killed!

Tempted to spur his horse, he realized that by the time he got down there in a vain attempt to stop the carnage, it would be over anyway. So disgusted he was that for once in his life he felt sick.

He angrily demanded that his troops show discipline in the future even to black troops. The Joint Committee on the Conduct of War, he warned, would catch up with them and find them all guilty of killing surrendering troops. Nor would the public accept that they had all fought up until the end, he also accurately predicted that the excuse that blacks wouldn't scow either "for being an inferior force." He knew that there would be backlash in the near future from other black troops in retribution to the Fort Pillow Massacre.

His reputation stained by the events at Fort Pillow, Forrest went on to achieve a stunning victory in June 1864, at the Battle of Brice's Crossroads. His men were ashamed, even the ones who were surprised that their fellow men had performed such atrocities. The unit as a whole was smart enough to know it was immoral and wrong and totally against military protocol.

They were all ashamed of letting their leader down and passionately promised never to let it happen again and maintained strict Christian discipline from that time forward!

He also gave a personal reprimand to the surviving Matlock brother who served under him, not excusing his feeble protest even though he was innocent. He reminded him of the time that he had spared his life and his brothers when his Uncle James Forest was killed by their clan. No excuses were acceptable in any given situation.

Of the above incident Sherman writes:

About this time, the early part of April, I was much disturbed by a bold raid made by the rebel General Forrest up between the Mississippi and Tennessee Rivers. He reached the Ohio River at Paducah but was handsomely repulsed by Colonel Hicks. He then swung down toward Memphis, and carried Fort Pillow, massacring a part of its garrison, composed wholly of Negro troops. At first, I discredited the story because, in preparing for the Meridian campaign, I had ordered Fort Pillow to be evacuated, but General Hurlbut had retained a small garrison at Fort Pillow to encourage the enlistment of the blacks as soldiers, which was a favorite political policy at that time. The massacre at Fort Pillow occurred April 12, 1864, and has been the subject of congressional inquiry. No doubt Forrest's men acted like a set of barbarians, shooting down the helpless Negro garrison after the fort was in their possession; but I am told that Forrest personally disclaims any active participation in the assault, and that he stopped the firing as soon as he could. I also take it for granted that Forrest did not lead the assault in person, and consequently that he was to the rear, out of sight if not of hearing at the time, and I was told by hundreds of our men, who were at various times prisoners in Forrest's possession, that he was usually very kind to them. No doubt the feeling of the Southern people was fearfully savage on this very point of our making soldiers out of their late slaves, and Forrest may have shared the feeling.

May 12, 1864 – Tragedy Strikes Heman and Lousia Albright Goodspeed of the Eastern Underground Station

The war touched the family of Heman and Louisa Goodspeed. One of their sons Theron, served in the Union Army and enlisted Aug. 14, 1862, for three years as a private in the Nineteenth Battery, Light Artillery, N.Y.V., at Lockport, N.Y. He was mustered in at Elmira Oct. 27, 1862, and promoted corporal on Dec. 6, 1863. He was killed by a gunshot at the battle of the Wilderness, near Spotsylvania, C.H., on May 12, 1864, and was buried on the field. After the war his body was removed to Lockport and buried in the family lot near the old homestead. Fortunately, from the description in the *Goodspeed Genealogy,* he was not wounded then burned to death by wild brush fires caused by dry conditions, wind and started by burnt discarded spent wads, as many other unfortunate souls were. Heman, the father and my Great-Great Grandfather, died March 31, 1869, and was survived by Louisa, his wife, also related, who died on August 30, 1883. She inspired Weston to start his research along with the historian Harriet, surviving daughter of Elijah and Olive Goodspeed. They kept the images and bitter indentured servant/slave memories, along with happier recollections of underground family triumphs of those very unique and sacrificing family members and friends of humanity for all times and all seasons.

During this time, and still today, there came the issue of lost family legacies in our tale of the underground blanket and Theron's Army or Navy Colt revolver. They were passed on through the generations from Heman and Louisa, through their son Herschel to his son John, this author's grandfather, and to John, this author's father, then to the author, D. N. Goodspeed. The blanket this author inherited, kept, and preserved for history. Theron's revolver the only other sibling and older brother "Jack" sold before he was informed, or otherwise he would have also purchased to preserve. The revolver would have been good proof that Corporal Theron had most likely not burned in the fire since the author can attest that the revolver was in great condition. The wooden handles were not scorched and it remained in good shooting condition, as once personally witnessed in the late 1950s. It was assumed to be functional at the time of sale either in the late 1990s or sometime before brother Jack died in September 2012.

The author's brother preferred to be called John after their father John died but this author prefers to call him Jack, affectionately but also to tick him off both here on earth and in paradise, where this author may have the opportunity in eternity to harass him once again and complain about the missing revolver! If it was a Navy revolver, beloved brother, it may have also been a gift from either Gideon Wells or Sherman to the Eastern Station. The author is leaning toward recalling a conversation with his brother that a shorter barrel on that revolver would have curiously meant it was a Navy not an Army revolver. That puzzled both of us at the time of our youth.

Author's Note: Heman and Louisa were my great-great-grandfather and grandmother and cousins of Elijah and Olive Goodspeed's Western partners in the Underground Railroad effort and underground Railroad Station keepers. They also worked closely with Mashpee, the family's Indian ally and friend to the end, who kindly helped after the war to transport the remains of Corporal Theron from the Wilderness battlegrounds to their homestead in Niagara County.

Atlanta Campaign

June 1864

The men were in a tent carrying the strong smell of paraffin previously dissolved in gasoline long before the same substance was discovered to be useful when engines were developed for horseless carriages. The idea was to mix waterproof tent fabric with a mix of paraffin dissolved in this substance, then poured over the raw tent fabric, and then the sun allowed to bake off the gas. It made a very waterproof surface to stay under in bad rains like they were now experiencing as Sherman's troops were now moving into the mountains overlooking the Kennesaw Mountains of Atlanta.

Sherman was giving a lecture the night they were advancing on the hills overlooking the valley of Atlanta. One handsome but awkward gentleman, Calvin Goodspeed's son, John C. Goodspeed, described from previous chapter dialogue, had entered the tent to find a seat to listen to their instructor Sherman.

"On the first of June our three armies were well in hand," Sherman started when the bang of a wooden folding chair caught everyone's attention. The awkward man, John C. for Calvin, sheepishly grinned good naturedly at Sherman trying to behave himself but his body wouldn't let him.

Sherman couldn't help but smile back at the man. Though awkward he had a way about him that made him stand out from the others as intelligent, fearless, and a leader in spite of his involuntary antics. The man also had a clipboard with documents which he almost dropped as he stumbled but finally made it to an empty seat, smiling all the while at the General who smiled back.

"Our armies were well in hand in the broken and densely wooded country fronting the enemy entrenched at New Hope Church, " Sherman began again when the man's repeater timer went off. He offered another embarrassed smile. "About five miles north of Dallas."

"General Stoneman's division of cavalry now occupied Allatoona, on the railroad, and Colonel W. W. Wright, of the Engineers, was busily employed in repairing the railroad and rebuilding the bridge across the Etowah or High Tower River which had been destroyed by the enemy on his retreat.

"There were constant skirmishes along a front of about six miles," Sherman finally continued with no more distractions coming from the apologetic soldier.

"By gradually covering our front with protective bulwark, and extending to the left, we approached the railroad toward Acworth and overlapped the enemy's right. By the 4th of June we had made such progress that Johnston evacuated his lines in the night."

Outside the tent a torrential downpour almost drowned out Sherman's voice, but he spoke on.

"Heavy rains set in about the 1st of June, but our marches were short, as we needed time for the repair of the railroad. On the 6th I rode back to Allatoona, found it all that was expected, and gave orders for its fortification and preparation as a 'secondary base.'"

By the 10th of June, Sherman's troops and the whole combined army, moved forward another six miles to Big Shanty, a station on the railroad, where they had a good view of the enemy's position. It embraced three prominent hills known as Kennesaw, Pine Mountain, and Lost Mountain. It was on these hills the enemy had signal-stations and fresh lines of parapets. Heavy masses of infantry could be distinctly seen with the naked eye. "Johnston had chosen his ground well and it gave him a perfect view over our field. We had to proceed with due caution," Sherman added.

On the 11th, the Etowah Bridge was done; the railroad was repaired up to our skirmish line, close to the base of Kennesaw.

Then next day and the next, the rains continued to pour, and the troops and awkward John C. Goodspeed made their way along the many footrails. The soggy forests made the going tough, for there were no roads in the dense forests unlike the broader fields. These had to be improvised by each division for its own supply train from the depot in Big Shanty to the camps.

"The enemy's cavalry was also busy in their rear, compelling us to detach cavalry all the way back as far as Resaca, and to strengthen all the infantry posts as far as Nashville. In my mind there was great danger that Forrest would collect a heavy cavalry command in Mississippi, cross the Tennessee River, and break up their troop's railroad below Nashville.

John Goodspeed had now gotten to know Sherman quite well. It was his father Calvin who Sherman remembered had saved Grant's career, although that stubborn Grant would never admit. Halleck would ever humbly remind him and again and again apologize to Grant, not so much in words or apology, but by way of friendly teasing the man.

Meanwhile, Sherman had sent General Sturgis to Memphis to take command of all the cavalry in that quarter. He was to go out toward Pontotoc, engage Forrest and defeat him, but on the 14th of June Sherman and the troops learned that General Sturgis had himself been defeated and had been driven by Forrest back into Memphis in considerable confusion.

"I ordered General Smith to go out from Memphis and renew the offensive, to keep Forrest off our roads. He finally did, defeating Forrest at Tupelo, on the 13th, 14th, and 15th days of July. That so stirred up matters in North Mississippi that Forrest could not leave for Tennessee. This left me only the task of covering the roads against such minor detachments of cavalry as Johnston could spare from his immediate army. I proposed to keep them too busy in their own defense to spare detachments. When I reconnoitered, to make a break in their line between Kennesaw and Pine Mountain, I noticed a rebel battery on it. At the time our skirmishers were engaged in the woods near the base of this hill between the lines. The distance to the battery on the crest was about eight hundred yards. General Howard, commanding the Fourth Corps, was nearby, and I called his attention to this group. I explained to him that we must keep up the morale of a bold offensive and force the enemy to remain on the defensive. I ordered him to direct a battery close by to fire three volleys. The next division in order was Geary's, and I gave him similar orders. General Polk, in my opinion, was killed by the second volley fired from the first battery referred to."

John C. Goodspeed then showed Sherman how he was able to break the codes as signal-officer should anything happen to him in the frequent skirmishes that attended them. Needless to say, Sherman was very impressed. "Like a chip off the old block," Sherman liked to say about John's dad Calvin. Sherman made a note to keep this man around like a good luck charm even after eventually taking Atlanta.

The signal-officer reported that by studying the enemy's signals he had learned the key, and that he could read their signals. He explained to Sherman that he had translated a signal about noon, from Pine Mountain to Marietta, "Send an ambulance for General Polk's body," and later in the day another, "Why don't you send an ambulance for General Polk?" From this they inferred that General Polk had been killed which was confirmed later in the day by some prisoners who had been captured.

On the 15th they advanced our general lines, where Pine Mountain was found to be abandoned, by Johnston. On the 16th Lost Mountain was abandoned. The right flank swung round to threaten the railroad below Marietta, but Johnston had further contracted and strengthened his lines, covering Marietta and all the roads below.

By the 19th of June the rebel army again fell back on its flanks as Sherman's troops pressed forward and found it still more concentrated, covering Marietta and the railroad. On the 20th Johnston's position was unusually strong; Kennesaw Mountain was salient and his two flanks were refused and covered by parapets and by Noonday and Nose's Creeks.

"We were also so far from Nashville and Chattanooga that we were naturally sensitive for the safety of our railroad and depots, so that the left (McPherson) was held very strong." Sherman later wrote.

"About this time reports came that a large cavalry force of the enemy had passed around our left flank, evidently to strike this very railroad somewhere below Chattanooga. I therefore reinforced the cavalry stationed from Resaca to Casaville."

While Sherman was engaged about Kennesaw, General Grant had his hands full with Lee, in Virginia. General Halleck was the chief-of-staff at Washington, and Sherman communicated with him almost daily. On the 21st of June Sherman gave this report.

"This is the nineteenth day of rain, and the prospect of fair weather is as far off as ever. The roads are impassable; the fields and woods become quagmires after a few wagons have crossed over. We are at work all the time. The left flank is across Noonday Creek and the right across Nose's Creek. In action and on the march, rain is favorable; but in the woods, where all is blind, it seems almost impossible for an army covering ten miles of front to act in concert during wet and stormy weather." Sherman had Goodspeed report.

On the 22d of June Sherman rode the whole line and ordered General Thomas in person to advance his extreme right corps (Hooker's). He instructed General Schofield, by letter, to keep his entire army, the Twenty-third Corps, as a strong right flank in close support of Hooker's deployed line.

"During this day the sun came out, with some promise of clear weather, and I had got back to my bivouac about dark, when a signal message was received, dated," John C. Goodspeed reported.

The March to the Sea and Beyond: November 15 to December 21 1864

John C. was there with them the night the strange fireworks started. They were able to walk down the hill, into empty streets and bars emptied of rebel soldier and take the city without any more conflict.

John C. was with them when soldiers rejoiced and wept when they went into Atlanta.

John C. was there when Sherman chased Hood and Forest until he realized that a defensive strategy wasn't working.

John C. was there when Sherman chased Hood in the forests of Atlanta, as futile as chasing ghosts. Then they came up with the best plan: Let them try to outguess us rather than us trying vainly to outguess them!

John C. was there to agree with him that the March to the Sea would be that key to make mad men that were too stupid to know that they had already lost the war and chase Sherman and his troops as the only way to distract mad men from destroying the infrastructure and supply lines that Sherman had created in surrounding Atlanta.

John C. was there when Sherman evicted the civilian population from Atlanta as a military necessity.

But most importantly, John C. was there to see Sherman work hard and prep hard to convince Grant, Halleck, and Lincoln that the March was the only way to win the contest and the War.

They left Atlanta secured against enemy invasion as Sherman had assigned and put key people in place to assure military stability.

Taking only the most able-bodied soldiers with him, they followed the trails diagonally toward Savannah and ran incognito until they came out at the sea. They foraged only what food and supplies they needed and spared the rest for the communities they marched through.

To spare communities and only destroy the war machine infrastructure, only if the civilian population got belligerent then would the troops become belligerent and torch their churches and storage facilities. Otherwise, they left them untouched. All the while Sherman used his troops to destroy the railroad links vital to the rebel war machine that caused some civilian distress but being largely a farming society, it didn't really matter as long as some friendly grain depots remained intact.

Staying in the beautiful garden-blocked and flowered plazas and Spanish moss decorated live oaks of Savannah, Sherman realized that with his strategy the war was already over. The civilian population of Savannah realized they held a crumbling war cause and were starting like Sherman and the others, and that was it madness to continue so bloody a conflict. Sherman and Goodspeed even staid ironically at the Mercer home and buildings where Gold Nathan's protégé Eli Whitney had stayed when he built that awful cotton gin that led to the whole Civil War tragedy.

Likewise, Sherman would not destroy the major cities like Colombia or even Charleston where that bloody war had started nor would he destroy anything other than the war machinery infrastructure.

The only time Sherman could be accused of anything was in Colombia where burning cotton bales which the fleeing Confederacy had ignited themselves. His soldiers and fire teams in conjunction with the municipal fire departments had been able to put out the fires during the calm daylight the hours. However, one horrible windy night reflashed those very same bales and started an inferno that took eighty percent of the buildings down because most in Colombia were dry ancient wood frame buildings. Sherman had friends and relations from more peaceful antebellum times and prevented their homes from being ransacked by their foraging operations, however sometimes that wasn't always the case.

A hard but gentle man, Sherman was the only one that could make such a reality possible. And John Calvin Goodspeed was there to witness the transformation of society and share it with the rest of the Goodspeed Underground Railroad families and friends.

Where war is hell and pure war is pure hell! He taught the South to suffer to the point of the populous to yearn to reject and go against their own leaders madness.

One Final Adventure

TELEGRAPH MESSAGE:
Elijah Goodspeed, Athens, Ohio

- Released this date December 21, 1864, the under-signed request submitted to us from August 02, 1863, Vis–Goodspeeds Landing East Haddam Ct. has been granted.
- Authorized Pilot Capt. E. Goodspeed
- Authorized use of two (2) 90 -day gunboats "USSS Kanawha" and "USSS Noname" As escorts Good-speeds Landing Pilots as designated by US Union Army Authority
- Authorized use of one (1) SS "Rebecca Jane" com-mercial / transport Capt. E. Goodspeed
- For purposes of navigational research and future celebratory activities has been granted on the OHIO and MISSISSIPPI RIVER, and ESTUARY AREAS
- 1ST Celebration of this date of MAJOR GENERAL SHERMAN NOVEMBER 15 TO DECEMBER 21 MARCH

TO THE SEA
- Fireworks permit granted
- Use of 24-pdr 1,300 pounds Dahlgren Cannons prohibited on inner waters
- Coastal waters of the Gulf of Mexico granted but make note fire away from the coastal areas seaward unless in national defense should a belligerent use of force from the enemy present itself. Use of rockets skyward launch for celebratory purposes only has also been granted specifically in said waters and underwritten by New Orleans local port authorities.

−WILLIAM STANTON SECRETARY OF WAR
DECEMBER 21, 1864

Elijah smiled. He laughed at the reference to rockets. He knew that he had been reprimanded by the coastal authorities of New Jersey from a previous transport of *SS Rebecca Jane* from East Haddam, Connecticut, to a destination at Pomeroy on the Ohio River. For unauthorized use of fire rockets.

"Sounds like you may be getting money for the research, but definitely both Goodspeed's Landing and the War Department want you to proceed on the celebration," Mashpee laughed. Elijah chuckled.

"Yeah, man, they even gave the celebration a name!"

"Yes... General Sherman's March to the Sea," Mash concurred. "I'm onboard with that one!"

"Apparently William of Goodspeed's Landing is too,"

Elijah responded. "It's sad that George isn't around to see this day!"

"I'm sad your wife's not here either, Elijah. She would have been so proud of you and honored!"

Elijah put his coffee down and looked hard at Chatham, but Mash could hear in his voice and see in his eyes, that he was a broken man missing his sweetheart girl and the woman of his life and dreams.

"Her memory is so honored. Trust me, Mash."

"Wow!" Mash replied, breaking down in front of Elijah.

Wednesday April, 12 1865 – Mississippi River, Memphis region

The war was over when Lee surrendered to Grant on a Sunday and the ship's celebration originally billed as "Sherman's March" was changed at the last minute to "Lee's Surrender." The event had attracted a large crowd of patriots and smaller crowd of protesters, but the protestors were subdued because of police presence and that fact that by this time, at the end of the war, most people in that region had seen enough of war and were convicted that continued hostilities were madness and everyone just wanted to get on and move on.

So, in general it was simply a nice celebration as planned by Goodspeed's Landing in conjunction with the War Department of Washington City. Circus tents were erected by P. T. Barnum who was also personally on hand. Boarding the two gunboats were mayors, council members, and delegates from New York, Connecticut, Ohio, Kentucky, and Tennessee, mostly in honor of the war's conclusion. A similar number of supporters from Goodspeed's Landing were serving as volunteers for the various other functions and entertainment host, food, and beverage responsibilities.

Stanton and Lincoln were briefly present and for once spoke agreeably with each other for a change, although both left to return to Washington long before the evening celebrations started, along with Grant, Sherman, and other well-wishers.

Elijah and his Indian sidekick, Mashpee Chatham were the center of attention when they boarded the *City of Rebecca Jane* along with Mashpee's wife Rebecca, dressed in the same beautiful Indian marriage dress she wore to her mother's funeral. Calvin and his son John C. Goodspeed also went aboard accompanied by the deceased Capt. Nathan's son Hiram, now age twenty-seven and long since estranged from his weak, over protective mother.

"Times sure have grown you two," Elijah laughed, but Hiram now was a disabled Civil War veteran as described earlier in this story. He used a crutch because of a leg amputation slightly above the knee that he suffered during the war when he was shot through his ankle during a charge. Allen, the younger son of Solomon and tag-along on the voyage, came with the diseased older brother Nathan, who was forty-five and bore a less serious war-related injury. That took Elijah by surprise, this added color to this celebration and small family reunion. The younger brother to Nathan was the one who found himself up to his neck in water in the Atlantic when he helped Mash catch the lobsters in that Florida reef.

"Boy, I'll never forget that adventure," he said. Elijah and Allen had a good laugh about that since Hiram didn't really know what fun they did have was only three at the time of his father's death. That trip had been the high point of the experience, their going down the Mississippi where Hiram, the son of Allen's older brother who died from yellow fever, had heard the tales. He could exchange war stories about how each of them had become disabled in battle, separated from then till this point in time.

The kickoff cruise started at Memphis and was headed all the way to the Gulf of Mexico, then returned to Memphis by that Friday in time for the Easter celebrations.

The high point of this particular event was that Allen realized how much more the ship creaked from wear, and how abandoned slave markets had dried up during the war, and how Elijah suddenly looked old to him.

But Elijah was still Elijah with a longing for following the sea. When they got to the Gulf of Mexico the warship *USSS Noname* was in front of them and the *USSS Kanawha* in tow behind them as they came out into the Gulf of Mexico's spangled waters. The salty breezes enamored them with delight, and for the first time found Hiram, himself an old farm boy, crowing with delight.

"Now watch!" Elijah announced with delight and blew the ship's horn twice then pointed. "Look!"

They watched two large gun boats, the *Kanawha* tacked to port while the *Noname* in front of them slowed down and tacked to starboard. The veteran without a leg and the other vet saw them falling behind as Elijah slammed the *Rebecca Jane* to "Full Speed Ahead" on the ship's telegraph. The men watched in awe as the gunboats fell further and further behind them, then each came to a full stop. Hiram and Allen turned and looked at Elijah who was holding a straight course ahead. He smiled then, winked and nodded at them. Further on he took the telegraph to "Slow," then started laughing as he looked back, now a mile out from the two stationary ships and two miles out from shore. The gunboats didn't move from that distance but looked closer and closer together as the *Rebecca Jane* played out.

Mischievously, like a schoolboy, the old man blew the steam horn with a prolonged blast, then full stop. Silence. The sea lapping quietly against the hull mesmerized the two observers and the rest of the audience aboard.

Then they heard a short blast of the gunboat on their right as the *Kanawha* sounded a signal to alert the other gunboat. The *Noname* on their left then gave two short blasts to acknowledge and take action on both parties' part.

KAAABOOOOOM! Simultaneously from both gunboats there was much smoke, flashes and two 24-pound cannon balls hurled right directly at them! Or at least so it seemed. Theses projectiles flashed past them like thunder on either side with hushed howls.

Then quickly the audience turned and looked ahead of the *Rebecca Jane*. They all cheered and clapped when two distinct plumes of salty sea water shot forty feet of foam up into the clear blue sky, then the twin projectiles touched down and skipped, hit, and sank just a couple of hundred yards ahead of them.

"Wow!" Rebecca exclaimed while Mashpee Chatham gave a full bodied authentic Indian war whoop and fired a Spring Rocket off the stern where the audience didn't even have to turn to see it. With ooohs and aaahs they saw it go straight up to 1,500 yards above their craning necks then...KAABOOM! and a flash!

Cheers and claps greeted that spectacle in fire power's exhibition, demonstrating its awesome destructive strength, energy and might! Then the steam pistons came back to life as Elijah skillfully drove the *Rebecca Jane* to hard port till they were heading shoreward. The paddle wheels churned up water in the leeward wind and caught some of the audience members on one side by surprise! The *Rebecca Jane's* and the *Noname's* horns were trumpeting away till the whole shoreline was awash with their mighty thunder of pure patriotism and energy.

For the first time since Olive's death, Elijah grinned, totally enjoying himself at his unsuspecting but good-natured audience's expense.

Now crew member Noname, for which one of the gunboats was named, skillfully and without fear went quickly up the ship's ladder, up a pole with other lines anchoring it, to the deck where he grabbed a line and jerked it to unfurl a long banner that brought tears to the strongest of men's eyes.

Whipping out into the wind blew a long white banner with stark red borders and blue lettering that spelled out a message that could unite rather than divide North with South!

UNION FIRST

They had traveled so many miles with positive thoughts to share with the community upon their return. It was late Friday night of the Easter week when they pulled back into Memphis to be told the terrible news.

Lincoln had been shot at Ford's Theater in Washington City, and the outcome looked desperate. They woke up to more terrible news. President Lincoln, whom they all knew personally, was dead from a bullet ball to the head from an assassin's derringer. The telegraph room in Memphis was packed and the subdued crowd flowed out into the muddy streets and nearby stores, anxious for more reports and updates. A few scoffed but most listened.

The Easter weekend celebration mood had been stolen. It seemed that just the other day Mr. Lincoln had been standing right next to them.

Marshall Goodspeed had been in Memphis that night waiting for the ships to come in. Marshall recognized

Elijah, Calvin, and John C. as they disembarked from the ship full of excitement. Elijah noticed Marshall whom he knew had a keen interest in politics but noted the crowd was very quiet.

It was then, and in the morning, when they heard of the tragedy from Marshall, then later news that the killer had been identified as John Wilkes Booth, an international favorite actor and darling of great plays.

"I don't understand," Elijah lamented. "We had such a good reception in the south, with cheers and plaudits. It was like Charles Dickens' second visit to America. We saw it as if the south had rapidly come to heal, but now this. What evil is still at work! Someone must have corrupted this actor that he should have done so terrible an act."

Mash stood by now and anxiously noted the change in Elijah, from once cheerful and uplifted, to the reception, to that uniting message of the banner. By whose evil will had it been stolen when its message had been one of love and unity?

"I hear church bells," Marshall observed, acknowledging their loss and recognizing the spiritual mood the tolling bells ushered in.

"Let us repair to attend service." he suggested after a pause and reflection.

"What else?" Elijah ventured. "It is Easter service after all. What harm would it do us?"

So into one church they entered where the brightest of lights shown as if some miracle was about to occur. Perhaps some message that would purposefully dispel that tragic moment in history and help the lost to find comfort and assurance from worldly cares.

"But no," intoned the minister, candid and to the point. "Satan is there just when victory from evil is most apparent. That ship's banner had a beautiful message!"

Elijah's heart jumped for he knew the minister and the public had noticed Goodspeed's Landing after all! The minister shook his head solemnly and continued.

"The following message from Christ so long ago is just as relevant now as it was then. Please turn to Matthew Chapter 25 and let us all read." The minister was measured and steadfast in his message about the Sheep and the Goats.

"When the Son of Man comes in his glory, and all the angels with him, he will sit on his glorious throne. All the nations will be gathered before him, and he will separate the people one from another as a shepherd separates the sheep from the goats. He will put the sheep on his right and the goats on his left.

"Then the King will say to those on his right, 'Come, you who are blessed by my Father; take your inheritance, the kingdom prepared for you since the creation of the world. For I was hungry, and you gave me something to eat, I was thirsty and you gave me something to drink, I was a stranger and you invited me in, I needed clothes and you clothed me, I was sick and you looked after me, I was in prison and you came to visit me.'

"Then the righteous will answer him, 'Lord, when did we see you hungry and feed you, or thirsty and give you something to drink? When did we see you a stranger and invite you in, or needing clothes and clothe you? When did we see you sick or in prison and go to visit you?'

"The King will reply, 'Truly I tell you, whatever you did for one of the least of these brothers and sisters of mine, you did for me.'

"Then he will say to those on his left, 'Depart from me, you who are cursed, into the eternal fire prepared for the devil and his angels. For I was hungry and you gave me nothing to eat, I was thirsty and you gave me nothing to drink, I was a stranger and you did not invite me in, I needed clothes and you did not clothe me, I was sick and in prison and you did not look after me.'

"They also will answer, 'Lord, when did we see you hungry or thirsty or a stranger or needing clothes or sick or in prison, and did not help you?'

The minister looked up at the entire crowded congregation for a moment.

"Final warning to the deep state of Slavery and so called 'friends of slavery and tyranny!'" Then he raised his voice up into a lion's roar.

"Line 45!" The good minister boomed. "He will reply, *'Truly I tell you, whatever you did not do for one of the least of these, you did not do for me.' Then they will go away to eternal punishment, but the righteous to eternal life.*"

The entire time Elijah was reminded of the age-old battle between liberty and tyranny as the black robe minister meant it; the banner with a uniting cry that evil vainly sought to silence! The minister pressed on.

"And readers think of a Lincoln that came into the

world to do good with a similar message for the nation 'of the people for the people and by the people... shall not perish from the earth!' Whose term in office was so uselessly and tragically cut short! Who could have gone on to heal the nation but his term was cut short[22] by an assassin's bullet once again threw the nation back into chaos and confusion! How indeed the devil hates that message of a bright shining light on the hill of a nation devoted to individual life, liberty, just laws and love!" the minister rightfully concluded.

"He will reply, *'Truly I tell you, whatever you did not do for one of the least of these, you did not do for me.'* Then they will go away to eternal punishment, but the righteous to eternal life," he spoke as he ended his message.

---

22 Author's note: Think of another leader that also came into the world over one hundred fifty-five years later, to also do good; another President whose term was also cut short who could have saved not just a nation but the earth itself from death and darkness... this time by a stolen election and a man-made plague 'from another enemy from within'... to Mathew 24, line 45...America?

Crabs in a Bucket

Sunday January 6, 1867 - Elijah's Old Station House

"Crabs in a bucket" refers to an old New England crabbing trick that if you put a crab in a bucket filled with water that it will quickly escape to freedom. But if you put several crabs in there is no need for a lid to contain them because in the escape attempt one crab almost out will get pulled back by the others also trying to escape.

And that's how Communism works, or more to the point has never worked and never will. Another way to say it is that if the system pays everyone equally for their work, at the end of the year there is always going to be one person richer than the rest!

The Communist Manifesto, is merely putting lipstick on a pig. Never has such a document led to so much filth, squalor, misery, and death as this bad economic philosophy, which leads us to this final chapter regarding how Woodrow Wilson slammed the American dream on its head. Never has this failed concept ever worked, but time and time again failed; that morons like him were given so much impetus from hell, as no better operational definition for stupidity or insanity, greed, corruption, and power with no regard for the individual, and no love for humanity or creation, has ever been found.

Thus spoke the good Minister from Memphis back in '65 to Elijah and his team:

Why do the heathen rage and the people imagine a vain thing?

The kings of the earth set themselves, and the rulers take counsel together,

against the Lord, and against his anointed, saying,

Let us break their bands asunder and cast away their cords from us.

He that sitteth in the heavens shall laugh: the Lord shall have them in derision.

Then shall he speak unto them in his wrath and vex them in his sore displeasure.

Yet have I set my king upon my holy hill of Zion.

I will declare the decree: the Lord hath said unto me, Thou art my Son; this day have I begotten thee.

Ask of me, and I shall give thee the heathen for thine inheritance, and the uttermost parts of the earth for thy possession.

Thou shalt break them with a rod of iron; thou shalt dash them in pieces like a potter's vessel.

Be wise now therefore, O ye kings: be instructed, ye judges of the earth.

Serve the Lord with fear, and rejoice with trembling.

Kiss the Son, lest he be angry, and ye perish from the way, when his wrath is kindled but a little. Blessed are all they that put their trust in him.

Very Early in January 1867, before Elijah's death January 12th

"Elijah, you have a special visitor!" The voice was Mashpce's and in less than a week, Elijah would succumb to the ravages of diabetes.

Propped up on his porch rocker, wrapped in a blanket, woken from a sound sleep, his mind was still active and curious.

"Who?" he asked.

"Nathan Bedford Forest," the visitor answered.

In spite of his deteriorating condition, Elijah laughed in genuine surprise. He smiled and spoke.

"A meeting of three great warriors."

They all laughed.

Elijah, forced himself to focus on that rare warm January day, and noted that Forrest had a "striking and commanding presence".

Nathan drew himself to full attention and saluted Elijah with all seriousness and compassion without pity, but reverence spoke.

"We who are about to die salute you! This is the only country in the history of the world that puts God and the individual first and guarantees those rights in the Bill of Rights, regardless of race, creed or color!"

"Jesus Christ!" Elijah humbly replied, not meaning to use the Lord's Name in vain, but rather to acknowledge His impact on the founders.

They all laughed knowing and understanding his intent.

"That's right!" Mashpee said enthusiastically smiling, then added, "American Exceptionalism as defined so eloquently by Forest just now!"

Elijah could feel God's presence and the peace of the Holy Spirit in this honorable company of humble men where, after the laughter, all three men had tears but maintained their brave composure.

After a brief time, Elijah asked Nathan what brought him all the way up to his door in Athens, Ohio, from Memphis, Tennessee.

"Elijah, I've got the same affliction that you have," Nathan gently informed. "It will one day, no doubt, also catch up with me."

It did, some ten years after Elijah's passing that year in 1867. Forest died in 1877 at the age of 56 in comparison to Elijah's life span of almost reaching 69.

"I was once cured by inoculation of whooping cough after my liberation," Elijah reflected, "but as you and I both know, Nathan, there is no cure for this one. However, my bags are packed and I'm ready to go and meet up with my sweetheart in paradise."

"I brought you a present, Elijah," Nathan announced and nodded.

"What's that? Elijah asked.

"I'm quitting the KKK and giving up my position as Alderman in the Memphis council. It is time for America to move on!" he said to Elijah's surprise.

"Sherman once said that I was a dangerous man; that my kind should be killed and were a danger to the world. Later he added rather than killing them, people should be employed."

Nathan looked off in the distance briefly, then smiled pleasantly and looked back at Elijah. He shrugged.

"I guess I decided that I had best change my attitude, stay alive and, as W. Tecumseh himself most wisely instructed, become 'employed'!"

All laughed except Elijah.

Nathan noting Elijah's quizzical look explained the "gift" in a short summary of his own life and how it related to Elijah's life:

"Elijah, I've been following you all my life, even before I knew it was you that I was following! Follow the money they say, in this case gold. I grew very wealthy in the slave trade, more so than in the stagecoach line and other businesses. I was a self-made man, but always of honorable spirit, in spite of my many sins. Funny, too, one time that I was following you I once observed a red-headed man waving to you in New Orleans. He was watching your ship either coming or leaving I recall, or rather recognized as the same man William T. who taught this old dog new tricks." Again he laughed and pointed to himself.

"Your team, Elijah offered solid gold wherever I sold

my slaves. Then I didn't know you were the captain of that boat, but I eventually figured out that wherever your ship landed gold, not printed worthless dollars, was the medium of exchange! That alone contributed most to my great wealth of over one-and-a-half million dollars and extensive land ownerships totaling over nine-thousand acres of good land," he continued.

"Then something unexpected happened in that antebellum era. In following your travels up and down the Mississippi, I kept looking for where you would deliver the gold next. I also learned at that time who you were, as well as your family's history and about Goodspeed's Landing where illegal covert rescuing operations were performed. I could have turned you all in at any point as I followed you from New Orleans to Memphis," the man revealed.

"Why? I loved the gold, and second, I especially hated how brutally the bondsmen was treated in contrast between New Orleans and Memphis, my original home state of origin, Tennessee". Nathan paused and laughed.

"Nor could Karl Marx convince the proletariat to buy into his tripe as long as that class was Christian, so he had to find a way do away with Christians, and he's been working hard at that ever since." Nathan's brow furrowed.

"State's Rights, although wrongfully applied to slavery, especially black slavery, became my mantra which took me through my career from a private to a fearless military lieutenant general in that conflict that damned near destroyed our Republic. During the war my men disappointed and disgraced me at the Fort Pillow Massacre for which I, as their leader took the blame. It was a crime that only Jesus Christ could forgive!"

He paused, biting his lip, then after only a moment continued after collecting his thoughts.

"Then after the war, as Alderman, I joined a Southern gentleman's club that morphed into the KKK." Nathan looked up at Elijah, directly into his eyes.

"Mashpee described your sister, Rebecca's troubles. Terrible indeed! I also know of the history about how Rev. Joseph Ruggles Wilson had poisoned his own father James. Did you know about that? They said it was cholera but that was crap. James ate bad oysters at a function, and it was definitely intentional. James knew Old Nathan and Joseph. Then later, Joseph, James and Thaddeus Stevens all worked on the steam transportation and waterway projects together. Good men all!" The story moved forward.

"Well, anyway before his father resumed room temperature, that bad Reverend moved South in the 50s and filled the folks, blacks and his own son, Woodrow's mind with poison; the kind of spiritual poison that puts bad oysters to shame!

"Anyway, I then followed the atrocities of the KKK, where I met your black privateer associates of Slippery Sam's, not once in my life but twice. The first time I received your gold in New Orleans was for the two sisters' sale, which I now deeply regret, but fortunately your team of Yankee cutthroats rescued." Nathan paused to laugh. "Quite a clever ruse you, P.T. Barnum, and Mashpee pulled off!"

"The second time was recently, during my involvement with the KKK. My path crossed with the older sister, a brave God-fearing Negro woman who literally brought my renegade band and me to Jesus.

"She was alone as we were pursuing her party and she deliberately stayed behind to stop us in the name of Jesus. What a shock that was when she boldly revealed her plan to offer herself to save her party and said more boldly that God Himself would strike us dead if we continued to persecute Negro Christians!

"Now I know warriors, and respect them deeply regardless of race, creed, or color. Call it professional courtesy if you will, but that older Negro woman was a bold woman and brave! She had that quality as you do, Elijah. The killing of your other family members, by another band of rival cutthroats that I also regret having been associated with even if only indirectly! So with that, I quit the KKK in disgust along with my band of men who stopped pursuing her group. Henceforth, I vainly made it my personal goal to terminate that hateful organization and as I opened this discussion will now end it... that it is indeed high time, in Jesus' Name, for America to move on.

Before this time no slave nation has ever survived but for our nation, as the exception, did miraculously survive!"

Elijah "You're not telling me something I didn't already know".

"What"?

Elijah coughed but laughed "We've been watching you too. Before Jesus, kings and judges ruled. After Christ, our God given conscience does... Allow me to get to the point... Scotland tried to warn Lincoln... but Lincoln was assassinated. So now, it will fall on some future leader".

Forest shook his head "I don't understand".

"I know you don't, Nathan, but a future generation will!

God gives us wisdom and common sense, shared by common heroes, just like you and me..."

Rebecca, now reborn as Thankful, her mother, came and stood by Mashpee's side.

"We knew as the children of God were sold into slavery that bound boys like you, Elijah, in those days had a hard time of it, and a bound girl worse. Too often we were made drudges in the masters' families and not infrequently were made to feel the sting of charity mincingly and tauntingly bestowed. The wrongs suffered under that early form of child slavery," Rebecca said in tears of joy, "are now a thing of the past for the time being!'

Mashpee tenderly put his arms affectionately around Thankful in support, and all present said "Amen!" as the meeting concluded.

On the following Saturday Elijah departed to meet up with the Maker Who once walked among us, and his partner in this life, Olive, never to be kept apart again, now permanently joined for all eternity.

1877

Only a Moral Nation shall not perish from the earth

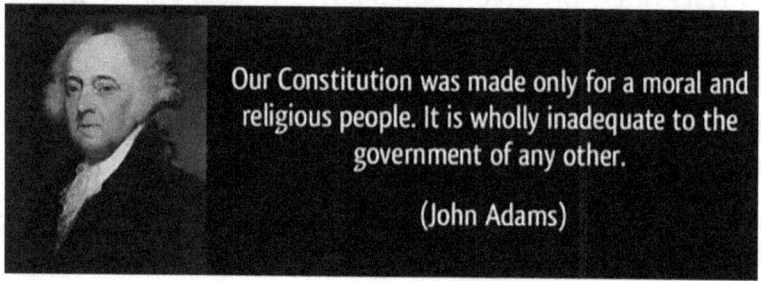

Our Constitution was made only for a moral and religious people. It is wholly inadequate to the government of any other.

(John Adams)

Ten years later over Nathan's own death bed, his survivors prayed.

"If my people, which are called by my name, shall humble themselves, and pray, and seek my face, and turn from their wicked ways; then will I hear from heaven, and will forgive their sin, and will heal their land." Second Chronicles 7:14.

Marshall Goodspeed completed his education, moved to Illinois, and became a teacher after graduating in 1849. He engaged in the nursery business during the so-called Christiana tragedy that started September 11, 1851. The press Whig rags portrayed the lawmen as honest men and the blacks as armed Negros. The Quakers that defended the fugitives and restored civility were jailed and framed by the same rags as ring leaders, murderers, and traitors to the US Congress. Yet oddly before the end of that month, they were all acquitted including the Negros.

But what really got Marshall's attention happened October 25, 1851, when editor Horace Greeley, after an embarrassed silence, came out with a twelve-page edition rather than their usual eight-page paper. Not once was it mentioned anything about Christiana but featured a new foreign correspondent named Karl Marx. He was hired by golden whiskered Charles A. Danna, Greeley's young managing editor. Karl, up until the Civil War, was the world news small talk contributor. Marshall studied these installments with interest which seemed to have quite a literary style, until it was revealed that Marx, a German, could only write in German and had an English journalist named Frederic Engles as a ghost writer. Marx eventually would learn to write his own pieces but by that time was earning less and was finally let go by Greeley just before the Civil War started.

Marshall learned later that Karl Marx in 1867, after Elijah's death, had written Das Kapital. But it was all in German. Marx planned to publish second and third parts. They were both completed from his notes then published after his death by his colleague Friedrich Engles, finally in English in 1883. Horace Greeley died in November 1872, a month afterward, his wife died, heartbroken. Marshall still faithfully followed the New York Tribune until 1883. He read Engles' second and third parts, then totally disgusted, Marshall promptly stopped his forty-year subscription to the N.Y. Tribune. Later he simply looked over at his wife and shrugged.

Marshall's wife was Cordelia Petty, the daughter of

John and Orinda Coffeen Petty, granddaughter of Rev. Michael Coffeen, who as a boy of seventeen, like Thomas Goodspeed, had fought at Bunker Hill earlier April 19, 1775. Afterward, he became one of the founders of the Universalist Church in America and was a contemporary and intimate friend of Rev. Hosea Ballou. Ballou's cousin Adin was an early free-enterprise critic along with fake journalist, Minister Joseph Ruggles Wilson, who both despised the Goodspeed's Landing successes and attacked his economic success model of every opportunity he got. They also did not like Goodspeeds and James Wilson's canal building efforts to help rescue the bondsmen. And after 1851, when James Wilson died, Goodspeed participated with many other bankers and industrialists to bring down the South with the coastal blockade strategy that Lincoln advanced for ending the dreadful war and slavery. We can now more clearly see where President Woodrow Wilson was coming from in his crusade against independent banking systems (with the FED) and independent industrialists and the middle-class machine (with the IRS) that had much to do with killing the enemies of the deep state of Antebellum slavery and made war on the American middle-class system. It was the first thing the Southern Democrat party (and the devil) did after the Civil War when they finally got back into power in 1912, make no mistake about that. With the neo-masons' support, that was also the group that murdered Thaddeus Stevens' whistle-blower friend Captain Morgan. But by then, with Nymphas Marston, Nathan Goodspeed,

Samuel Goodspeed, the other Nathan in 41, James Wilson, Joseph Goodspeed and Abraham Lincoln's death, there is nothing new under the sun!

Final Note from this author's business partner and editor J.R. Gork: A Glance into America's Future

The turning point of freedom in America occurred under Woodrow Wilson's presidency, which began in 1913. The three Central Events are:

Passing of the 16th amendment, which is what enables the income tax to exist in this country. This was opposed by many as it violates one of the tenants of the United States Constitution (I see article 1, section 9 as powers forbidden to Congress, "no capitalization, or all the direct tax shall be laid...)

(*Author's Note: Actually, the dirty little secret is that it really never passed on ratifying... But never let the facts get in that way of a good fraud!*)

Passing of the 17th amendment, which changed how United States senators are elected. Prior to this, U.S. Senators were elected by the state houses. The 17th amendment changed this allowing the people to elect senators, similar to how the House of Representatives are elected. This change minimizes the power of the states and creates more central power and thereby essentially federalizing the elections further. As the deep state has figured out how to "rig" elections this has become an even more concerning amendment.

Finally, the Federal Reserve Act was put into place in

November 1913. The book, "The Creator from Jekyll Island" lays out a lot of insights into this act. This now nationalizes inflation. One of the central figures that benefited from this is JP Morgan. JP Morgan became famous, as one of the benefactors who bailed the federal government out as one of the key robber barons. There are actually books written about the idea that JP Morgan intentionally sank the Titanic to form the Federal Reserve Act. Some of the wealthiest people who died on the Titanic were opposed to the Federal Rescue Act. JP Morgan was booked on it's fateful voyage but canceled at the last second. John Astor III, who died on the Titanic, opposed the Federal Reserve Act and was from one of the richest families in the world.

> *There are no conspiracies but there are also no coincidences.*
> **STEVEN K. BANNON**

> *Even the smallest person can change the course of the future.*
> **J.R.R. TOLKIEN**

C.S Lewis and J.R.R. Tolkien met weekly, Inklings meetings, at the Eagle and Child pub in Oxford, England from the 1930's through the 1940's. This fellowship group was largely for the purpose of reading, debating the ideas, and entertaining themselves through sharing stories. Two notable seeds that took root at this pub were C.S. Lewis's conversion from an atheist to a God-fearing Christian, inspired in part from debates with his devout Catholic friend, J.R.R. Tolkien. The second, the novel, *Lord of the Rings*, a book that was published in part from the encouragement of C.S. Lewis. The clash of good and evil is the theme of this inspiring epic-like story. But, one idea is clear, a seemly meek hobbit, Frodo, and his loyal friend Sam, are uniquely positioned to resist the temptations of power and riches to confront and defeat the evil Sauron.

God works in mysterious ways to confront evil, not only in the fictional world of Middle Earth, but throughout history. The young David defeating giant Goliath, Joseph prevailing after being sold into slavery by his brothers, Moses leading the Israelites out of slavery, Gideon defeating the Midianites, Daniel surviving the lion's den, Christ defeating death through resurrection, Paul's conversion from killing Christians as Saul to being inspired by God to write the majority of the New Testament.

Karl Marx and Friedrich Engels created an evil idea in 1848 with the creation of the *Communist Manifesto*: the abolition of God and the family and centralizing power within the State has been and continues to be in conflict with the Judeo-Christian ideas that are the foundation of freedom of Western civilization.

Unfortunately, these ideas resonated with Woodrow Wilson and he made it a centerpiece of his administration to introduce legislation that would weaken the family structure financially through taxation 16th amendment, reducing their influence over the election of Senators via the 17th amendment, and manipulation and devaluing the currency via the Federal Reserve Act.

Freedom is about removing the shackles of taxation and representation and killing inflation by repealing the 16th and 17th Amendments and the Federal Reserve Act. This will begin the process of killing the Marxist ideology woven into Globalism that threatens the freedoms and standard of living of Western civilization. Doing so, God willing, will significantly help restore the family financially and will restore the idea of life, liberty, and the pursuit of happiness.

Additional thoughts on these points:

God uses the seemingly weak and the least expected people to fulfill his vision.

In addition to the Biblical figures (listed above) here are a few political figures:

George Washington: courage and military skill during the Revolutionary War to lead his troops during the battle of Trenton, including the crossing of the Potomac. Additionally, his willingness to give up power when his presidency ended.

Andrew Jackson: courage and military skill during the battle of New Orleans in 1815 that prevented the British from securing the Mississippi River and invading the interior of the United States. Additionally, his ability to prevail against the aristocracy, the deep state of the time, thus earning the label, the People's President. (President Donald Trump identifies with Andrew Jackson and has visited the hermitage in Nashville, TN several times during his first term to help point out this connection.)

Abraham Lincoln's presidency encompassed the Civil War and took a huge toll on this amazing leader. Yet he kept his faith in God as he seemed guided in creating the Gettysburg Address and his second inaugural address.

John Fitzgerald Kennedy who was assassinated due to his intention to expose Lyndon Baines Johnson and the Military Industrial Complex and the corruption that continues unabated to this day.

Richard Nixon who remains the most popular American President to this day, chose not to challenge the 1960 election against JFK that was stolen from him. Similar to JFK, President Nixon intended to expose LBJ and the Military Industrial Complex and was forced to resign due to being set up by John Dean and other advisors. Watergate was orchestrated by the CIA and FBI. The "Deep State" is way overdue for being dismantled.

Ronald Reagan who inspired this nation from the brink of disaster created by the incompetence of Jimmy Carter. His Morning in America campaign, disarming wit, and great communication skills guided this nation back to greatness.

Donald J. Trump made America Great Again! He withstood unimaginable attacks by the military industrial complex, the national security complex, and the Uni-party of Dems and RINOs who coordinated to protect this out-of-control corruption. And he is not done. God appears to be calling on President Trump to Make America Great Again, Again!

All of these great leaders seemed guided by God to serve the greater good of this nation and all Americans. But as important as these great leaders were (and continue to be in the case of President Donald J Trump), The Song of Freedom is about highlighting some of the millions of unknown Americans who have stepped up courageously and unselfishly to help preserve the freedoms of this great nation.

Song of Freedom was written in hopes of inspiring another generation of Americans to stand up for life, liberty, and the pursuit of happiness.

The End

Appendix

Ben Goodspeed's Final Poem
Friday, October 30, 2020

Godspeed

in warm sands, you awake.
as awareness acclimates,
your mind dwells still, upon a last recollection...

the forest.
mountainous and vast
sacred and quiet.
the sun beams down through boughs,
onto a carpet of pine needles.
there is a smell of tree sap,
and in the autumn air,
a stillness.
as if a place protected from the world outside
and the world outside;
of oblivious, defiled people.
where no one could understand your love
and every road, a dark pathway, from your heart,
leading from a place of virginity,
into a place of ruin

lingering memories
fading...

a bullet

flash of light
no sound
your feet stir against the sands
eyelids illuminated with cathartic glowing light,
strange at first, the air here soothes.
echoing faintly, from over the edges of your bed in the
dunes,
your ears pick up faint static, the sound of rolling waves,
one after another, in a tender trance
the air shifts gently with a breeze,
and you come to
lifting your head, the waves now fill your ears directly
as your senses behold... an ocean, without boundary
never ending shore, bordering another world.
those who follow the paths of the world
are forever lost at sea
for the meaning of love hides in plain sight
too obvious to see
and yet,
you find yourself, now,
here.
castaway survivor
on the shores of your heart
re-entering a dream long forgotten

now the idea seems to have no meaning
you've always been here. you never left here.
time passes like a stream, slowing and speeding,
cycling and swirling and returning whence it began
the darkness of that place in your dreams,
no more
the trauma is gone.

it's alright...it's over.

it's over

and laying your head back down...
the dunes muffle the waves back into the background
safe and warm, gazing upwards,
a pressure builds in your lungs...tears in your cheeks.
for far above you, the expanse of blue sky unfolds,
filling every inch of your mind
an infinity, unbounded by the limits of human capacity
like an awareness stretching out
and touching every star in the universe
and every inch of it is full of light.
and love is written across the cosmos

and like dams bursting open,
your war-torn heart suddenly overflows with belonging
a wholeness you never knew, and never knew possible
rivers of tears, impossible to repress, flowing through you
as your soul orbits the warm center of the universe
from lifetimes forgotten, the arms of a thousand

reaching out to you, in unreserved contact

you're home

one day you awoke
and I knew you were the one
i've been waiting my whole life
a hundred thousand lives,
as a thousand different people
and in every one of them, I was alone
sometimes a soul, so noble and radiant,
just has enough
and cannot be contained any longer.
no chains in existence have the power to hold her
no force on earth, nor god in heaven above.
and for one moment, the eyes of all creation turn to fix
upon her.
and she spreads her wings; and the mystery of love is
revealed

you, god among mortals,
you were everything I ever wanted
every single day of crushing isolation
every night of emptiness & despair,
you were the one
and there is no more need of false worlds and false
dreams
for there is nothing else
that will ever keep us apart again.

Self Portrait – September 27, 2020

Benjamin Karas Goodspeed

DECEMBER 7, 1984 – OCTOBER 30, 2020